Haunted Ground

The Ghosts of Laskin's Farm

By

Cailyn Lloyd

Haunted Ground: The Ghosts of Laskin's Farm

© 2023 Land of Oz LLC

ISBN: 979-8-218-17465-1

Cover design: MiblArt

For Jennie.

And Max.

One

Kat Lundquist felt an inexplicable unease.

Something was wrong.

The warehouse was dark, silent. Dank and disused. A rusty remnant of a bygone industrial era. The perfect spot to do the deal.

The cops didn't patrol this area much. Almost like they had an unspoken agreement.

No gunfire? No homicide? We'll leave you alone.

Besides, they didn't have the will or resources to tackle the drug cartels, and it was easier to chase the little guys.

Per their arrangement, the black Tahoe pulled through the open door, lights out, and crept forward until it reached the point where she stood. Kat was a regional distributor for the Campo brothers, a smaller cartel that controlled parts of Wisconsin and Illinois—though calling it a cartel was generous. She waited with two dudes, Theo and Mike, her trusted bodyguards and muscle. They would handle the actual product transfer.

They weren't alone. Jesús lay up in the rafters with a sniper rifle, ready to handle any unexpected issues. Stefan and Paul, armed with

AR-15s, had slipped into dark corners of the warehouse. Harven, her boss, had sent them as backup, but she expected no trouble. Tony Roberts, the buyer, was a regular, reliable customer—though this was an unusually large transaction.

It all went like clockwork—

Until it didn't.

Tony stepped out of the SUV with a wave. "Hey, Kat."

Something about him felt off. She didn't understand it. She and Tony had concluded plenty of deals and she trusted him—as much as you could trust anyone in this business, especially when dealing large quantities of coke, meth, heroin, and other sundry items. Everything but fentanyl. Kat refused to touch the stuff. It was simply too dangerous and killed too many people. Dealing it would draw unwanted attention to her operation.

As they walked toward her Yukon, she knew. Tony didn't make eye contact when she asked how he was. Firm eye contact was his thing. Instead, his gaze slid away.

Fuck!

A moment later, two armored SWAT vehicles flew through the open bay door and converged on their location. Tony and Mike dropped to the ground. Theo pulled his gun while Kat dropped her Glock in the shadows and sidestepped away, raising her hands. She was not getting killed over a drug deal. Theo followed suit as helmeted cops swarmed into the building with assault rifles and night vision gear.

Cops appeared behind them and rounded up the dudes lurking in the shadows. Other cops with flashlights spotted Jesús in the rafters. He surrendered without a fight.

It played out in seconds, like watching a movie on an IMAX screen. Dazed, Kat stared into infinity. She knew this moment might come.

But she had operated successfully for so long, it had become a minor worry, one rarely examined. Nobody planned for this. How could they?

A cop cuffed her and shoved her toward a waiting squad. Kat felt a powerful hankering for a fat line of coke.

That wasn't happening. She was going to prison forever.

Ha!

That was the least of her worries.

Cut off from an endless supply of cocaine, she was about to detox the hard way.

Unless Harven killed her first for blowing the deal.

Two

Five Years Later

Kat smiled.

A tight, joyless expression.

The place looked perfect. A sanctuary. A haven away from the world and the people pursuing her.

She discovered the farm after hours spent poring over satellite images and a plat map of individual land parcels on a library computer.

Standing in the shade of an oak, the farmhouse was a silhouette beyond the dense brush. It was invisible from the road. Mischievous crows bickered somewhere nearby. Kat wrinkled her nose at a whiff of manure as the branches overhead creaked in the stiff south wind. It was hot but tolerable with the breeze.

The house was a half mile from the next farm in any direction and surrounded by untamed trees and shrubs. The driveway had disappeared beneath wild brush. On a little used road a mile from the nearest highway, it was too far from town to attract teens looking for a party shack. Kat had run a search on the property and learned only one detail. The owner, Adam Laskin, lived in California and paid the property taxes yearly in advance.

But how bad was the house? Was it truly empty?

Only one way to find out. Kat pushed her bike, an old Trek splattered with mud, deeper through the thick brush. One hundred feet in, she broke through into the open, standing amid long grass waving in the breeze. The surrounding fields had reverted to wild prairie with stands of second-growth trees, some over forty feet tall.

It looked sound. The roof was old and weathered but otherwise intact. The finish on the wood siding had mostly peeled, a rough grey surface flecked with remnants of white paint. That was fine. More surprising, the old double-hung windows looked undamaged. Not a broken pane anywhere in sight. How was that possible? Trees had fallen over the years, but somehow the house had been spared. The barn was less fortunate, a ruin that may have collapsed in a windstorm. No matter. She didn't need it.

Kat scanned the yard for watchful eyes and pulled up to the porch, leaning the bike against the railing. Pushing her way through the tall grass, she circled the house, assessing the structure while keeping a wary eye open for hidden hazards in the grass. The house looked sturdy: the doors, the windows, the foundation. She saw no evidence of recent visitors or maintenance, nor an alarm system of any sort.

Kat marveled at her apparent good fortune.

This search could have taken weeks. Visits to dozens of potential sites. Miles and miles on the bike. Plenty of frustration. Instead, she found the house in two days after a painstaking search on Google Earth for places just like this: an old farmstead where the fields were no longer plowed or cultivated.

It seemed perfect in every respect. Maybe she should question that.

Until her recent parole, the previous five years had been difficult.

When anything went well, she viewed it with suspicion. This seemed too easy. What was she missing? What were the hidden problems or dangers?

Clearly, the inside had to be a disaster.

After looping the house, she stepped gingerly onto the wood-framed porch. It felt solid. Not a wiggle or shudder. She opened the screen door, surprised to see only a residential-grade keyed doorknob. No deadbolt. She peered through the dirty glass but the interior was too dark to visualize.

On a whim, she gave the knob a twist. Locked of course. What did she expect?

She pulled a screwdriver from her backpack, shoved it between the jamb and door, then pried and shouldered the wood in a practiced move. The door popped opened with the whine of a creaky hinge.

The interior was funereal, the windows covered with heavy blinds. Her eyes took a moment to adjust.

Holy shit!

It was still furnished. Old-fashioned stuff though. It looked a little like her grandmother's house. A couple of recliners and a sofa. A book-shelf. Some kitschy decor. An old TV, console style, maybe a Zenith. To the left, a half bath and a narrow staircase running up the wall.

A thick but pristine blanket of dust covered everything, including the floor. Spider webs crisscrossed the room. Kat brushed them aside, unfazed. Her shoes left prints in the dust like a walk through freshly fallen snow. She walked toward the back into a dining room. The layout was basic with a dining table and sideboard.

Someone had set the table for three. The silverware lay in casual disarray. On the plates, clumps lay beneath the dust. Old food? Curious, she grabbed a fork, poked around, finding old bones from a steak or pork chops. Two wine glasses had a black residue. Remnants of red wine?

Creepy.

A family dinner with a peculiar twist. Almost like those stranger-than-fiction tales where the people fled and disappeared. But she sensed no urgency to leave—as if they finished dinner and just wandered off into the night. In the kitchen, two dirty kettles sat on the grates of an older gas range. Dirty dishes lay in the sink. An empty bottle of burgundy on the counter. No one had attempted to clean up.

Weird.

But nothing more. She wasn't superstitious. Didn't believe in alien abductions. It was just odd. And there might be a rational explanation. Staged maybe? A prank to scare off intruders? An abandoned set from some low budget horror movie? Kat shook her head. It wasn't important.

Walking full circle, she peered out the front door, her hypervigilance an ingrained trait. Still no evidence she had been observed or followed.

A creaky staircase led to the second floor. Kat found three bedrooms, all furnished. She saw no water damage on the ceilings. In two of the bedrooms, the beds were made and grey with dust. Identical tallboys stood in each room, one covered with toy cars and trucks—a boy's room—the other a blank slate. A flag from Arizona State University hung next to it.

The third bedroom looked like the master. The furniture was dark, heavy, and old. Dated, but not yet retro. A suitcase lay open on the unmade bed. Here she sensed urgency, a scramble to flee.

The closet stood open, half-filled with clothes in drab greys and blacks. The dresser drawers were open and partially emptied. Clothes lay scattered across the floor, covered by the ubiquitous layers of dust, mostly work clothes in denim and flannel. Someone left in a hurry and didn't return. The mystery deepened. Kat couldn't imagine a scenario that fit the situation. Unless they left for some mundane reason and were killed in an accident. Still, why no clean up?

Did it matter? They were gone now.

She walked downstairs and peeked out the window again.

All clear.

Kat shook off her unease. Despite the eerie presentation, the house was perfect for her needs. A place to escape Harven and his henchmen.

Here, hidden from the world, she could relax. Feel safe again.

Stay alive.

Three

The rest of the day was arduous.

Kat rode two miles to a bike trailer hidden in the woods that held her worldly possessions. Hooking the handle to a latch under the seat, she pedaled back to the farm. She rode on secondary roads to stay out of sight, limiting her exposure to the observant or the curious, but mostly to hide from Harven and his men.

The kitchen was large. A window over the sink looked out to the back yard. Wood-stained cabinets mounted over the countertops reached to the ceiling. They looked like hickory. Good quality stuff. An old gas range sat in the middle of the west wall, a small breakfast table in the center of the room. The fridge sat opposite on the east wall. Kat opened and closed it quickly. The smell wasn't terrible, but the interior was black with old mold and looked disgusting. It had to go. Next to the range, cafe doors led to a pantry that was stocked with food. Mice had pilfered most of it, but some canned goods that might be salvageable—soup, beans, and vegetables—remained.

Ferreting around, she found a broom and dustpan, a mop, and other cleaning supplies in a cabinet.

She swept the countertops, amazed to find quartz beneath the dust. This was looking less and less like an ordinary farmhouse. Someone had done a fairly expensive renovation in the kitchen.

Stepping outside, she unloaded the contents of the trailer onto the porch. A Yeti cooler—her refrigerator. Two pairs of Silver jeans, a flannel shirt, and tees from Salt Life, Hard Rock, and a trip to Antigua. Underwear, socks, sandals, Merrill hiking shoes, a winter coat with liner. A TracFone. A can of almonds, beef jerky, and trail mix. Bottled water, a lantern, and a Glock 19 with two magazines and a box of ammo bought illegally from an old friend on the street. A bedroll and pillow. A basic first-aid kit and a small set of tools. A start.

Now she needed supplies.

She slipped three hundred dollars from her money belt into her pocket and hopped on her bike.

The nearest town, the Village of Walden, was seven miles away. A small, friendly community of eighteen hundred people, she had looked it over before biking to the farmhouse. Evidently, crime wasn't an issue. Security cameras were rare and there were no police street cams. Still, she kept her head down in case she had missed one to avoid facial recognition software.

Kat was once almost beautiful. She could be again with enough effort, but she had no desire to stand out. Of average height, she opted for bland clothing and looked older than her actual age, a consequence of a hard life and purposeful neglect. She had shoulder-length brown hair and no distinguishing marks that suited her need for anonymity. Plain women were seldom noticed. She spoke quietly and seldom made eye contact.

There was a convenience store, Quik Stop, on the edge of town with a steady stream of customers. The teenagers working the checkouts looked disinterested. A perfect store for her basic needs. She grabbed a six-pack of Blue Moon. Cheese. Lunch meat. Mayo. Jerky. Donuts. Some Red Bull until she could figure out how to brew coffee. A small bag of charcoal. Chicken breasts. Ice. It all fit nicely in the trailer.

Riding out of town, she passed a little free library, stopped and grabbed a Lee Child book. She'd started reading the *Reacher* series in prison but hadn't yet read this one.

She unloaded her groceries and packed the ice and perishables in the cooler.

Taking another walk through the house, she opened any windows with screens still intact. The breeze swirled the dust about as she swept and cleaned, uncovering narrow-width maple floors. They looked beautiful, pristine, protected by the dust and a lack of traffic over the years. The house was looking like a gem in the rough and again, she wondered, what was the catch?

Kat took a second walk around the yard. Noted a set of storm doors that probably led into the basement. She thought she had spotted an old-fashioned hand-pump well in the back yard.

Yep, about thirty feet behind the house. The handle barely moved at first, stiff with the inertia of rust and age. As it loosened up, she heard noises and gurgling. A moment later, rusty water burped out: first a few sad drips, then a steady flow of brown, smelly water. After fifteen minutes of effort, the stream cleared as she flushed the rust out of the system. Another five minutes and the water was cold, crystal clear, and odorless.

She spent the last hour of daylight clearing the master bedroom of dust. She threw everything out the window: clothing, sheets, decor, knick-knacks, shoes, the shitty art hanging on the walls.

The walls were plaster and cracked, but easily repaired. Some drywall tape and mud. Texture. Paint. All skills learned when she and her ex-husband, Josh, had flipped a house early in their marriage. She could make the rooms look new. Despite her hand-to-mouth existence, style still mattered. She had spent almost five years in prison and longed to make something her own again.

This bedroom would be her first project, painted some bright color other than white. Pale blue? Green? Some Florida colors? Yes. She wanted to dream of the beach as she slept. She'd gone to Clearwater with Josh. So long ago. Sometimes losing him still stung. Or was she just lonely? Such was her fate, destined to be a solitary soul, unmoored from anyone in the world.

Kat shook her head. Enough self-pity.

Tomorrow, she would ride to town for ammonia and supplies to start repairs. Maybe buy a grill to cook on. Eventually a solar panel for lights or a coffee pot.

Who was she kidding? Kat didn't even know if she'd be here next week.

Kat was dead tired, and the room grew dark as the western sky faded to black. She spread her bedroll out and quickly fell asleep. Slipped away with a worry that even here, hidden from the world, she would never feel fully safe.

Somewhat later, she had a dark dream about a beast. A fearsome creature with an enormous head, a snaky body with little T-Rex hands, and a down-turned mouth filled with pointed shark-like teeth. No legs or feet though. It was underground, clawing its way to the surface. Coming for her.

The nightmare was persistent until she startled awake, rolled over, and fell back asleep.

By morning, it was forgotten.

Four

Kat wiped the sweat from her brow.

The day was sunny and hot, especially on the second floor. The air was still, dead. A fan would be nice, but she had no electricity to drive it. No matter, the heat was bearable and she was no wimp. The bigger question? How would she heat the place in winter?

She slapped the trowel of drywall compound at the top of the wall and drew it downward, leveling the goop over the rough first coat.

The master bedroom was the first step to making the house comfortable. The walls were plaster, cracked in places but in otherwise good condition. She repaired the surface with drywall tape and mud. Doing the work made her think of Josh, a flash of sadness she dismissed with a shake of the head. Josh was gone and never coming back.

Kat had picked up the materials the day before at the hardware store, along with a rich sage-green paint. So much for Florida colors. She liked them, but they were wrong for this old house. Again, she silently thanked the dealer who talked her into the bike trailer. The amount of stuff she could haul was amazing.

With the second coat complete, Kat grabbed a beer from the cooler and stepped outside. She had a deck chair now, courtesy of a rummage sale in town. She also bought a machete and a chainsaw from the hardware store to clear the yard behind the house.

Maybe she would plant a garden next year. Too late to grow much this year. Still, there were plenty of wild raspberries out back and an apple tree in the yard.

She sat in her chair and decided to work outside for the rest of the day. A tangle of brush, trees, prairie grass, and weeds; clearing it would keep her busy for a few days. The goal? To create a small area to sit and relax. Nothing in front of the house would change to maintain the look of neglect.

Kat spent an hour cutting the field grass down, hauling piles of clippings out two hundred feet, and dumping them. When her arm grew tired from machete work, she grabbed the chainsaw and cleared bushes, junk trees, and cut-up fallen branches, leaving an assortment of maples and spruces standing. During her time at the Susan B. Anthony Correctional Facility—aka the Hotel Anthony—she had worked on the grounds crew, learning the skills and developing the muscle necessary for the job.

Kat worked until dark, ate two granola bars, brushed her teeth, and slipped into her bedroll, falling asleep as her head hit the pillow.

★　★　★

In the morning, she worked in the bedroom, then spent the afternoon laboring in the yard.

By the time she quit, Kat was exhausted. She had cleared a grassy area roughly forty feet wide and sixty feet deep. Too tired to cook, she grabbed some jerky, string cheese, and a beer. As she sat, she glimpsed an animal moving in the longer prairie grass. It looked like a dog. Or a fox maybe? She blinked and looked again, but it was gone. Playing it safe, she stepped inside, grabbed the Glock, and chambered a round.

The creature didn't return but left her wary. She had no idea what kinds of wild animals prowled the countryside.

Kat nibbled at her dinner. It was more filling if she paced herself. She finished her beer and grabbed another, settling into a relaxed mood, feeling more at peace than she had in years. Still, her eyes occasionally scanned her surroundings, alert for any changes or disturbances. Getting *too* comfy could be the death of her.

She had to believe Harven and the crew wouldn't find her here. That her solitary existence in this hidden farmhouse would draw no attention. She was comfortable alone, especially after fifty-two months in prison.

She sighed.

Almost five years of her life gone. Vanished. Time in which she lost her freedom, her choices, her dignity—much like the three years that preceded her conviction, a fuzzy period she now recalled only in bits and pieces of hazy memory. All a consequence of her addiction to cocaine. She had sold her soul to the Campo brothers to keep the white powder flowing.

Never again—though the resolution came far too late. She had lost her husband. Her parents. A comfortable if boring life in the suburbs. All gone forever.

Kat had long ago decided she wasn't a good person, and now doubted she deserved this bit of luck, this haven from her failed life.

She tossed her empty bottle into the grass and stood up sharply.

Enough!

Kat had learned one very useful skill from Jamie, her only friend in prison: mindfulness. No worrying about the future. No wallowing in the past.

She had just slipped up.

To avoid dwelling further, she threw herself into cleaning the kitchen. The dust, cobwebs, and grime were endless, but a useful diversion from pointless rumination. Going through the cupboards was like a treasure hunt: cups and glasses, dishes, cookware, serving ware. Stuff she had imagined buying, bit by bit, but here it was, ready to go. Old, yes. Cleaned up, it looked fine. She picked off one cabinet a day, washing and rinsing the contents with water and scouring the cabinet with an ammonia solution.

A question gnawed at her.

Who had lived here? Why had they left everything? It made no sense. A story gradually evolved in her head. The family had died in an accident. Adam Laskin, who still paid the property taxes, was the sole remaining family member. He had left the house undisturbed as a shrine, like some parents refused to disturb a dead child's room. But if so, why wasn't the property better maintained?

For whatever reason, they were gone, and it wasn't worth the energy to solve the mystery. Maybe she would go to the library and google the name sometime.

Ironically, even though the house had no electricity or running water, she had flush toilets if she filled the tanks with well water. The septic system seemed to function just fine, and why wouldn't it? It was a simple drainage bed, buried somewhere in the yard.

The front door glass, visible from the kitchen, reflected flickering candlelight in the house. Two candles in the kitchen and one in the dining room lit the first floor, a yellow atmospheric light and a vision of how the farmhouse looked before electricity.

Kat was musing about that when she saw movement, a reflection of somebody moving toward the half bath by the front door. No sound. No footsteps. Just a brief vision.

Had she imagined it?

She had put in a long day. Her eyes were tired, but Kat needed to investigate. She grabbed a candle and the Glock and crept down the hallway.

"Hello?"

The house remained deathly silent. She looked left into the living room, then eased up to the half bath door. It was open. Kat sensed no one but felt her hackles rise anyway.

This was ridiculous. She was the only one here.

Glock leading, she swung around and found exactly what she expected, an empty bathroom.

She hadn't cleaned it yet and the layers of dust remained undisturbed.

Fatigue.

Had to be. Time for bed.

She locked the doors and carried the candle upstairs to the bedroom. Blew the candle out and slipped into her bedroll.

As her eyes adjusted, there was enough moonlight to see vague outlines of her work. Wide ghostly white stripes of drywall compound. One more coat and she could sand and texture the walls and paint them. The maple floors needed no work. Some new curtains and this room would be done.

Kat felt a vague sense of accomplishment as she fell asleep.

Sometime later, she was back in the warehouse. Just her and Harven. An unassuming man, people underestimated his deadliness. Five-ten, mousy brown hair, a bland face; he looked like an insurance salesman. If only that were true.

His leering face loomed over her, brandishing a Black and Decker cordless drill.

"You know how we feel about snitches, Kat."

He laughed and went to work on her kneecaps.

She awoke in a cold sweat, screaming. As her heart rate settled, she stared at the ceiling and spoke aloud.

"Wonderful life you've carved out for yourself, Kat."

Five

Over the next two days, Kat finished the bedroom.

After sanding and washing the repairs, she sprayed aerosol texture on the ceiling and walls. When that dried, she painted the room in the same order: the ceiling white, the walls sage-green. She scrubbed the wide baseboards and the maple flooring. Both were in good condition. She oiled the maple dresser and tallboy. Washed the windows. Cleaned the screens. She just needed curtains and a little decor.

All in good time.

Late in the day, she grabbed a beer and stepped out onto the porch. The day was still hot, oppressive. Thunderheads grew and spread in the west. Good. They could use some rain and she loved a good thunderstorm.

Tonight, she was having a hot dinner. Chicken and an ear of corn.

On her trip to town this morning, she bought a tabletop Weber grill at the hardware store. The small amount of smoke from the grill should attract no attention. She wanted a gas grill, the closest she would ever come to owning an actual range. Again, all in good time.

Looking out, she saw movement in the grass. A shadow. The grass swayed atypically. Kat reached for the Glock at her side.

A moment later, the grass parted and a large, bushy canine stepped out, a strange looking creature with a thick tawny coat. A golden retriever and St. Bernard mix maybe? He stopped and stared, sizing her up. No one followed or called out for him.

A stray.

A male, Kat thought of Cujo. He displayed no expression, no hint of whether he was friend or foe. With no foam around the mouth and a passive stance, he didn't look rabid. He sauntered forward and stopped again, seemingly aware this was a dance of sorts.

Kat maintained eye contact and eased the Glock aside. He continued the slow waltz forward, his posture relaxed. He looked like someone who needed a friend. Then she noticed a collar: light blue with a white stripe. A lost family pet? But she saw no tags.

A few paces more. His nose neared her foot. He took a tentative sniff and waited. She eased her hand out. He sniffed it and glanced at the grill. Had his stomach rumbled? Of course, he was looking for food. His eyes were bright and clear, but he looked thin and had burrs in his tangled coat. He had been running loose for a while. Reasonably certain he represented no threat, she stroked behind his ears and under his jaw. He leaned into the attention.

Kat spotted a name on the collar. Someone had inked it into the fabric with a black pen like a Sharpie.

Max.

She understood. No tags? The cheap collar? Someone had tossed him out, hoping he found a home. Maybe they had been evicted. Or couldn't afford him. Or just grew tired of him. Some people were just that shitty.

She eased off the chair onto the wooden porch, coaxing him forward, sitting next to him. Suddenly, he lay down, rolled over, and plopped his large head onto her lap. He gazed at her with an expression of gratitude.

Aww.

Friends at first sight.

Kat rubbed his chin and belly. He groaned appreciatively. After he settled in, she filled a bowl with water and set it down. He emptied it. She sat in her chair and Max lay down like he belonged there, exuding an air of contentment.

As the sun sank in the west, she fired up the Weber and cooked the chicken and corn, giving Max a third of it. Grateful for the warm food, he nuzzled against her but didn't pester her for more.

After dark, she cleaned another cupboard in the kitchen. She had nothing but time and oodles of patience; a form of escapism, really. What would she do after? She shook her head. There was plenty to keep her busy for months—if she stayed here that long.

Max lay on the floor and watched her move about. She pulled out a piece of jerky and gave him half of it. He settled and slept. She wondered how long he would stay. Would he wander off later tonight? Or did he feel safer here too?

She had few friends and trusted no one—other than Jamie, her roommate at the Hotel Anthony—but this mangy mutt was a companion she could live with. If he stayed, she would need to buy dog food and clean him up. Take him for a rabies shot at some point.

Suddenly, he lifted his head, stood, and walked to the hallway leading to the front door. He let out a low growl. As he did, Kat glimpsed the familiar figure floating across the hall to the half bath.

Holy shit!

It was something tangible. Max sensed it too.

Three times now she had spotted the reflection in the door glass. It was growing hard to ignore the nightly routine. Until Max reacted, she had written it off as a trick of the candlelight. Now Kat knew it was real. A presence that felt female—though she couldn't explain why.

A ghost? Was she seeing a ghost?

She felt no fear. Confusion maybe. She had never given the subject serious thought.

Max stood for a minute, watchful, and returned to his spot to lie down.

Time for bed.

Without a word, Max followed her up the stairs. At the top landing, she spotted lightning flickering to the west. She loved nighttime storms but she was too tired to wait for this one. Kat slipped into her bedroll. Max curled up on the floor next to the bed. She thought about her grandmother and the ghost stories she told when Kat was young. They were spooky but always ended on a funny note. Having no prior experience with ghosts, she didn't really believe in them. She wasn't opposed to the idea either. Whatever or whoever it was, she seemed harmless enough. Perhaps the ghost was happy to have company again.

She thought about the person who paid the taxes on the farm, Adam Laskin. With that, Kat dubbed the nightly visitor Mrs. Laskin.

Far to the west, the clouds flickered with light as she fell asleep.

A few hours later, the strident crash of thunder shook her awake. Max stood next to the bed, staring at her. He looked intelligent and seemed to recognize in Kat another loner, a kindred spirit.

The sky sparkled with dazzling flashes. She slipped out of her bedroll and stood at the window, watching the violent display of lightning arcing cloud-to-cloud or striking the ground. The thunder was a near-constant roar. Chinks of hail struck the windows while Max stood next to her, unperturbed. When the storm subsided, she slipped back into the bedroll.

As she drifted to sleep, the house shuddered and continued to shake for several seconds. Downstairs, glass shattered.

Kat jumped up, grabbed the Glock, and eased into the hallway. Peeked down the stairs.

Nothing visible.

Silence.

She crept down the stairs holding the gun two handed, cop-style. Max followed warily, looking ready to pounce.

Glancing left, she saw the problem. A glass bowl had fallen. The shaking probably.

It felt like an earthquake. She had spent time in Italy. There was no mistaking the sensation.

She walked a circuit of the house, found nothing, and returned to bed.

Strange.

Was an earthquake even possible here?

Six

Justin Sommerfeld jolted awake.

What?

He stared at the white ceiling of his bedroom, trying to orient himself.

Thunder detonated nearby with a boom that reverberated across the sky. Seconds later, a bright flash of lightning and a clap of thunder were followed by an intense blue flash. The streetlights and the power light on his cable box went dark. He sat up.

Oh great. A transformer blew. The power was gone, maybe for hours. He grabbed his phone, searched for the utility hotline, and reported the outage. Three in the morning? He should just go back to bed, but he didn't feel tired. Maybe if he read for a while. He reached for his Kindle—

The room shuddered slightly. A moment later, it evolved to an erratic rumble. He jumped out of bed and planted himself in the doorway—basic instinct for any experienced geologist who understood the significance of the shaking house.

The tremor ran for almost six seconds.

He guessed the quake was a magnitude four and about V on the Mercalli scale, and truly odd. The possibility of an earthquake anywhere in Wisconsin was near zero. The nearest active seismic zone was over a hundred miles away in central Illinois. Justin tried to wrap his head around the idea.

It would take several minutes for the US Geological Survey to report the event, but people must be talking about it. He grabbed his phone and tapped over to Twitter. No activity yet.

Eight minutes later, an email notification arrived from the USGS:

M4.1 Earthquake – 10km NE of Walden, Wisconsin. Depth: 17km

The message included the date, time, and latitude and longitude of the quake. He sent a group text to some friends. Several were awake and replied. They too were puzzled. The depth and duration suggested a fault, not hydrostatic rebound. Northeast of Madison, Wisconsin, the crust was thick and seismically stable. Buried fault lines existed but they had never shifted in recorded history. He knew the geological and seismic terrain of Wisconsin well. There had been few significant earthquakes in the past. In the last hundred years, only the 1947 Milwaukee earthquake was comparable. The cause of that event had never been determined.

He wanted to work. With the power out, he couldn't, so he lay down, hoping to sleep a little longer.

It wasn't to be. The anomalous quake felt important to him, an unquantifiable hunch. He needed data but felt frustrated lying here in the dark.

The lights snapped on.

He got up and showered. Trimmed his rather short brown beard, stooping a little to clip his brows. He really should move the mirror higher to accommodate his height. Dried his hair. Brushed his teeth.

Brewed coffee.

Justin owned an original Craftsman home just outside of Madison. Modestly furnished, he had converted the dining room with its built-in maple cabinets to an office that overlooked a lush garden on the side of the house. Self-employed—or unemployed, depending on the point of view—this room, painted slate blue, was his place of work.

The glass-faced cabinets displayed a substantial collection of antique devices: an antique spy glass on a tripod, several brass compasses, a sextant, nautical astrolabes, various hour glasses, glass Galileo thermometers, Franklin barometers, antique rock hammers, magnifiers and glasses, knives, and old field notebooks.

On the opposite wall, he had hung two world maps: a current topographical map, and a canvas map from 1682.

His desk was a large slab of oak on sturdy bases and a long right-side return that hosted a portable seismograph. Cables from large dual monitors ran to a powerful desktop beneath. A laptop sat on one side.

In a secluded neighborhood, the house was silent beyond the slight hum of the computer fan and the fridge.

With a mug of hot coffee in hand, he sat and set to work. Within the last hour, his Twitter had blown up with questions and comments about the event. Though relatively minor, the quake might be the event of the year by virtue of location, especially if aftershocks followed.

While Justin had little interest in routine earthquake studies, he wondered if he should examine this event in more detail. It might qualify as a test case to support his esoteric theories. One aspect of those theories posited random earthquakes in unexpected locations. This event certainly fit.

Or was he grasping at straws? Seeking a positive outcome without sufficient data to suggest the event was relevant to his research? Still, it was right in his back yard. He wouldn't have to travel far to evaluate the possibility.

His EMF gauges showed a slight dip in voltage. Interesting, but nothing significant statistically. No change in the local ground temperature—though he was too far away to observe thermal effects. Looking at a map, he was about thirty miles southwest of the quake location. The nearest town, the Village of Walden, lay in the middle of a cluster of farms. There were no parks or public land anywhere in the area. Maybe he could get permission from a farmer to set up equipment, though they were seldom willing to allow strangers onto their property.

He performed a grid search at the epicenter using Google Earth. A few farmsteads looked abandoned, but the fields were still plowed and cultivated. He spotted a larger farm to the southwest that looked like an industrial-sized operation. They had probably bought all the smaller farms for the land. A shame, but following an inevitable and irreversible script. The little operations were no longer profitable.

Then he spotted a promising location. The property looked abandoned, the fields overgrown with shrubs, trees, and prairie grass. A place where he could slip in and set up some gear unnoticed. He bookmarked it.

The million dollar question? Was magma creeping upward in that area? Could he be that lucky? He would only know by taking local temperature readings. Mantle plumes—bubbles of magma or lava— were large-scale features, like the plumes that fed the Hawaiian Islands,

Iceland, and the Yellowstone supervolcano. Justin believed they also occurred on a smaller scale as local events. So far, his theory had attracted little but ridicule. No matter. Many of the most robust theories about geological and seismic activity had started as fringe theory and were mostly ignored, like plate tectonics. It didn't help that he had also posited electrical currents created by the plumes could induce criminal and antisocial behavior nearby, like the Heaven's Gate suicides in California.

Justin was pragmatic and doubted a test case would appear in his back yard. Still, there was no harm in spending a few days researching the quake and eliminating it as a source. The past few months had been unproductive, with few tangible leads. Even if desperation figured into the equation, did it matter? He wasn't working on anything else of importance right now.

But as he finished his coffee, he decided a trip to the site was premature. The event wasn't worthy of study until one or more aftershocks occurred or he noted a substantial shift in the strength of the telluric currents or a complete reversal of polarity. He could be more productive here, watching and searching for earthquakes in seismically quiet regions followed by aftershocks at decreasing depths.

Really, what were the probabilities a test case would pop up in his back yard?

Justin knew the answer.

Zero. A big, fat goose egg.

He sighed and returned to the USGS site, looking for other recent quakes that would meet his criteria.

Seven

Max was standing by the bed when Kat awoke.

She assumed he was house-trained. He probably had to go out. They walked downstairs and Max trotted out into the yard. She grabbed a Red Bull from the cooler and followed. The early morning was bright and fresh. The air smelled clean with scents of flowers, growing vegetation, and damp earth. Max sniffed around at the edges of the yard, marked a few spots, and trotted over, nuzzling along her leg. So he was staying. The warm chicken last night probably sealed the deal.

Kat lit the grill. She wanted a proper breakfast today. Fifteen minutes later, sausages sizzled as she scrambled eggs. Max moseyed over, gave the grill a casual sniff, and looked at her.

"Yeah, I made some for you too, buddy."

After breakfast, she pedaled into town for supplies and information on caring for a dog.

Kat felt nervous. She had been doing this too often. People would note and remember the odd woman towing a bike trailer around town. Today, she left the trailer in the woods and made several trips to various stores, shuttling stuff back and forth after each stop.

The Village of Walden sat at the intersection of WI 196 and County Highway H. A typical small town, there were two churches, a high school, and combined middle and elementary schools. Plenty of houses, new and old. A good side of town and a blighted section with older apartments and a trailer park. A bunch of small shops that looked like they were just surviving. An old-fashioned Wisconsin supper club. A medical center and a dental clinic. The usual assortment of taverns. A new bank building across from the Quik Stop. The ubiquitous storage center just down the street. The rich people lived out of town in big houses on Walden Lake.

She biked into town on Kelly Road, which approached WI 196 at an angle from the northeast. The Quik Stop sat at the long angle where the roads met. Just before the Quik Stop, she turned right on North Avenue and left onto Kleiner Street. The hardware store and grocery were just a couple of blocks over. The library was two blocks south and the pet store was one block east, all in the northeast quadrant of the village. Thus she could make her normal stops without venturing onto or crossing either highway in Walden.

At the pet store, she bought a brush, a comb, cordless clippers, a flea collar, and a bag of kibble and rode back to the trailer.

Passing a rummage sale, she wandered around until she found the perfect addition for her home, a turkey fryer. She had no intention of cooking a turkey. The fryers had a tendency to boil over and catch fire. But that big pot would be perfect to boil water. Hot water? That would be a delightful luxury. She struggled out of town with it rested on her hip then returned for a propane tank from the Quik Stop.

She went to the library to learn about dog grooming and the issues she might face. While she read, she surreptitiously charged the clippers and her phone.

She had owned a Sheltie years ago, but was high most of the time and did a lousy job of caring for her. In a sober moment, she realized it would be best to take the dog to the humane society for adoption.

Glancing at the newspapers, she saw last night's earthquake made the national news, then noted with curiosity that the quake occurred near Walden.

Wow! What were the odds? The event baffled geologists, who were abuzz with ideas and explanations. Some felt the quake occurred on an extension of a fault from the Wabash Seismic Zone to the south in Illinois. Others felt that a failed rift or scar in the crustal rock below had caused the quake. The subject was interesting but Kat had more pressing things to do.

The grocery store was the last stop. She loaded her bags with all she felt she could handle and pedaled out to the trailer, then spent five minutes organizing things before it was stable enough to tow without tipping.

After packing the perishables in the cooler, she started heating water and sat with Max on the porch, working on his coat. At first hesitant, she grew more confident, working through the long, matted hair. She didn't bother with style, clipping the fur short. His coat looked better after the trimming. She checked his skin for ticks and combed out the few she found. Kat then found several circular wounds healing on his rear flank. He recoiled when she touched them. She then realized what they were. Poor guy had been pelted with buckshot.

He looked better but still smelled bad. She washed him with warm water and soap.

Cleaned up, he looked quite handsome, a weird mix of golden retriever and something else. He drooled a bit like a St. Bernard. He accepted the grooming affably, shook his coat off and dried himself on the porch in the late afternoon sun.

Lifting her arm and sniffing, she wrinkled her nose. Ugh. She was pretty ripe herself. Tomorrow, she would clean the tub and take a bath. The idea sounded decadent after a week of roughing it.

Kat fired up the Weber and prepared a gourmet meal: a baked potato and a small fillet. Max ate kibble with a little steak and seemed happy with it. They watched the sunset and moved to the kitchen where Kat took on the next cupboard, one filled with drinking glasses and coffee mugs. Old stuff but perfectly usable.

Max stood and walked to the hallway. Growled—a grumble really—as if he objected to being disturbed. A moment later, she saw the familiar reflection. Staring intently, she thought it might be a woman in a robe, though only her right arm and torso were visible. The rest was hazy, more impression than fact.

"Evening, Mrs. Laskin. Nice of you to stop by." Apparently, she intended to be a nightly visitor. She seemed harmless enough.

When Kat returned to the task at hand, she stopped with a start. The clean glasses she just placed in the cupboard had flipped over. She always placed her glasses top down to keep them dust-free inside. Now they were sitting top side up.

What the hell?

It shook her confidence. The glasses didn't just flip. Was she that tired? Absent-minded? What had she been thinking about? She couldn't remember.

She started to turn them, then shut the cabinet in frustration and muttered, "Fuck it."

Time for bed. She would deal with the glasses tomorrow.

"Let's go, buddy." Kat grabbed the candle and the Glock, walked up to the bedroom, and slid into her bedroll. Max curled up on the floor as she blew the candle out and pinched the wick to ensure it was fully extinguished. The heat barely registered through her calloused fingers.

Kat fretted about the glasses. She must have placed them upside down in a distracted moment. Only that wasn't like her.

Exhaustion soon trumped anxiety and she fell asleep.

Her sleep—disturbed and uneasy—devolved into a nightmare. Trapped in the basement, she saw no way out. Beneath her, a beast clawed and chewed its way to the surface. It looked familiar. A snaky body, a fat head with spiky teeth, and creepy little reptile hands. She could see it through the concrete floor. It meant to kill her.

It spoke. "I'm coming, Kat."

Harven's voice. She woke with a start.

Christ! Would she ever escape the anxiety that he would find her?

The man was ruthless. Relentless.

She feared the answer was no.

Eight

It was raining.

One of those midsummer Wisconsin days when it poured from iron-grey skies all day. Kat opted to finish exploring the house, starting with the attic.

In the second-floor hallway, she pulled a set of folding stairs down from the ceiling with a dry screech of metal. She climbed with a flashlight in hand but didn't need it. Like most foursquare houses, the attic had dormer windows that provided plenty of natural light, even with the gloomy weather outdoors. The wide pine plank flooring was covered with a thick layer of dust. It smelled musty with a hint of cedar. Virtual spider cities spanned the room. A splendid set for a horror movie.

With a broom, she pulled down the webs and balled up the silk. The attic was empty save for an old steamer trunk and a box of toys from an era before electronics.

The trunk was solid but empty and told her nothing about the former owners of the house.

She poked through the toys and wondered if she could donate them. At the bottom of the box, she discovered a hardbound notebook that looked like a journal or such. On the light brown cover, someone had written *Michael Laskin* in a loopy, unrefined cursive at maybe a sixth-grade level.

It wasn't a diary. On the first page, Michael—presumably—had drawn a woman's face in charcoal. A decent effort, it was better than the handwriting suggested. The next page was a pencil sketch of the house, drawn with obvious skill. She paged through the book, impressed with the artistic talent. About fifteen pages in, the artistry floundered, the sketches edgier with angry strokes and less finesse.

The sketches turned perverse and violent. One drawing showed a boy stabbing a man in graphic detail, including spurts of blood from the wounds. The next page was frightening. He had drawn a church with a crowd out front, a Sunday morning maybe. A boy was shooting at them, rapid fire with a long gun, bullets popping out of the gun in a long string.

Holy shit!

This was beyond angry. It suggested a serious psychosis based on the little she knew of the subject. The pictures were disturbing and hard to look at. It raised new questions about the state of the house when she arrived but answered none.

She flipped through the remaining drawings, barely glancing at them, until they ended abruptly. The last page appeared unfinished, but what he had sketched was horrible. A limp body hung from a half-drawn noose, the torso stabbed with knives. Two legs lay severed on the ground, blood dripping from the dangling stumps above.

She shuddered and slammed the book shut.

Sick.

The kid was a monster. Did the parents know? Who hid the book in the attic? The kid or the parents?

Probably not the parents, who usually saved the idyllic art with bright yellow flowers, box houses, and lollipop trees, not sketchbooks filled with mutilation and murder. Maybe the kid was planning a career in horror cinema, but she thought not. The progression from mundane drawings to violent imagery alluded to mental illness.

Kat dropped the book back into the box, clambered down the stairs, and slammed them shut. Out of sight, out of mind.

No need to revisit the attic.

The basement was the dank, dirty mess she expected. The floor and lower third of the walls were damp, the smell of mold and mildew pervasive. Spider webs stretched everywhere. Mice and possibly rats certainly lurked down there. A cistern sat in one corner, a messy pile of gardening gear in another. The junk had to go, and the basement needed to be scrubbed and bleached.

Not today. She would tackle that project when the house was finished—if she was still living here.

The thought hurt a little. She was just settling in. Feeling comfortable.

Outside, the rain continued falling.

The day was warm so she and Max sat on the porch. The big mutt had become her faithful sidekick. A companion who asked for nothing but food and water. He was also an independent soul who enjoyed his own space. Someone had trained him. He sat and heeled on command. Stayed off the furniture. Seemed to appreciate her efforts to clean him up and dress his wounds.

Occasionally, he would go to a window or door, just to observe. Rarely, he growled softly. Kat found it unnerving initially, but realized

Max had seen or heard something she hadn't and thus recognized his value as a guardian. And a reminder to stay alert.

Another unexpected gift. What was the catch? There was always a balance due.

Kat had an idea. She made a loop out of an old necktie from the upstairs and tacked it to the screen door. She got down on all fours, grabbed the tie with her teeth, pulled the door open, and slipped through the opening. Max watched her intently. She repeated the process and sat back. Max bit the tie and tugged on the door, but it closed before he could step in. The second time, he yanked it open, caught the door with his snout, and walked into the house.

He trotted back out with a blasé expression.

No big deal.

Kat laughed. The first time she could remember laughing in months. He was smarter than some people she had known.

Dinner was simple. Jerky and string cheese for Kat and kibble for Max. They watched the grey sky darken to near pitch black, then moved in for the nightly ritual in the kitchen.

She had solved the mystery of the shifting glasses in the cabinet the other night the following morning.

They were back where they belonged. But was it absent-mindedness or something more? The drawing book had left her unsettled and now she saw portents and perils in little things, like her nightly visitor and the glasses rearranging themselves. The house was perfect for her but it had a personality—some of it spooky.

She lit two candles and dug into the next cabinet under the counters. Beneath a bunch of worthless pans with damaged non-stick surfaces, she found a couple usable cast iron skillets. Perfect.

Each night, Mrs. Laskin made her nightly visit, her reflection gliding across the front door window. Even Max accepted her presence. He no longer bothered to growl at her reflection.

She sat in bed and read for twenty minutes before blowing out the candle and falling to sleep.

Somewhat later, she dreamt of the beast underground again, the details exquisitely graphic: the sharp teeth glistening with saliva, the grasping little hands. The creature broke through the basement floor and pursued her up the stairs and out the backdoor. No Harven voice tonight, just a monster relentless in the chase as she ran from tree to tree, trying to hide. Kat could find no safe haven in the nightmare that ran for hours.

Waking with a start, clammy with sweat, Kat sat up. Max stood by the bed, watching her. The rain had stopped and moonlight bathed him and the room in eerie grey light.

She didn't understand the sudden rash of nightmares. She rarely had them, even in prison. Why did it feel like her mistakes were coming home to roost now? Because she knew Harven was still hunting her? Because the house felt a little off?

Improbably, her insane life stemmed from an occasional but debilitating depression she suffered from as a teen. A college friend introduced her to cocaine during their freshman year. She felt better at once. Kat recognized the danger and steered clear of the stuff, but never sought help for her mood swings.

She met Josh. They married and life was perfect until she went off the rails three years into the marriage. They tried to have a child but after two years, she saw a gynecologist who diagnosed her with severe endometriosis. Her chances of getting pregnant were near zero. She fell into the worst depression of her life, angry with her flawed body and feeling she had failed Josh, who wanted children badly.

Cocaine came to the rescue, but this time, she couldn't walk away. Kat became a heavy user, stealing money from their joint accounts to pay for it. She was in charge of the household finances and diverting funds was easy. But her dealer also allowed her to run up a tab until it became a debt she couldn't repay.

The final descent into hell began the day her dealer introduced her to a dude named Harven. He offered to clear the debt if she worked for the Campo brothers. They liked her suburban mom look and squeaky clean criminal background.

Soon, she was dealing coke and meth and making big money, but failing in her personal life. She had confrontations with her husband over her drug use and the hours she spent away from him. But he refused to draw a firm line on her behavior and, in ways, enabled her. He must have loved her very much to tolerate her dreadful behavior. When she finally tried to turn her life around, it was too late. Josh snapped. He threw her out of the house, started a divorce, and filed a restraining order against her. Still in debt and out of options, Kat then went to work for Tomas and Antonio Campo as a full-time asset.

And continued doing coke.

Harven was a dangerous man, trained in multiple disciplines including Krav Maga and Tae Kwon Do. He taught Kat guns, weapons, and self-defense. The drug business was treacherous and the Campo brothers trained their people to manage "difficult" situations.

Then she was arrested and faced a long list of charges. Kat gave up the brothers and Harven for a lighter sentence. She had been facing at least twenty years, but the DA agreed to a deal when the cops failed to link any drug-related deaths to her dealing enterprise.

In the end, Harven walked due to a lack of evidence. As an enforcer, he handled no money or product. Kat had never actually seen him use violence, and no one offered to testify against him. His reputation was terrifying. Kat felt certain everyone feared what Harven might do to anyone who talked.

The brothers were tried, convicted, and received lengthy sentences. The details weren't important.

Harven was still out there and would settle their grievances.

As long as that remained true, she would never be safe.

Nine

A sunny morning, the heat rose early, the humidity thick like Florida in July.

Kat tried to shake the unease over the nightmares and the drawings, spending a few hours clearing additional brush in the yard. She biked to town for groceries. The checkout clerks remembered her. She could tell by their greetings and small talk about the weather. Kat didn't like it, but concluded it was inevitable and that the risk of wider recognition in a small town was negligible.

Her face had been on the news a few times during the trial. She had looked attractive and elegant, but five years had passed and she now looked older, nondescript, plain. The media had lost interest in the case and her release went unnoticed.

Still, in her last year at the Hotel Anthony, she began to view the future with fear.

Her attorney had pressed for witness protection before the trial during the plea negotiations, but the prosecution resisted. They argued the cartel was broken and the kingpins would receive long sentences, eliminating the risk of reprisal. Kat knew better but ignored the advice of counsel. Depressed and sober for the first time in years, she saw herself as worthless. An addict who had lost everything through bad choices, lack of willpower, and an inability to handle the normal stresses of life. A loser who lacked the will to do the right thing and kill herself. Kat wondered if her true motive in ratting out the brothers was the hope they would murder her—in effect, suicide by testimony. She had never expected to see the light of day again, certain Harven would kill her.

In prison, she waited for the fateful moment when a shiv would appear. But the Hotel Anthony was nothing like media portrayals of female prisons or brutal male prisons with their cultures of violence. There were dangers like poor medical care or sexual harassment from guards, but no gangs willing to commit contract killings. No way for Harven to get to her. Early on, an inmate told her that women would rather hug each other than shank each other, and she learned it was true. When Jaime became her roommate and helped change her attitude, it was too late. The DA who approved the deal was gone. No one in that office would discuss the case or witness protection.

Kat knew Harven and the crew would be waiting when she was freed. When they found her, they wouldn't be content with just killing her. No, they would send a message by raping and torturing her and leaving a mangled body in a ditch somewhere. Even though she had been a valued asset, Harven had shown her photos of several cartel killings lest Kat ever forgot who she worked for.

From prison, they released Kat to a halfway house for three months of supervision. She lived in constant fear, waiting for a dark shadow and the glint of a knife blade. She took a job nearby to minimize her time in public. Wore baggy clothes and disguises and otherwise stayed indoors. When Harven failed to make a move, she concluded he was waiting for her parole. It made sense. She was less likely to be missed.

Kat remained vigilant and careful as she concocted a scheme to disappear forever.

The day of her release, certain she hadn't been tailed, Kat checked into a motel and set the plan in motion. She pulled fifty thousand dollars out of a bank account, proceeds from the divorce. A stack of hundreds just over two inches tall, it was the maximum amount she could reasonably conceal in a money belt. She paid cash for the bike and trailer at a bike shop, then looked up an old friend who sold her the Glock and ammo. At a hardware store, she bought the Yeti cooler and other supplies and camped out at the library for days as she compiled a list of towns with populations of around fifteen hundred in the central part of the state.

Kat had just ten days before the first meeting with her parole officer to find a place and disappear. Visiting that office would be the death of her. Kat settled on Walden and disappeared the following day. Thus began her life on the run.

In retrospect, perhaps she should have taken the twenty years and kept her mouth shut.

Max lay sprawled on the porch when she returned, looking like he owned the place. Kat smiled. While she had no desire for attachments, human or otherwise, the big mutt was growing on her. Beyond meals and a roof over his head, he asked for nothing. The perfect companion, he listened intently, sometimes tilting his head with curiosity as she spoke. She never considered herself a dog person, but Max had quickly convinced her otherwise.

He was just the friend she needed. People were shit. Unreliable, insincere, only interested in what they could extract from a relationship or situation. She was the worst of all. On cocaine, she had been a manipulative bitch, only interested in clearing a path to her next high.

What had she done to deserve him? What payback awaited?

Kat shook her head and decided to clear the dining room. A first pass anyway, pulling down the cobwebs and sweeping the dust into an impressive pile. She wasn't certain why she left this room until last—though that wasn't exactly true. She hadn't cleaned the half bath either. Had she been avoiding this space?

Maybe.

As much as she tried to dismiss the implications, the room was creepy. It even felt a few degrees cooler, a sensation that might exist only in her head.

It was hard to ignore the odd presentation at the table: the three place settings with discarded bones on the plates. When she lifted the first plate, she found a Tarot card beneath it.

The Moon.

There were cards under the other plates. *The Lovers* and the *Death* card. *The Fool* lay beneath the dust in front of the fourth chair.

What fresh hell was this?

Kat knew nothing about Tarot cards, but the discovery was unnerving. Another quirk in a house that grew stranger every day. She knew the cards had paranormal associations. Maybe a family game or joke? A daily card reading akin to fortune cookies perhaps?

Enough of this creepy shit. The Laskins were gone.

Or were they?

Weird occurrences and coincidences kept adding up. The sudden surge of nightmares. The sketchbook. The glasses turning upside down. The nightly appearance of a ghost she had dubbed Mrs. Laskin.

Was that the catch? That her perfect hideout was haunted?

No matter. Creepy she could handle. And for now, she *had* to live with it.

Kat bunched the tablecloth, wrapping the dishes, silverware, glasses, bones, and the Tarot cards into a ball, and hauled the mess to the dump in back, tossing it without ceremony.

She heated water and washed everything. The table and sideboard were oak. The people who lived here had been affluent based on their choices. She took the heavy curtains down and carried them outdoors to beat the dust out of them. They remained useful to keep the ground floor dark, so no light crept out at night to draw attention to her presence. Cleaning the room helped erase the unease she felt.

As the sun set, Kat grabbed a beer and sat on the porch. It was a warm night, the air ahum with crickets, the moon near full, casting a pale fluorescence on the yard. She wasn't supposed to drink alcohol. Kat went through a psych evaluation during her prison intake and was required to go through drug and alcohol rehab. She pretended to care. But she wasn't addicted to alcohol. She had never sold her body and soul for a drink. Life was better now. She wasn't happy, but she wasn't tormented either. She had read somewhere that an addiction to drugs killed the capacity for joy, and it seemed true in her case. But she was mostly at peace.

For now, it was enough.

The porch bumped a little. Kat turned to see if Max had moved. He hadn't, but sat alert, looking as bothered as she felt. A moment later, the porch juddered and shook for three or four seconds. Her beer tipped over and something crashed in the kitchen.

Another tremor, no doubt about it. She was no geologist, but she knew earthquakes in Wisconsin were rarer than honest politicians. Now there had been two in less than a week. She had read about fracking causing quakes, but Kat didn't think there was any oil in the Midwest.

A hint of something darker? Kat had a sense the world was going to hell. People were ruining the planet. Overcrowding, pollution, exploitation of resources, climate change, the list seemed endless. While people fretted about extinction level events like massive volcanic eruptions or killer meteorites, Kat suspected humans would do it first.

Were the tremors another sign of an impending global collapse?

But she also ruminated on the location of the first quake. Ten kilometers northeast of Walden was right under her feet! Really, what were the odds?

That was exactly the problem. It was another disturbing issue to add to the growing list of oddities about the farm.

Was the house itself the retribution she feared?

Ten

Justin poured a glass of chardonnay and sat in his office.

Plotting a series of earthquakes in northern Oklahoma, he suspected they were caused by fracking and unrelated to his work. The last month had been dismal. He had found little fresh evidence to bolster his theories. He continued to hope for an aftershock from the recent quake near Walden—not only his most promising lead, but his only active lead.

Wishful thinking, he decided. He expected to travel a great distance when a proper test case arose. One wouldn't pop up thirty miles from his front door. He needed patience. Somewhere, activity would ramp up again soon.

He spotted a new quake to the east of the area he was monitoring in Oklahoma. As he set his wine down to reach for the mouse, the room jolted. He fumbled with the glass and knocked it to the floor.

"Damn!"

The room trembled for several seconds as he jumped over to the kitchen doorway and assumed the position. Glassware crashed behind him. The canvas map fell off the wall. Suddenly, the spilled wine was a non-issue. One earthquake in Wisconsin was improbable but not impossible. Two seemed inconceivable. An aftershock probably. Or a quake on a second fault triggered by the first tremor. He would know the details soon.

He wiped up the wine and grabbed his laptop, refreshing the page for updates from the USGS.

Seven minutes later, he had an answer:

M4.3 Earthquake – 10km NE of Walden, Wisconsin. Depth: 14km

Holy moly!

An aftershock, surprisingly close to the initial quake.

The common cause of minor tremors around Lake Michigan was hydrostatic rebound. During the last glacial period, the weight of the massive ice sheets had pushed the lithosphere or crust downward. The ground was still rebounding thousands of years later. But two tremors greater than four was something different, the very definition of atypical—exactly what he was searching for.

About time.

Until now, he had pursued cold cases and had some promising leads. Jonestown was the most convincing and central to his theses.

In 1978, the Reverend Jim Jones, a self-styled prophet, established Jonestown in Guyana, South America, a community he described as a socialist paradise and sanctuary. Accusations of fraud and child abuse followed. In November of that year, Congressman Leo Ryan headed to Jonestown with a group of journalists to investigate. The visit went south and Ryan rushed his people and a few residents to an airstrip to escape. Jones' gunmen intercepted the group and killed them. Jones then commanded his followers to drink a cyanide-laced punch and they willingly complied. Soon after, the outside world discovered the rotting bodies of over nine hundred people.

Beyond the sordid statistics, Justin knew little of the story until he read a couple of obscure papers by Dr. Miguel Carneiro.

Carneiro was a Brazilian geologist who retired to Guyana in 1974 and kept a log of seismic data recorded at his home near Jonestown. In 1978, he noted an uptick in seismic activity in the area, a region that wasn't geologically active. The data showed an increasing pattern of focal earthquakes in the Jonestown area with steadily decreasing depth. The scientific community dismissed his initial paper as insignificant, then ridiculed Carneiro when he published a second paper suggesting a tie-in to the nearby Jonestown mass suicide and a general increase in lawlessness in the area.

Carneiro noted, among other things, that his well water grew warmer over a two-month period, a clear sign of heated rock or magma below. He also tracked the water temperatures in the wells of his neighbors and wells farther afield and noted a rapid drop off in warming. From this, he proposed a theory of microplumes, thin channels of magma that rose through the crust to near the surface. He also posited that changes in electrical or telluric currents associated with the phenomenon caused people in the area of the plume to act in strange and unpredictable ways.

Justin found the work fascinating. Through his studies in philosophy, he had always been intrigued by the question or problem of evil. Why did it exist? Why was suffering necessary? If there was a God and he was omnipotent, why did he do nothing to alleviate pain and misery? They were age-old questions.

When he read Doctor Carneiro's papers, a light bulb lit up.

Justin was intrigued by the second paper and the correlation with evil acts like Jonestown. What if some evils were a measurable, quantifiable value? Could flux in telluric currents cause behavioral changes in the brain the same way the phases of the moon affected people to varying degrees?

A fascinating question.

In that case, evil might simply be a negative energy flux or instability without intent, purpose, or consciousness. Not the work of the devil. Or demons. No fallen angels required. Maybe the ancients had it right in that hell lay below—but for the wrong reasons.

Over time, Justin added the mass suicide at Heaven's Gate, California, and the March 2000 mass suicide in Uganda to his list of potential related events based on patterns of anomalous seismic activity in those areas. Next, he planned to drill down on smaller events and locales that were considered unlucky or cursed like Donner Pass or Dudleytown, Connecticut. He had a long list of possibilities.

Justin also spent a year becoming an expert on telluric currents, the natural voltage that flowed upward from the core of the planet and across the surface of the earth. He further elaborated on Carneiro's ideas to formulate a series of more formal theorems based on existing theory about mantle hot spots and plumes.

Right at his front door, this was an unbelievable gift. Justin pulled up Google Earth and located Walden, a small town he remembered passing through once or twice. He zeroed in on the farm he had bookmarked. It sat right at the quake epicenter.

Too excited to sleep, he gathered up his field gear, checked the batteries, and packed it into his Land Rover. Somewhat frugal, this vehicle was the one luxury he allowed himself. The Defender X was a superb off-road vehicle and loaded with every creature comfort.

Excited or not, he needed rest. Justin popped a melatonin and laid in bed, running scenarios through his head until sleep came.

With luck, he was about to become famous.

Eleven

Natalie Schaal shook her head and flicked the TV off.

Some scientist was explaining why they suddenly had earthquakes in Wisconsin. As far as she was concerned, it was merely another sign the end times were near. She didn't trust media scientists much. They all had agendas. Crazier explanations had flooded the internet, but Natalie ignored those people too. The internet was mostly a cesspool overrun by all manner of crackpots and lunatics. Reliable news was hard to find these days.

She had better things to do anyway.

Natalie set her Ouija board on the kitchen table, a small chrome and wood-toned set she bought at a Goodwill. The room was cramped with a brown fridge and range from the last century, three feet of counter space, and no dishwasher. The walls were a bland yellow, the floor grey.

She placed four ruddy brown pieces of hematite in each corner of the room—grounding stones to keep her safe during her spiritual journeys. After lighting a candle and closing the blinds, she positioned her scrying mirror behind the board, a divination instrument that allowed her to speak to spirits. It was a family heirloom passed down from Great-Grandma O'Reilly. Almost two feet tall, the oval mirror was mounted in a dark mahogany frame with an ornate cross-stretcher between the legs of the stand. It was worth thousands of dollars, but she would never dream of selling it.

It was just after noon, often the best time of day to conduct a séance. The downstairs neighbors were at work and the neighborhood was relatively quiet. The scent of the candle—subtle notes of sage and amber—replaced the stale smells of cooking in the room.

Natalie sat and faced the Ouija board. It was one thing she had spent serious money on, almost four hundred bucks on Etsy. Otherwise, she lived paycheck to paycheck. Had no health insurance. Her apartment was furnished by Goodwill. This was the only adventure she could afford: leaving her shabby apartment to travel amongst the spirits. Observing, learning. There was so much more to the world than people realized.

The board was a solid chunk of black walnut—a wood preferred by discerning mediums for its beauty, weight, and ability to resonate with the spirit world. An instrument like a quality piano, it played beautifully when handled properly. The planchette, also walnut, was inlaid with a sliver of clear quartz. She placed it in her favored starting position on the word OUIJA at the top of the board.

There was considerable argument in the community about the dangers of using the board alone. Natalie was an experienced medium and had never encountered a problem operating solo. People also questioned the results, arguing it was too easy to influence or manipulate the conversation. Her trick? She never touched the planchette other than to close the board at the end of a reading. She placed her hands on each side of the board so her thumbs formed a triangle with her heart. When she concentrated, the planchette moved on its own, driven by whatever spirit spoke to her.

The board was a gateway, an antenna for spirits. The mirror acted like a smart phone. On their own, they were only modestly effective. Together, they created a synergy that gave her an unparalleled ability to connect with the spirit world—not her words, but those of another medium describing her unusual technique.

Concentration was the key. No distractions internal or external. It was often difficult in this apartment. Her neighbors with their loud TV and bickering were a constant issue. Complaining did little good. They settled down for a few days before they were back at it.

Today, the silence was bliss.

Positioning her hands, she relaxed. Cleared her mind. Left her heart open and felt the familiar resonance of the spirit world, a dimension separate from this world but existing in the same space. In this small town, she knew most of the spirits who called it home.

They were appreciative that she was available and willing to talk. And talk they did. Natalie listened. Everyone had a story. Some were dull, others fascinating, but most were sad. Many of these spirits had lived arduous lives filled with pain. In fact, her crappy life looked fabulous in comparison. Still, she had a wistful thought that someday, a spirit would tell her about a hidden cache of money or valuables that would change her life like a lottery win.

They had certainly upended her ideas about the spirit world. They weren't in the world willingly, but unlike the common misconception, they weren't chained to the place of their death or any particular location. No, they were free to roam the world, but most chose not to. They stayed in their hometown, in their old neighborhoods where they felt the most comfortable. They were stuck in a separate plane they didn't understand. One Natalie struggled to explain herself, though she had some theories. They could communicate with each other and were aware of the living world but couldn't interact with it in a meaningful way. They could haunt the living, but most chose not to, wanting no complications and worried about the implied dangers of an exorcism. Already trapped in limbo, where would an exorcist send them?

Ten minutes later, the planchette moved.

"Who do I have the pleasure of speaking with today?" She always opened formally, an effort to show respect. Many spirits had lived in eras of politeness and manners, traits sorely lacking in the world today.

The planchette spelled out ALICE.

She was an old friend. "How are you, Alice?"

NOT GOOD.

"Would you like to talk?" Natalie always spoke with an empathetic air. The spirits told her that and she didn't fake it. That was her nature—with them, anyway. She never used the word ghost. They preferred to be called spirits. Being a ghost implied they weren't real, that they didn't exist.

The planchette moved to YES.

Natalie gazed into the mirror. Cleared her mind and defocused, relaxing as she slipped into a meditative state.

Soon, the mirror was all she could see. The space she gazed into became three dimensional and deep, like a tunnel. A woman appeared in the distance, her grey hair up in a bun, wearing a blue ankle-length dress of rough cotton or calico that looked handmade. They had spoken many times and Alice always looked the same. Perhaps she had died in that garb but Natalie wasn't about to ask.

"Hello, Alice. What's troubling you?"

Things are strange here. People are upset. I feel on edge myself.

Alice's voice had an eerie quality to it. Thin and diffuse, it sounded like she was in a large building, a church maybe—strange since the voice was in her head. She had recorded a few sessions to confirm that.

"What has everyone riled up?"

We're getting shocked.

It was an odd description. Natalie herself sensed something off in the spirit medium today, some disturbance she hadn't experienced before. A kind of pressure.

"I didn't know that was possible. To feel, I mean."

It happens, but it's rare. Now it's happening almost all the time.

Alice sounded agitated, distraught. Unusual for her. Like most spirits, she existed in quiet acceptance of her circumstances. Usually, the only issues that arose between the spirits were boundary issues. They were protective of their little plots in the ether. Natalie wasn't sure how they could feel in the spirit world. They never talked about physical sensations and she assumed they had none, being dead and all.

"Can you describe the sensations?"

Like static electricity on the fingertips—except we feel it all over. It's very unpleasant.

"That sounds awful."

Very much so.

"Has this ever happened before?"

Once maybe, long ago. Some of the old timers remember something. They're not sure.

"Any idea what's causing it?"

We think—

With several sharp raps on the front door, the connection to Alice snapped.

Natalie shook her head and walked to the door, grumbling a curse as she opened it.

A young guy in a uniform stood there. "We're checking for gas leaks, ma'am."

"Why?"

"Because of the quakes, ma'am."

Crap.

She had to work soon.

Her conversation with Alice would have to wait.

Twelve

The afternoon was sultry.

Kat and Max lounged on the porch, taking a break. He gnawed on a chew toy while Kat sipped an ice-cold Coke Zero.

Max stopped, looked up, and growled at a rustle in the brush line west of the house. Then he jumped to his feet and barked as a man broke through the foliage and stopped. After putting a hand on Max's shoulder to quiet him, she grabbed the gun and edged toward the corner of the house.

Of average build, the guy stood about six-two with dark hair, a trimmed beard, and glasses—a nerdy professor type with an anxious look on his face. Was he waiting for an attack from the unseen dog? After a minute, the man reached back into the brush and grabbed a case. It looked like a big tackle box. Probably not a hired assassin working for Harven.

So what then?

The man, perhaps in his late thirties, ambled toward the house with the halting stride of the wary, his head swiveling side to side.

Oh great! Some idiot was about to ruin her perfect sanctuary. Kat grew mad and, for a wistful moment, considered shooting him, but she was no killer.

When he was twenty feet from the farmhouse, she stepped out, assumed a stance, and pointed the gun at his chest with a steady two-handed grip. "Stop right there!"

The guy stopped, dropped the case, and threw both arms up, locked rigid with fear. "Don't shoot! Sorry if I'm trespassing. I thought it was deserted."

"Who are you?" Her eye remained focused along the sights.

"Jus— Justin— Justin Sommerfeld."

His manner and body language weren't threatening. She lowered the Glock but kept her finger on the trigger guard, ready to react.

"What do you want?"

With a gun no longer aimed at him, he relaxed a little. "I'm a geologist."

"The tremors?"

"Yes. The tremors. The earthquakes."

"You're trespassing."

"I know. I'll leave. Sorry I disturbed you, ma'am." He spoke nervously, then turned and reached for his case.

She should send him packing but her curiosity was piqued. Talking to him was a risk, but more practical than a couple wasted hours at the library. Besides, she didn't want him leaving and talking about the crazy woman with a gun at Laskin's farm.

"What about the quakes? Tell me what you know."

His shoulders relaxed a little more. "They're an anomaly. It's an oddity—"

"I know what anomaly means," she said more sharply than she intended.

"Sorry." His nervousness returned. "Wisconsin has no active fault lines. The last notable tremor was back in 1947, near Milwaukee. Most of the seismic activity here is due to crustal rebound after the last ice age."

"What does that mean?"

"That two-mile-thick sheet of ice weighed a lot and pressed down the earth's crust. It's still bouncing back."

"That I didn't know. Tell me more." Kat relaxed her grip on the gun.

"Sometimes, there are minor disturbances if the level of Lake Michigan changes significantly. In the winter, we can get frost quakes, but they're not seismic. The recent quakes, as I said, are an anomaly. They're definitely seismic—like you'd see along a fault line. There are fault lines buried across the state, but they've been stable for a long time. Maybe millions of years. So just now, I don't really know. Nobody does."

"Do you have a theory?"

"In fact, I do."

"Care to share?"

"Microplumes," he said. "Do you know what a mantle plume is?"

"Not really."

Max moseyed over and joined them, sitting next to Kat.

"Is he friendly?"

"He is." Kat smirked. "To me."

He eyed Max nervously. "A mantle plume is a mechanism of convection or movement of material within the planet. They develop where super-heated material forms deep in the Earth and then rises through the mantle as a series of hot bubbles. Reaching the upper lithosphere—the crust—they form diapirs or hot spots. The plumes partially melt when they reach shallower depths and are associated with volcanic hot spots like Iceland or the Yellowstone supervolcano. They can also create time-progressive chains of volcanoes that extend out from the plumes. The Hawaiian Islands are the visible portion of a long string of volcanoes spawned by a large persistent plume of magma. That's the theory."

"Okay, I understand that. But you said microplumes."

"Much smaller versions, obviously. A local phenomenon that's been overlooked. So small, the magma never reaches the surface. As yet, I don't have a fully developed theory for how such small plumes can exist and remain hot and fluid. Logic suggests the magma would cool deep in the lithosphere. That microplumes wouldn't carry sufficient latent heat to rise anywhere near the surface. I think superheated magma follows natural fracture planes in the crust, or remnants of volcanic dikes and sills from ancient activity and—" He stopped, looking self-conscious. "Probably more than you needed to know."

"Something that small could cause the tremors we've had?"

"Absolutely."

"But it's not a volcano?"

"No."

"What else?" He was holding something back. Something in his tone. She was getting half the story. "What aren't you telling me?"

His manner changed. He looked excited and yet reserved or nervous. He used his hands a lot when he talked. "This is where the scientific community and I diverge. I'm a geologist but I also have a Master's in Philosophy. Over the years, I became fascinated with the big questions. Why are we here? Why is there evil in the world?"

"Religious questions. How is that related to your microplumes?"

He eyed her for a moment, weighing a decision. "I believe when these plumes rise, they bring something with them. A negative force, with negative influences, what some people would call evil. Think of the bigger picture. Volcanoes bring death and mayhem, they always have."

"That's not evil."

"But it is. Volcanoes are natural evils. I believe in those cases, it has a quantifiable, measurable value."

"I can see why the scientific community might take issue with your theory."

He tilted his head. "Now you're an expert?"

"Sorry, but it sounds far-fetched."

"Think of it like this: the sun shining down is mostly beneficial, giving life, delivering energy to power planetary flora and fauna. Why wouldn't there be some opposite force, a negative energy, destroying life, degrading the environment? In philosophy, they're considered natural evils."

Kat felt caught in a bind. She didn't want the guy here, nor did she want him running back to town and talking either. She knew this place was too good to be true.

"What do you want?"

"To set up a tent and some instruments to monitor ground movements, voltages, and temperature."

"And if I say no?"

He looked around and adopted a challenging tone. "You're squatting here."

That caught her off-guard. The guy was some kind of savant? "No, I'm not."

"Yes, you are. No vehicle. You're not using the driveway. No mailbox. The rough manner in which you've cleared the yard. Shall I go on?"

"No." With a little snark, she said, "So?"

"I don't care. Whatever your secret is, it's safe with me."

"You know, I could just shoot you. Problem solved."

"I don't think you're a killer. If you were, I'd probably be dead already."

He was rather cocky suddenly. "Why should I trust you?"

"It's a situation where we both benefit," he said. "I need to be close to the plume and this farm is near ground zero. There isn't any public land nearby and I may have trouble getting permission from the other property owners. This way, I can do my thing. In return, I don't talk about you or this property."

She observed his facial expressions. She considered herself astute and particularly good at sensing lies and dishonesty. In the drug business and in prison, she had honed the skill as a matter of life or death. "Frankly, you sound a little crazy, but I'm interested in what you're doing."

"I can pay you if that'll help persuade you."

"I don't need money."

"Then why are you squatting here?"

"None of your business."

"Understood. Do you have a name?"

"Kat. With a K. We have a deal with the following conditions. You stay away from the house and keep your vehicle out of sight somewhere off the property. I can suggest a spot for you. I'll wander out for a daily update and that'll be the extent of our interaction. Any problems? Ms. Glock and I will show you off the property."

"Fair enough."

He extended his hand. Kat took it and shook. The deal was done.

She hoped she wasn't making a mistake.

Thirteen

Kat spent the rest of the afternoon turning soil for a small garden.

There were a few fast-growing vegetables she could plant yet: radishes, lettuce, spinach, spring onions. She mulled over the decision to let Justin set up here. It might be a mistake, but she would keep her distance and tell him nothing about herself. They wouldn't be friends—though, as off relationships as she was, she found him rather attractive. An appealing mix of intelligence, natural curiosity, and boyish charm.

She ended the thought. No connections. No entanglements. Nothing. Max was already a bigger commitment than she imagined accepting. What if she had to leave suddenly? But she knew the answer. Max would go too. They were a team. Someone had abandoned him once and she wouldn't do it again. Besides, he was the ideal partner: a loyal companion and more vigilant than any alarm system.

As for Justin, it was possible the guy was certifiable.

She stopped and laughed. She had been seeing and talking to a ghost for a week and he was the nut? Perhaps she should try being less judgmental.

Still, searching for the source of evil? It was a touchy subject for Kat. She had been Catholic once. Then came the pedophile priest scandal. She walked away and hadn't thought about faith much since. People needed little help or encouragement to do evil deeds. And she couldn't talk. Her cocaine habit? Dealing drugs? Destroying her marriage? The trial judge had called her actions evil. And they were.

Kat didn't commit to a fancy rehab facility to beat her addiction. She detoxed in jail and went through the standard prison programs. With enough money, she could buy drugs on the inside but didn't. Getting clean followed by endless hours of introspection while she lay awake nights had drawn a stark picture. She had hit bottom and had only one more chance to get things right.

Losing everything to her crazy addiction had left her stunned and struggling to comprehend how her charmed life had run so far off the rails.

Kat had an unremarkable childhood. Her parents, loving but distant, seemed to favor Trevor, her brother, but that was okay. Trev was better. Her home life had been safe and pleasant. She had never dealt with abuse. While popular at school, she was a bit of a loner. She graduated high school with honors and earned a degree in Economics at UW-Madison.

As a young woman, she had imagined a carefree suburban life with friends, parties, the requisite number of kids, and a great husband. Free time to plant a garden and landscape the yard. Write poetry. Have lunches with the other moms. Josh was that wonderful man. The first few years were rough, but they were in love. They worked hard, flipped their first house, and upgraded to a bigger place in an upscale neighborhood. But something was missing. Kat couldn't figure it out. A vague malaise or ennui. Then her infertility diagnosis and the subsequent depression hurled her off a cliff into drug abuse.

When she went to prison, her parents disowned her. The message had been simple: don't call, don't write. Just go away. Their rejection stung too much to admit she missed them. Parents were supposed to be more forgiving. Trev had stayed in touch and visited her occasionally in prison. She called him once from the halfway house but told him nothing of her plans. The less he knew, the better.

She missed Josh. He was a good husband and a great guy. She wrote letters to him, begging for another chance. He never replied and took none of her calls. In the throes of deep self-loathing, she didn't blame him.

Kat shook her head. Enough recrimination.

As she pondered it, she regretted giving Justin access. She was stuck now and couldn't say no. He knew the property wasn't hers. If it became a problem, she would have to move on. A shame, really. She was growing attached to the place. It had been perfect until Justin stumbled out of the bushes.

No undoing that. Despite her misgivings, Kat cleared an area for him a hundred yards south of the house and called it a day.

★　★　★

Justin drove home, replaying his encounter with the strange woman named Kat.

Beneath her plainness, he detected an attractive woman in her late thirties. The flat, unstyled, mousy hair and the lack of makeup was a purposeful mask. Her speech was too refined for some roughneck laborer or blue-collar worker. The gun, the wariness, the whole off-the-grid business? Kat was a woman on the run, he felt sure of it. From what? It was easy to imagine, the story almost a cliché. A battered woman, a predatory husband. Kat looked tough enough to take care of herself. A fighter. A survivor. He found himself attracted to her flinty independence. Then he cut the feeling short. If that was her story, she wouldn't welcome his attention. Actually, she had been very clear on the subject.

For now, he was happy to have her cooperation. Other than the lack of an access road, the site was ideal. He could work there discretely, but now wished he had started today and taken some baseline measurements. Tomorrow was soon enough. Having a clearer picture of the site, he would repack the vehicle.

Mostly, he was excited. The two quakes could have several causes, but they fit neatly into his theory. If they continued, his papers were already out there—mostly ignored, but presented—and he could point to them as prescient research. He would be on the leading edge of the investigations that followed. And it was happening on his front doorstep.

He stopped at Lowe's, buying a tent, a canopy, and tarps to set up an outdoor work area, then stopped at the store for groceries.

Justin threw together a grilled ham and cheese for dinner, and sat in his office, going backward in time through earthquake data. He realized he may have missed earlier minor tremors. The USGS site and their email notifications only reported events greater than M2.5, but he could search their database for quakes between M1 and M2.5.

Bingo!

There it was. A pattern. Four quakes in the past month: M1.3, M1.5, M1.9, and M1.6, occurring at decreasing depths in the same location, ten kilometers northeast of Walden. Probably written off as glacial rebound—if anyone had noted them at all.

He jumped up, ecstatic. This was a legitimate case and a potential gold mine.

Justin walked into the kitchen and prepared his favorite drink. He measured reposado tequila, Gran Marnier, freshly squeezed lime juice, agave sweetener, and ice into a cocktail shaker. Shook it vigorously and poured it into a glass with a salted rim. Toasting his reflection in the kitchen window, he stepped out onto the patio to enjoy the warm summer evening.

He called out, "Alexa. Play Jimmy Buffett. 'Margaritaville'."

Fourteen

Kat made a steak and a small salad of wild greens and shared them with Max.

The evening was hot and still. They sat and watched the sun slide behind the trees in the distance.

A little tired tonight, Kat picked a smaller cabinet filled with dusty bottles of dried-up spices and sauces that had turned various strange and disgusting colors. She threw it all into a box to dump behind the house.

The kitchen looked newer and better. Half of the cabinets were cleaned and polished, the floor and countertops washed. Running water would be nice but wasn't an option. Going to the well wasn't a big deal, though she might think differently in January. She still needed a plan to heat the place.

Kat was thinking about sleep when Mrs. Laskin wafted past the front door toward the half bath. She was about to say hello when the glass in the front door shattered.

Fuck!

Had someone thrown a rock through it?

Kat grabbed the Glock and ducked into the pantry. Max barked and stood guard in the hallway. Heart pounding, the gun gripped tight in her hands, she waited.

Had they found her?

But the house stayed silent, as did Max. If someone had stepped onto the porch, he'd be growling still.

What then?

She felt certain someone had thrown a rock through the window. A strange coincidence on the same night Justin showed up. When she peeked down the hall, she saw nothing. She slid down and crawled along the hallway floor guided by dim candlelight bleeding out of the kitchen.

No one. No movement, nothing.

The setting looked wrong. There was no glass or rock on the floor. Kat slid to the door. The remaining glass fragments in the frame tilted outward. Whatever hit the glass had come from inside the house.

Mrs. Laskin? That seemed ridiculous.

Still, she needed to check the yard. She scuttled around and crawled to the back door, blowing out the candle as she went. Max nudged ahead of her and padded out, but didn't growl. They walked a loop around the house, but he reacted to nothing in the yard.

Kat returned to the porch. The glass scattered outward from the door. There was no sign of the object that broke it.

What the hell?

Was Mrs. Laskin angry about something?

What a crazy thought. It was an old house. An old window. An old door. Maybe something had settled. She didn't quite buy it, and the uncertainty unnerved her. Suddenly, Justin's plume theory didn't sound quite so crazy.

Kat went to the kitchen, grabbed the bottle of Patrón, and poured a shot.

She downed the tequila in one swallow and climbed the stairs to bed.

Sleep eluded her. A freight train of circumstance was bearing down on her. Mrs. Laskin. The sketchbook. Her nightmares. The scientist who said evil was seeping out of the ground. Nothing seemed dangerous until the window broke. It felt like a message.

When sleep came, her dreams were disturbed and restless and filled with visions of monsters. The snaky creature with the glistening teeth and little hands clawing its way to the surface; Harven with his drill and a box cutter; her ex-husband dead on a slab, his neck slit—

Kat startled awake and sat bolt upright. She hugged herself, shaking with fear, trying to erase the horrendous images from her mind. She wondered about Jason's plume and her awful nightmares. Could such a thing exist? Was it messing with her head?

As she calmed down, that thought gave her solace. If a physical explanation existed, Justin might have a solution. Did that make sense logically? But she was reluctant to talk to him about anything. Of revealing anything about herself.

Kat lit a candle and read for a bit.

Her perfect little hideout was looking decidedly flawed.

Of all people, her father's *basso* voice echoed in her head.

Careful what you wish for.

★   ★   ★

Justin awoke at six. He rolled over, grabbed his phone, and checked his email. A message from USGS indicated another earthquake overnight of M2.5 at a depth of 13km in the same location near Walden. He jumped out of bed. As his theory predicted, the quakes were occurring at increasingly shallow depths. He had been cautiously excited by the first aftershock. This second aftershock, along with the earlier string of minor quakes, was huge. While it was too early to crow publicly, he felt vindication coming.

He had published several papers outlining his theories in obscure journals that had still drawn substantial ridicule. He knew his ideas were esoteric. Well-meaning friends had warned him he was committing professional suicide by publishing his work. That was the beauty of wealth. He didn't care and was beholden to no one. He had the luxury of chasing his ideas because he didn't have to worry about the fallout. In his mind, the mentality of the geological community at large stifled innovation and original thought. He would change their minds and acceptance would follow.

Justin spent an hour packing his vehicle and arrived at the farm at nine.

He parked across the road, clambered through the brush, and approached the house cautiously until Kat stepped off the back porch without the gun. The big dog ambled beside her.

She must have sensed his hesitation and said, "He's fine, relax."

The woman was all business and quickly showed him where to set up, where to park, and strode off without a word. He detected reluctance in her manner, but he was here and only that mattered.

Justin ferried his boxes and cases through the brush as instructed and set up in the spot Kat had cleared of brush and grass. It was an excellent location, secluded, and hidden from the road.

He had seen a group from UW-Madison talking to a farmer farther up, obviously looking for a place to set up portable seismic gear. Soon, there would be more.

He pitched a small tent and a pop-up canopy, and laid a tarp down. Situated a portable power station, one of two he would exchange every other day. A work table and a deck chair. A small cooler with water, Cokes, and a sandwich for lunch. A bag with snacks and power bars.

With his encampment set up, he pounded a four-foot aluminum rod into the ground, leaving a foot exposed. Measuring eight feet due west, he pounded another rod into the ground. He created the same arrangement aligned north and south. He ran wires to all four rods and connected them to separate voltmeters, one for each directional array. With them, he could measure the telluric currents that flowed through the soil on the farm.

Connecting the voltmeters to his laptop, he could record the readings continuously. He had written his own software to tabulate and chart the data. After setting and calibrating the equipment, Justin watched data stream in. The current was flowing away from the house as he suspected. A rig on the far side of the house would provide more clarity.

The plume should act like a positive terminal, pushing strong telluric currents outward.

After observing for several hours, he set up a third array, pointing from northeast to southwest to confirm the predominant direction of flow at his position.

Justin grabbed a post hole digger from the Defender and dug down three feet, placing a portable seismic sensor in the ground for detecting movements in the earth.

With everything arranged to his liking, Justin popped the top on a Coke and sat back.

Around three, Kat wandered over for an inspection.

With a sweep of the hand, she said, "What is all this?"

Pointing to the array of poles and wires, he said, "That gear measures telluric currents. They're flowing away from the farm as I would expect."

"What are telluric currents?"

"Telluric or earth currents are electrical flows across the planet's surface, through the sea, or underground—the product of both natural causes and human activity. They travel over sizable areas and can interact with each other in complex patterns. The currents that flow between the earth's mantle and the surface are the ones I'm most interested in. I'm hoping those flows will help prove my theories about microplumes and the spontaneous occurrence of antisocial and criminal behaviors caused by natural disruptive forces arising from deep within the planet."

"Sounds complex, but interesting," Kat said.

"I think so. I'd like to put a sensor on the other side of the house, if you have no objection."

"Wait a day or two until I'm convinced this is going to work out."

"Fair enough."

"And the rest of it?"

"A seismic monitor, a weather station, and ground temperature sensors." Her gaze remained intent and curious. His work seldom had that effect on people.

"Hmm. Anything yet?"

"Not here, but a minor quake overnight."

"I didn't feel it."

"You wouldn't have."

"Okay, Doc. Have fun." With that, she walked away. He noted she had a rather nice ass.

The rest of the day was uneventful, but he started thinking about the plume and the farm. What if he was right? What if this was the one? Was Kat safe here? His theories suggested potential risks going forward. He hoped his knowledge and awareness would protect him from the effects of the plume. But what about Kat?

She could be in danger—though he doubted she would believe him.

Fifteen

A dewy morning, the air smelled fresh and crisp.

Justin arrived just as Kat finished breakfast. After directing him to the designated spot, she monitored his progress surreptitiously as she went about her day. She still felt certain it was a mistake, but he was here, and unless he caused trouble, she would leave him be. He asked about bathroom facilities and she told him the house had no running water. She had no intention of letting him inside the house.

She took a piece of heavy fabric from a curtain upstairs and nailed it over the window frame in the front door to keep bugs out. Sheltered by the porch, it should stay dry. The window business was puzzling and upsetting. Not one to dwell, she didn't like loose ends and yet, more cropped up every day. Still, if the house *was* haunted—

If?

It was no longer a question. Mrs. Laskin was real and Kat scarcely believed she accepted it as fact. But it was like Occam's Razor, where the simplest explanation was usually the correct one. Nothing else fit.

So why break the window? It frustrated Kat that they couldn't talk about it. How did one talk to a ghost? She could handle the presence though. What choice did she have? Hopefully, breaking things wouldn't become a regular occurrence.

Grabbing her bike and trailer, she ran to town to buy supplies. The day was hot but comfortable, the ride pleasant.

First stop, the library.

Researching the Tarot cards, she found little of interest. Aside from their use in divination, a full Tarot deck, either fifty-four or seventy-eight cards, was once used to play various antiquated card games. That didn't seem relevant. People played a modern version to improve memory, but there were only four cards in the house.

Kat found the descriptions of each card vague and ominous—superstitious nonsense like horoscopes. She shook her head. The cards had to be a unique family game, not a sinister message to be deciphered.

A search of the Laskin name in the newspaper database revealed only two local articles: a marriage notice for Alan and Vera Laskin in 1958, and an obituary for Mildred Laskin in 1969. On a whim, she spent another hour looking for disappearances in the area and found two. One from 1962 and one from 1985. Neither had any obvious connection to the farm. The time wasted on research hadn't been worth the trouble. The cards were a silly diversion. Did it really matter what happened to the Laskins? With no evidence of foul play, they were best forgotten.

So why was she fixated on the question?

Simple. The dreams, the odd occurrences, Mrs. Laskin's nightly appearances? It all meant something but she couldn't figure it out. It fell outside her wheelhouse. She had never believed in the paranormal. Now, she did so reluctantly and with little insight or understanding.

Kat picked up groceries at the store, then stopped at the Quik Stop for ice and beer. She worked in the kitchen all afternoon and snooped on Justin.

Later in the afternoon, when he sat and relaxed, she strode over for the first update.

He had set up a tent and a canopy to keep the sun and rain off his gear. The equipment looked impressive, technical, and geeky. After talking to him, his studies sounded even more arcane and far-fetched. The seismic stuff was obvious. But she knew nothing of telluric currents and didn't understand the explanation. She missed having a computer, having the ability to search any subject on a whim. And electricity, running water, actual bedding—

Ironic thought. She had made her bed. Now she had to live with it.

Justin left without a word or nod. For dinner, she grilled a small piece of salmon and sat on the porch.

So far, so good—

Max growled and jumped up, peering across the yard. Kat saw nothing but instinctively grabbed the Glock. He leapt and bolted into the long grass. She heard a bark and a snarl and the grass shook vigorously as some hidden drama played out. Kat crouched, ready to fire in a double-handed grip, fearing the worst.

A moment later, Max emerged with a dead creature in his mouth. He trotted over and dropped it at her feet. A woodchuck, a dangerous animal in a fight. Max had handled it like a pro, answering one question. In a scuffle, he was a brawler.

Only now, she needed to have him vaccinated against rabies. Kat hoped cash would dissuade the vet from asking too many questions about the dog.

After dark, they moved indoors.

Kat had finished the exterior surfaces in the kitchen. Every inch of the cabinets, flooring, and walls once coated with layers of dust and grime, dead bugs, and mouse droppings had been scrubbed with an ammonia solution. Except for the lack of running water and power, the room looked comfortable and inviting.

The last drawer on the west end of the counter was stuck. Kat grabbed a claw hammer and pried it open by the handle, protecting the cabinet surface with a block of wood.

She blinked at the mess for a moment before realizing she had uncovered their junk drawer. It was full of loose paperwork and clutter: canceled checks, bills, a checkbook, and some photos, plus various odd tools, batteries, and screws.

Holy crap! Pay dirt.

Kat pulled the drawer out and dumped the contents on the counter, eyeing it like a treasure trove. Finally! Something tangible on the former owners. She set two candles nearby and dug in.

The checkbook belonged to Alan and Vera Laskin, presumably the couple who had married in 1958. The most recent check had been written in 1979. There was the standard assortment of bills: electric company, oil company, car insurance. Some farm bills for feed, seed, and various chemicals. The title for a 1976 Ford F-150 pickup.

On the surface, an average American family.

She found a dozen photos—kids mostly. In one, a good-looking young male and a preteen boy stood in front of the house. The boy was probably Michael Laskin. He looked so normal, so nice. His eyes did not reflect the darkness hidden in the sketchbook. The thought sent a shiver through her.

There were letters from Mildred Laskin, with a return address in Madison. Alan's mother? A few letters from someone at Arizona State University signed Adam. Adam Laskin was the name of the person paying the taxes. Was he the twenty-year-old in the photo?

Maybe if she called him—

And said what?

Hi! I'm squatting on your property. Why did your family just up and leave?

Not an option.

The rest was mundane. Receipts. Coupons for some weird food items she had never heard of: Danka toaster snacks and Mug-O-Lunch. Some fifteen cent stamps. But no official documents. No passports, licenses, or Social Security cards. No Tarot cards. When she looked again, she realized what was missing. There were no school items. No notices, schedules, report cards, or school pics. The Laskins had children, that was obvious. Had they been homeschooled? If so, how had Adam gotten into Arizona State without a high school diploma?

It occurred to her the house was weird in that respect. There were no family photos or personalized items anywhere. It made no sense. While it was nice to put names and faces to the people who had lived here, the drawer shed no actual light on them and only created more mysteries.

The truck was gone, yet they hadn't taken their checkbook or their clothes.

Why?

Kat shook her head, downed a shot of tequila, grabbed the candle, and walked upstairs, Max at her side.

Her anxiety rose at bedtime. Kat was exhausted and needed sleep, but some nights, the monsters in her head had other ideas. What would she dream of tonight? The snaky beast with the T-Rex hands? Harven and his drill? Or her dead ex on a slab—and where had that horror show come from?

Instead, she dreamt of Justin.

Justin naked in her bed. The two of them engaged in wild sex. He was indefatigable and creative, more so than her memories of sex with Josh. Not a nightmare, but an unexpected and welcome respite.

She awoke in a dark room and discovered she had pulled her panties off and tossed them on the floor.

Apparently, she had some unresolved sexual energy.

Or was that the house too?

Sixteen

A week passed.

Kat tended to her yard and garden and finished deep cleaning the half bath and dining room.

After dark, Kat spent most of her time in the kitchen. She pulled the best armchair from the living room, beat the dust out of it, and washed the fabric with hot water and upholstery cleaner. Placed with a small side table where the fridge once sat, she could sit and read until bedtime. The rest of the furniture really needed steam cleaning. She preferred the kitchen to the living room anyway.

Mrs. Laskin failed to appear for a few nights until, on a whim, Kat grabbed a framed mirror from upstairs and attached it to the front door. That night, she returned, gliding toward the half bath while Kat was adding finishing touches to the kitchen. Kat noted the time of her arrival. After a few days, it was clear Mrs. Laskin haunted on a schedule, arriving at 9:47 each night. Odd. And inexplicable.

To Kat's relief, she had broken nothing since the window. Still, she wondered if Mrs. Laskin had been trying to tell her something.

Her nightmares continued in vivid, wretched detail. Maybe it was her Catholic upbringing, but Kat felt she deserved them as punishment for her sins. Even if the plume was responsible—which seemed absurd—she was stuck here. She had violated her parole and imagined Harven conducting a vigorous manhunt for her this very minute.

Max kept her company and guarded her, always parking himself somewhere in her line of sight. She wondered if he sensed her hyper-vigilance. The visit to the vet was uneventful. A small office, they were happy to take cash and didn't question the bogus address she gave them to record the vaccine.

As promised, Justin stayed in his encampment. The daily updates were mundane. Apparently, there had been a steady stream of minor quakes, but nothing Kat actually felt. All day he sat there, watching his gear, reading a book, and taking naps. How was he not bored out of his mind?

To each their own, I guess.

Each time she biked to town, she saw more people gathering in the area. Mostly college kids with monitoring stations, but a few amateurs too. Yesterday, she saw a news crew parked on the side of the road.

Noting the steady uptick in traffic, Justin presented her with a handful of **No Trespassing** signs and a stapler when she walked over for an update.

"Here. Put these up around the property. Might keep the rabble out."

It was a good idea. Why hadn't she thought of it?

"I hope so. I saw a TV truck yesterday."

Justin said, "I've seen speculation about the 'big one' coming from the lunatic fringe and the End Times people."

"Same thing, aren't they?"

He shrugged. "More or less."

She had tacked the signs up and, so far, no one had ventured onto the property.

Today, Kat sat on the porch reading a book. Her right knee had ached for the last two days. Either she had pushed herself too hard or age was catching up with her. She popped three Advil and opted to take a day off. Max snoozed nearby.

She let herself doze. Justin appeared to be doing the same.

Though loathe to admit it, she enjoyed having a man around, even at a distance. Actually, from afar seemed best.

★   ★   ★

Justin napped beneath the canopy. The sounds of birds and the breeze in the trees lulled him into periods of light sleep.

He should be bored, but he wasn't. The results wouldn't be spectacular until they were. There had been a steady stream of low-level quake activity, all minor but highly unusual. The activity drew the interest of the scientific community at large, and more groups were showing up with sensing equipment. Thank God he found the farm first. He was invisible from the road and could work on his research without speculation or ridicule.

After confirming the farm was ground zero for the seismic activity, he moved the telluric current-sensing gear with Kat's permission, placing one at each corner of the property. The results were unequivocal. The surface and near-surface voltage flowed away from the property as expected. He then placed a sensor at his house, thirty miles away. It showed the same directional pattern.

He explored most of the property while moving the sensors. Populated with deer, a fox, ducks, and a few pheasants, it had great potential as a hunting ground. The deer were a minor interest—he preferred stalking elk in Colorado, but he loved hunting and eating pheasant. Hopefully, by October, when the season arrived, he would be in her good graces and Kat would let him hunt on the farm.

On the day he established camp, he buried a thermal sensor in the ground nearby, one in a clearing in the woods where he parked, and one at his house as a control. Throughout the summer, the ground would warm but do so evenly in areas of similar sunlight, soil, and vegetation. The sensors in the woods and his house had gone up a degree. Here, the sensor had risen five degrees—more physical evidence to support his theories.

During his morning siesta, Justin decided to buy Kat a gift to repay her for the access to the property. He drove to town for lunch, grabbed a burger at Wendy's, and stopped at the hardware store. Perusing the grills, he bought a two-element unit with a side burner and added two propane tanks to the order. Only the floor model remained, and he was thrilled to nab a fully assembled unit. Kat had mentioned wanting a gas grill after he noted her charcoal grill on the wooden porch was a fire danger.

He parked and hauled the gear to his camp and waited, monitoring the equipment until she went inside. He huffed the grill and a propane tank over to the house and set them on the porch. She walked out the door and stopped short as he tightened the propane connection.

"What's that?"

"I believe it's called a gas grill."

"I don't want to borrow your stuff."

"It's not mine. It's yours. A gift for putting up with me."

She looked sideways across the yard, lost for words, or choosing them carefully. Finally, she said, "That's very nice of you. I have a steak and some potatoes. Would you care to stay and eat dinner with us later?"

He gave her a look of surprise. Some invisible boundary had been crossed. "I'd love to."

"Be here at six and bring a chair."

He nodded, smart enough to leave it at that.

Seventeen

Kat was prepping the steak when Justin knocked.

The evening was perfect. Warm but not too humid, a light breeze wafting rural smells across the porch: loam, fresh-cut hay, a hint of decay. Somewhere in the distance, a tractor worked the land.

Potatoes were baking on the grill. It thrilled Kat to simply turn a knob and flick a switch. She remained ambivalent about the gift but couldn't deny it was perfect and would make life easier. She also felt ambivalent about inviting Justin to dinner, but it was a reasonable response to his thoughtful, if unnecessary, gift.

He popped his head in and looked suitably impressed by the kitchen. "Wow! Very nice."

She raised a hand to stop him. "Have a seat on the porch. I'll be right there. Beer?"

"Please."

She had set up outside, using the breakfast table from the kitchen. She had no intention of giving him a house tour—or a glimpse into her life.

After putting the steak on the grill, she grabbed two beers, handed a bottle to Justin, and sat.

She lifted her bottle in a toast. "Thank you. It wasn't necessary, but I appreciate it."

"You're welcome. And thank you." He tipped his bottle in return. "You've given me a front-row seat here."

"Do you have a life outside of that?" She pointed to the encampment. "A wife? Kids?"

"No, and no."

"What do you do for fun?"

"I hunt in the fall. Snowmobile in the winter. I fish some. That's about it." He eyed her. "And you?"

"This is it. Living a quiet, contemplative life."

She got up and pulled the steak and potatoes, regretting asking a personal question and leaving herself open to one in return. She let the steak rest, split the potatoes, then sliced the meat across the grain and carried it out on a platter.

Their dinner began as a quiet affair with basic small talk about the weather and such. As they relaxed, the conversation shifted to his research.

"So, are you any closer to proving your theories?"

"The microplumes, yes. Too early on the rest of it."

"How did a study of microplumes lead to a search for evil?"

"It's the other way around. I became interested in the problem of evil first. Then I read two obscure geology papers combining the two that became the basis for my theories."

"The problem of evil? Evil is bad. What's the question?" She knew a little about the subject but considered it an abstract topic only explored in college and theology classes.

"Not that simple. Not everyone agrees on a definition of evil. Some people deny it exists at all."

"They do? Who?"

"Christian Scientists for one. They believe that evil is an illusion."

"That's ridiculous."

"I agree. It's an impossible position to defend." He stabbed a piece of beef, ate it, then looked up and said, "Do you believe in God?"

"I guess. You don't?"

"Let's say I have a troubled relationship with him. If he's all powerful, why doesn't he alleviate the suffering in the world?"

"Suffering's a part of life. A consequence of free will—something like that." Kat said offhandedly, "I took some philosophy in college."

"Your degree?"

"Economics."

Justin gave her a bemused look suggesting her degree didn't count. It was probably true. "Okay. But if people suffer because of free will, what about animals?"

"What do you mean?"

"Suffering in the absence of free will." He framed an imaginary stage with his hands. "Consider this. A doe is caught in a forest fire and horribly burned. It lays in terrible pain for days until it dies. What purpose does that serve? Why does God allow that suffering?"

The image was disturbing. She glanced at Max and couldn't imagine him suffering through something like that. "I don't know. That's awful, but how is that evil?"

"A forest fire is a natural evil."

"Not a great subject over dinner. Can we stick to your plume theory?"

"Right. Sorry."

She raised a fork and pointed it at him. "If electrical currents near the plumes are the cause, then what about the Hawaiian Islands? Why aren't they hot beds of crime? How about all the other places near active volcanoes?"

"One, people in the vicinity get used to it. Two, the currents aren't the problem, it's the changes in the currents. I believe strong changes in direction and intensity affects people in various ways. During major eruptions, outbreaks of looting and other forms of lawlessness often occur."

"Are you trying to find an excuse for evil? To give people an out when they do bad things?"

"Not at all. I'm just trying to understand it."

"Most of us are capable of evil under the right circumstances."

"A proven fact."

"I think that's enough for one night." She reveled in the discussion but worried about growing too comfortable with him.

"Indeed. Thank you for the stimulating conversation."

He talked with passion, but Kat wondered if he wasn't a little nuts too. The line between genius and insanity was thin and his theories sounded so implausible.

But aside from that, he was circumspect, asking no questions about her family or personal history. After dinner, he insisted on washing the dishes. She let him in, enjoying the company. He didn't comment, kept his eyes on the task, and said goodnight without lingering. He was considerate and empathetic—the kind of man women sought but seldom found.

As he disappeared into the trees, Kat felt she had just been on a date.

The feeling was magnified later that night by the wild sex they had in her dreams. When she awoke late that night, her bedroll was bunched up and she was hugging it like a lover. Max stood and stared at her with a look of concern.

Like she was losing it.

Was she?

Wanting a man in her life wasn't crazy, but it wasn't an option either. He would never accept her past. No man would, not one worth dating anyway. That was the reality and there was no escape from the guilt engendered by her Catholic upbringing.

She deserved to be alone.

Eighteen

Natalie finally had a day off.

Her job at the Quik Stop was tedious and barely paid a living wage. She often worked fifty hours a week to make ends meet. She should clean, but her shabby apartment wasn't that dirty and she never entertained.

The neighbors had been unusually loud the past few days. When she finally complained, they told her to fuck off. She didn't care for that word. After she called the manager, they settled down, but for how long? She understood why people occasionally freaked out and killed their neighbors.

She wished she could move but didn't have the money. She could barely afford this dump. But unlike some people who struggled with poverty and loneliness, Natalie rarely drank and never took drugs. They interfered with her abilities as a medium, the only useful skill her mother had given her—though, more likely, it came from her grandmother, who had the gift and knew how to use it. Until the day she died, Natalie would never understand how that sweet, gracious woman spawned the grumpy, sarcastic bitch her mother had become. She and Mom rarely spoke now. Her mother groused about her own life and belittled Natalie's. Her crummy apartment. Her divorce. Her lack of children. If she gained weight, she was fat. If she lost weight, she was anorexic. Right now, she was fat. Oh well, she had given up caring.

Most of all, she disparaged the time Natalie "wasted" talking to the mirror.

You'll never made a buck talking to spirits, Natalie.

Her mother was wrong. She could hang a shingle out and make money. She had genuine talent, a gift, but she didn't want to make money from it. A purist, she had no intention of exploiting the spirits she met. Their circumstances were difficult enough. She preferred the spirit world to the real world and didn't want to risk harming her relationship with them.

She sometimes wondered how much like her mother she really was. Maybe that was why Bob left. She had strived to be better—to be the polar opposite of her mother. Maybe it wasn't possible to escape bad parenting.

Natalie shook her head to clear it and push the negativity away. Such thoughts weren't conducive to making spiritual connections.

Natalie laid the walnut Ouija board on the kitchen table, then placed a grounding stone in each corner of the room. Over each, she intoned the words *Salvum Iter,* Latin for safe journey. Lit a candle and closed the blinds. Slid her scrying mirror into place behind the board, then sat, clearing her mind. Some days, it was easy. On others, like today, she struggled. She was dying to know how Alice was doing and more about the shocks. She'd never heard of anything like it. Ironically, her excitement prevented her from achieving the proper mindset. With a deep breathing exercise, she lowered her heart rate and slid into a light trance.

She never knew who was going to show up. Sometimes she made no connection; sometimes several spirits would clamor for attention—though she could only converse with one during each session. It came down to who was available and willing.

Ten minutes later, the planchette moved.

"Who do I have the pleasure of speaking with today?"

ALICE.

Perfect. She could finish their conversation from the other day.

"Would you like to talk, Alice?"

The planchette slid to YES.

Natalie gazed into the mirror and cleared her mind. She worked a ritual. She couldn't just sit down and start a conversation with a spirit. They established a connection through the Ouija board and conversed through the mirror. Only then could she hear them speak.

She unfocused her eyes, relaxing as she slipped into a meditative state. Soon, the mirror was all she could see as she gazed into the three-dimensional space within. Alice appeared in her usual form: hair in a bun, wearing the blue ankle-length dress. Again, she sensed some disturbance in the ether, an odd sensation like the last time she talked with Alice.

"Hello, Alice. Are you still having trouble with shocks?"

Yes. If anything, they're worse.

Her voice sounded like she was lost in a warehouse. Crackly too, like an old AM radio.

"Any idea what's causing them?"

No, but it feels stronger on the northeast corner of town. Lester McElroy thinks it's coming from Laskin's farm.

"I don't know where that is."

It's about seven or eight miles out of town, off Kelly Road. Mildred Laskin resides there.

"Have you talked to her?"

I've never met her. I won't leave town. You know that.

"What about Lester? Why does he suspect the farm?"

He never liked Mildred. They never got along. He doesn't trust her.

Figures. Lester McElroy was a curmudgeon who died penniless after being cheated out of his money in a scam. He didn't trust anyone. It seemed odd to Natalie that such petty emotions carried through to the afterlife.

"Why?"

Because she's a woman. Lester doesn't like women much.

"Is he gay?"

That old grouch is never happy. You know that.

"I mean, does he prefer men?"

Good Lord, no. What a queer thing to say.

Natalie shook her head in frustration and changed tack. She sometimes forgot how little the spirits knew about the modern world. "Does Lester have proof?"

No.

"What can I do, Alice?"

If you can figure out where it's coming from, maybe you could do something about it?

"I don't know, but I can try."

I'm tired. I'm going now. Please help us.

"I will. Goodbye, Alice. We'll talk soon."

Natalie sat for a moment, feeling the sensation on the spirit level even after Alice left. It was stronger today, almost like a breeze. When she turned her head, she sensed directionality, from northeast to southwest. As she closed the connection, she felt a little shimmer, similar to a shock.

Weird.

For a moment, she wondered if she could talk to Mildred Laskin from here. She never summoned people by name and had never tried. It was a matter of respect, about not invading their space. Besides, she didn't know where to start.

Natalie then thought about the disturbance arising or emanating from the northeast. What was it? A flow or disturbance in the ether? Was that what they felt? Where was it coming from?

She put little credence in Lester's hunch, but locating the farm might point her in the right direction. If she could find it. She had an old Walden phone book but found no Laskins listed. She went into the living room and grabbed her ancient Dell Inspiron. It weighed almost ten pounds and took several minutes to start up, but it served its purpose. To read the news on the BBC website. She also talked with her paranormal friends and bought stuff on eBay and Etsy, like her Ouija board.

A statewide search revealed dozens of Laskins, but none within thirty miles of Walden. Maybe it hadn't been called Laskin's farm in years. Alice mentioned Kelly Road, but it was fifteen miles long and there were houses and farms all along it. Not much help.

She then went to her group on a private message board and posted a description of the situation. Made up of a diverse collection of mediums, psychics, and clairvoyants, the board was a great place to exchange ideas, experiences, and to post questions.

One person replied and suggested that earth currents or stray voltage in the soil might be responsible. A few others then agreed, but no one had personal experience with it. The mention of voltage piqued her interest. But when she googled *earth currents*, she didn't really understand the subject.

Natalie thought about the earthquake the other day. Didn't it happen somewhere out there? Were they related? Could that be the source of the stray voltage?

Off tomorrow, she was going to investigate and see if she could figure it out.

She closed the board and set the mirror inside the wooden carrying case her grandfather had built for it years ago. A rectangular plywood box, the lid had a metal handle and four clasps to secure the carrier shut.

A road trip.

A little one anyway. It might be fun.

★   ★   ★

After breakfast, Natalie loaded her stuff into an older Honda Civic. With only a vague sense of what she hoped to accomplish, she drove up Kelly Road, planning to wander around aimlessly, hoping to locate the source of the disturbance causing the shocks. On the surface, it sounded illogical, desperate even, but she had no better ideas.

Two miles out of town, she pulled onto the shoulder and rolled down the windows because it was hot and her AC had died. She sat and left herself open to any sensations in the ether.

Nothing.

She set up the board and mirror on the passenger seat even though it was less than ideal. It was harder to concentrate in the car, but she managed. After ten minutes, the planchette moved slightly, though oddly, she felt no presence. For a minute, the planchette drifted slowly northeast until it fell off the board.

Whoa! If that wasn't a sign…

Natalie drove another two miles and pulled over. Now she felt a faint sensation without the board or the mirror—a strange, ethereal breeze. Not an actual wind but something felt only in her head. On Kelly Road, it blew from the northeast to southwest. She had never experienced anything like it.

Fascinating.

She turned to the east and drove for several miles. The flow shifted in direction, blowing from the northwest, suggesting that it emanated from a single point. Her excitement rose. If this panned out, she would have one heck of a story for the group.

After another hour of driving, she honed in on one location by triangulating the sensation in her head, a spot just off Kelly Road. She saw nothing of interest when she stopped. No houses, no outbuildings, no farm, just a dense wall of trees and brush. She wasn't the outdoorsy type and the idea of stumbling around in the woods wasn't appealing. But she was here and wearing old clothing and walking shoes. If she found the source, it would be worth the inconvenience.

Would it? What about bugs? And snakes?

Ugh.

Natalie stared at her reflection in the rearview mirror and said, "Suck it up and get out there!"

She took a deep breath and stepped out of the car. Other than stray bird calls and a light breeze in the tree branches, it was quiet. She walked through the ditch, eyed the trees one last time, and plunged into the brush at the edge of the woods.

The sensation grew stronger.

She was in the right place.

Nineteen

Another hot day.

Kat spent the morning weeding her garden and tending to the yard. Enlarging it, pruning the trees she wanted to keep, cutting down the junk, and hauling the debris to her trash dump. She thought about her dinner with Justin and the hypothetical injured doe in the forest. It had been years since she engaged in a deep, meaningful conversation, and she had never mused about the nature of evil. Now she couldn't stop.

She kept an eye on Justin as well.

Beneath his canopy, he appeared to be lazing and monitoring his various gadgets. Occasionally, he stole a glance at Kat, trying to be discreet but failing. She sensed he liked her. She liked him too, and thought he was good looking, sexy even. Or was she less discerning now?

Kat thought little about sex. It wasn't an option, so why dwell on it? Some women were bisexual, but she wasn't wired that way and avoided the lesbians who flirted with her in prison. She decided she didn't miss it. Maybe she was lying to herself. Her sex dream last night had been vivid, and Justin was fabulous in bed. She snickered. Of course he was. It was a dream! But it had also been a lovely distraction from the nightmares.

Her and Justin?

She shook her head. No need for that complication.

Max jumped up, walked to the edge of the porch, and growled.

"What is it, buddy?"

She reflexively looked for the Glock.

Damn!

She had left it in the kitchen. She was getting lax with Justin around. It was a bad idea to forget who she was. Or why she was hiding here.

The foliage rustled along the brush line. Then a frumpy, dark-haired woman parted two branches and stepped out, looking lost before her gaze settled on the house. Justin spotted her and looked at Kat with a questioning expression and a shrug.

Kat muttered, "Jesus Christ."

She leapt off the porch with Max at her side. She didn't need a gun. The silly bitch was probably lost.

With a pointed finger, Kat yelled, "This is private property, ma'am. You need to leave."

The woman raised her hands in a sign of submission. "I know. I'm sorry. I'll leave. Can I just ask you one question?"

Kat knew the woman from somewhere. "You work at the Quik Stop, right?"

"Yeah. You're the bike lady."

Shit! She had been noticed in town and now this woman knew where she lived. "What's your question?"

"Have you noticed anything odd here in the past week or two?"

Oh no. Kat feared where this was leading.

"Odd? Like what?"

"Disturbances." The woman eyed Kat warily. "Hard to explain. I'm a psychic medium—if you believe in that sort of thing."

"What kind of disturbances?"

"I speak with a group of spirits on a regular basis. They say there's a problem here. I can feel it myself."

Kat heard Justin amble up. This woman appearing based on a feeling was disturbing. First Justin, now a medium? What had she stumbled into here?

Justin spoke. "What did they tell you exactly?"

"They've been getting shocks. They think they're coming from somewhere in this area."

"Electric shocks?"

"That's what they say."

"That's ridiculous," Kat said, alarmed and frustrated, wanting to end the conversation and send the woman on her way. What had drawn her here? Justin's plume? Or Mrs. Laskin? Could someone sense a ghost from a distance? A month ago, she hadn't believed in them. Now she had a medium knocking at her door.

"No, it makes sense," Justin said, eyes skyward, looking thoughtful while he spoke. "People have speculated that ghosts are an electromagnetic phenomenon. If so, a strong shift in telluric currents would affect them as well. The shocks make sense. I think it's fascinating."

The woman looked at Justin and said, "I didn't understand a word of that. And they don't like being called ghosts—" She paused and frowned. "Did you say telluric currents? Is that like earth currents?"

"Yes. Why?"

"Those currents might be the problem—"

"No matter. You're leaving," Kat said, hands on hips. She saw the situation spiraling out of control. The earthquakes seemed to be drawing the wackos out of the woodwork. After finding the perfect hideaway, crazies would overrun the farm and force her to move. She should have refused Justin from the start—though it seemed people were being drawn to the farm anyway. Maybe she was overreacting. How many mediums could there be around here?

Justin said, "Wait. She might be the perfect addition to what I'm doing."

The woman looked to Justin, evidently sensing an ally. "So you have noticed something?"

"I don't want people hanging around," Kat snapped in frustration, seeing her sanctuary crumbling before her eyes.

The woman turned to Kat and said, "I'll do whatever you ask. I'll set up in the woods—"

"No. You should leave."

The woman continued as if Kat hadn't spoken. "You won't even know I'm here. I'm only interested in the spirit world. I want to find out what's going on. Those earthquakes, the sudden upset in the spirit community? Something's happening, I can feel it."

Justin did a little pleading routine with his hands. "Kat, this woman might be the missing link to understanding the plume fully. You want to know too. I know you do."

She did. Kat saw little upside to fighting it. Either way, another person knew she was here. If she kicked the woman out, she faced the same risks she had with Justin. If the woman left feeling angry, she was more likely to talk about the crazy bike lady at Laskin's farm. It felt like a lose-lose situation. She just might have to plan to move on. This house was too perfect from the start. Nothing in her life would work out. She deserved no happiness and the universe was making sure she remembered the score.

Still, she couldn't give in too easily either.

"You say you won't talk about this place? What assurances do I have? You'll tell your husband."

"Don't have one."

"Your friends then."

"Don't have any."

"Not even at work?"

"Not really."

"Your mother."

"We haven't spoken in months. We don't get along." The woman shifted her stance. Trying to look humble? Trustworthy? "I just want to talk to the spirits. I'll do whatever you ask."

Kat recognized in this woman a kindred spirit, another loner. Maybe this could work out.

"Okay, but I have rules."

Twenty

The following day, Justin looked toward the house when Natalie arrived.

Kat paced on the porch, arms crossed, and watched them with a suspicious gaze. He felt certain she believed him responsible for Natalie's appearance. It looked far too convenient.

The morning grass was dewy. Overhead, a hawk looped about, looking for breakfast. Another day in paradise.

To humor Kat and keep the woman away from the house, Justin brought a second table for Natalie to use. Her role as a medium was fascinating. He considered himself a skeptic, though he had never thought much about the supernatural. His theory of evil didn't require a paranormal element. It was about energy levels, positive and negative, and the related energy flows. No monsters, ghosts, or demons need apply. But he didn't dismiss them either. Even though he'd never had an experience with the paranormal, he couldn't rule out the possibility of its existence. Still, he was a scientist and found scant rigorous evidence to support the claims of a supernatural world.

Her set-up looked interesting and ridiculous in the same breath. She set an old wooden Ouija board and an antique mirror on the table and placed brown stones at each corner of the tarp while she muttered something in Latin.

"These okay here?" she asked.

"Yes. Do what you have to do."

A mirror and a Ouija board? Maybe Kat was right. This might be a silly distraction.

But many considered his ideas crazy too. He needed to remain open-minded. If ghosts existed and this woman talked to them, they could describe problems unique to their world—like the electric shocks—and reveal novel aspects about telluric currents.

But what was normal for ghosts? A fascinating angle in itself.

Natalie's appearance was almost too good to be true. Assuming his theories were true, wouldn't people with special skills like mediums and psychics be drawn to the plume because they sensed the changes in energy? Her presence seemed to confirm that. He was amazed that Natalie sensed the current in her head. Was it further proof of his theories? Or evidence he was sliding off the deep end into the realm of pseudoscience? Was there a way to test her ability? Would anyone believe the results? Being on the vanguard of scientific discovery was often a lonely place.

"I need quiet while I work."

"You won't hear a word from me."

Justin watched his gear silently, then stood and walked around the field to stretch his legs. His thoughts drifted to the dinner with Kat the other night, as they had the day before. She was tough, attractive, intelligent, curious, and unlike any woman he had met before. Intrigued but frustrated, he saw no path to a relationship with her. Her defenses were impenetrable. Maybe in time she would open up.

He slipped into his tent to read, and maybe nap for a bit, but mostly to eavesdrop on the psychic lady.

For the longest time, she was silent.

He peeked. The woman was just sitting there, staring into a mirror. If she announced afterward that she had presided over some big ghostly conclave, he would have to call bullshit. If it all happened in her head, it was patently unreliable. Unscientific. Not amenable to analysis.

Then he heard a faint sliding sound. The Ouija board? But she wasn't touching the planchette. How did that work?

Still unreliable. As he lay back down, he heard her speak.

"Who do I have the pleasure of speaking with today?"

After a flurry of scratching sounds, Natalie hissed, "There's no need for that kind of language!"

Justin peeked out just as Natalie slammed the board shut, looking primed to explode.

"Want to talk about it?" Justin asked.

"Not really."

"I thought the idea was to work together."

"Not much to report." Natalie stared ahead and wouldn't make eye contact. "She wouldn't talk to me."

"The comment about language?"

Natalie turned. "She told me to eff off. Spelled it right out on the board."

"Game over?"

"No, I'll try again tomorrow. I'll come up with a strategy."

Justin crawled out of the tent and sat next to her. "How does this work?"

Natalie looked at him with an indeterminate expression between frustration and anger. "Are you going to mock me?"

Justin was surprised by the question but realized she had probably been ridiculed for her beliefs. He knew how that felt. "No, not at all."

Her response was terse. "The board is the portal. The scrying mirror and my powers as a medium are the method of communication."

"You talk and they move the planchette?"

"Just to start. Then we speak through the mirror."

Hmm. He wasn't convinced. Still nothing he could measure.

"You said they don't like to be called ghosts. Why?"

"They feel more real as spirits." Evidently to reciprocate interest, she pointed and said, "How does your stuff work?"

"I'm monitoring several things. The seismograph registers earth-quakes. This array measures electric current flows in the ground, and this one records soil temperatures." He detected zero curiosity, her expression blank.

"Where'd you get all the gear? You work for a university or some-thing?"

"No. I work independently and buy my equipment."

"What'd that all cost then?"

"About thirty grand."

"What?" Natalie did an exaggerated, wide-eyed startle. "Rich boy, huh?"

"Yep." He nodded and shrugged. "Sorry."

"Figures. You look like a dandy."

"What?"

"Your hands are soft. You don't do much physical labor and your clothing is expensive. Your casual bumming-around clothes are all designer labels. You're wearing about a thousand dollars in grubby gear." She stood and twirled. "Goodwill. Eight bucks. The shoes were three. Jesus, people like you have no clue."

"People like me? What does that even mean? I'm not allowed to wear nice clothes? They happen to be comfortable."

"Yeah, yeah. You could feed a family for a month with what that getup cost," she said derisively.

Was she trying to provoke him? A snarky sense of humor? An effect of the plume? He couldn't tell, but he was growing angry. "What are you? A member of the people's proletariat? I won't apologize for wearing nice stuff."

"I wouldn't expect you to. Rich white guy? Figures."

"Fuck you."

"No thanks."

What a nasty woman. He seldom encountered difficult people and had little experience in dealing with them. She seemed more angry with humanity than with him personally. A deflection? Was she angry her attempts to communicate had failed? No matter. They needed to work together.

"We don't have to like each other to work together."

"Good thing, huh?"

"I'd say."

Casually, she said, "So what's with the lady of the house?"

"Now you want to gossip?"

She rolled her eyes. "Whatever. See you tomorrow."

With that, she grabbed her stuff and stomped off.

Justin stared after her, mouth gaping. What was her problem?

Had the plume lit that fuse?

Twenty-One

Emily Novak flipped the eggs, careful not to break the yolks.

Her husband, Matt, demanded over-easy perfection. She really needed new pans and a spatula. He wouldn't hear of it even though they could afford it. They had a nice house on a big lot out of town on Kelly Road. Her range and the kitchen itself were state-of-the art. They had money.

In the past few days, he had been unusually grumpy. When he got that way, he yelled and pushed her around and called her vile names. Once, he had been her Prince Charming. Then he lost two fingers in a work mishap. The hand still didn't work right. He remained on restricted duty two years later. They had medical bills and the insurance company fought them at every turn.

Matt drank and gambled to cope. He felt depressed and quit taking care of the house and yard. In truth, he wasn't disabled, he was lazy. And he treated her like crap. Like everything was her fault. So she cut the lawn, unclogged the drains, fixed the stuff that broke, and changed the furnace filter.

She should just leave.

Sigh.

Emily had been thinking that for a year. One of these days, he would hurt her bad. She just knew it.

But what could she do? Where would she go? The one time she threatened to leave, Matt promised to burn the house down and blow every last buck at a casino before she got a dime.

She had no skills, no degree, no serious job experience—

God, these stupid thoughts recycled every morning while Matt bitched at her, then went to work. She cleaned the house, did the yard work, and drank chardonnay all afternoon. She often complained of a migraine and went to bed early. The kids had grown up and moved away. Her life had purpose when they were here, but now her life was pathetic. She was pathetic.

Maybe today she would break the cycle. Pack a suitcase, steal money from their account. Just leave. Matt probably wouldn't even miss her.

Ha!

Who was she kidding? Who would cook his meals and do the laundry and clean the house and lay in bed like a corpse when he demanded sex?

He barked, "Hey, dumbass, those eggs done yet? I'm gonna be late."

Oh shit. She'd been daydreaming. They were burning. Matt would be furious.

A strange feeling possessed her.

Not today.

She opened the junk drawer, shuffled around, and found the hammer. Looked at it. Held it in her hand. It had a good heft and she knew how to use it. Lord knew he never did.

Emily eyed the back of his big, fat head. Vacillated.

A little voice in her head spoke.

Do it!

With a swift, powerful swing, Emily swiveled and buried the rusty hammer head in the bald spot on his crown, spattering herself with blood.

He exhaled and pitched forward into his empty cereal bowl.

Served him right.

"Who's the dumbass now?"

Emily dropped the hammer, dialed 911, and explained the situation to the operator. She poured a glass of chardonnay, sat, and took a long drink.

Waited for the police to arrive with hands clasped in her lap.

Twenty-Two

The next morning, Justin sat under the canopy checking his instruments and girding himself for Natalie's arrival. He didn't know how she had gotten under his skin, but she had. He had never faced ridicule over his money before.

Being rich wasn't his fault. He wasn't extravagant with money. The trust paid him the proceeds of the investments each year and he donated a third to various charities. A third! That was good, wasn't it? The trust was a stroke of good fortune, nothing more. He didn't act entitled. Or did he? How would he know? Was it because he was male? White males weren't popular right now, and it seemed unfair, painting all men with the same brush. He didn't harass women. Supported women's rights. He was a nice guy. At least he thought so.

His arrangement with Julie, his friend with benefits, was fully reciprocal. It was Julie who had suggested it first. He wasn't sure he would have initiated such a relationship on his own, but agreed it was a perfectly logical idea, handling a natural urge in a safe, practical manner.

Still, men were paying for the sins of their fathers and grandfathers. Men used to be bastards, no argument. Some still were. He wasn't and didn't like being marked as a Neanderthal simply because of his Y chromosome.

Maybe guys simply couldn't understand the female perspective. A full understanding of the issues eluded him.

He sighed. These musings were wasted energy. Natalie didn't have to like him. She just had to work with him, and had agreed to do so. The situation had given him a migraine. He checked his waist pack. He had Advil but no migraine meds. Between the crows bickering in the trees and Natalie hanging around, it could be a long day.

He took four Advil and went back to work.

★   ★   ★

Natalie stumbled through the woods to the rich boy's tent, wondering why the heck they couldn't just use the driveway—an overgrown strip of gravel running toward the house. But when she drove up the road, she couldn't find the driveway, a mailbox, or any sign of the farm. It was strange. The excuse he had given her about keeping his research quiet didn't ring true. Why was he there? What did earth currents have to do with earthquakes? What was the real issue?

She was fascinated by her brief interaction at the Laskin farm with a spirit who proved to be vulgar and cranky. She had spent the evening in her group, talking with other mediums on the best approach to take. If a spirit didn't want to talk, it was considered rude to force a connection. Here, it seemed one spirit was creating a disturbance and bothering the others in the area. Interceding for the community seemed appropriate.

She came armed with the standard items that might facilitate a connection: candles, incense, and a food offering—fresh dinner rolls from the bakery, something she never used otherwise. It felt like a waste, but if it worked, maybe not.

Natalie decided to be nicer to Ritchie Rich. She had been rude yesterday and wasn't sure why, surprised by her reaction to him. Sometimes, her circumstances and lack of money bothered her. She struggled to make ends meet. It was hard to see people who had been given everything. Still, she needed his help and would have to apologize.

Ugh.

She should have gone to college, but her mother said she was too stupid for school. Then Bob came along. They got married and there was no reason to bother—until they split up. Bob made good money and she didn't. At forty-five, she believed herself too old to start school again.

Despite her bitchiness yesterday, she hoped he was agreeable to giving her the tent, a more isolated spot; it would be darker and more conducive to a reading.

He looked wary as she approached.

"Sorry if I was grumpy yesterday. Mind if I use your tent today?"

"Go ahead, help yourself."

He seemed relieved she wouldn't be sitting at the table.

She stopped and said, "So why are you here? What are you looking for?"

"I'm a geologist. I'm following up on the quake."

She nodded. "Tell me about the earth currents."

He did, but she still didn't understand it. Voltage in the ground? It meant nothing to her—except that it might be upending the spirit world.

Inside the tent, it was warm and stuffy. She set up and ignored her discomfort. Soon, the sweat beading on her forehead no longer registered.

Sometime later, the planchette moved an inch.

"Who do I have the pleasure of speaking with today?"

Silence. But no profanity—a promising sign.

She waited a minute and asked, "Can I talk to you? Please? I'm here to help."

Not entirely true, but it might get her foot in the door.

The planchette meandered to YES.

"And who am I speaking with?"

MILDRED

She gazed into the mirror and centered herself, connecting with the glass and the world beyond. An old woman resolved out of the haze. Short and stooped, her hands crabbed with arthritis, she had permed brown hair, a slightly unnatural color from too many years of dye. The sensation or ethereal breeze that she traced to the farm felt stronger today, suggesting the situation was intensifying. No one in the group had understood the feeling she described. She waited for Mildred to speak, applying no pressure. She would work slowly to establish and build a rapport.

Finally, Mildred spoke. Her voice crackled like a bad radio signal.

Sorry about the other day. Things have been difficult here. I was testy.

"Quite all right." Natalie meant it, having just apologized for the same thing. Mildred didn't realize it had just been yesterday. Spirits had little sense of time. She paused, not wanting to push. This was progress. Finally, she said, "When you're ready, tell me what's going on."

Mildred spoke in a rush. *Everything's kittywampus here. I get shocks all the time. I feel like I'm losing my mind.*

"I'm sorry to hear that. The same thing is happening in town." Natalie then explained what Justin had told her about the currents, even though she didn't understand it. Mildred seemed satisfied with the explanation.

Is there anything I can do about it?

"I don't know, but I'll certainly ask." Of course. Why hadn't she thought of that? Though she only now knew the shocks were also occurring on the farm. "So what do the shocks feel like?"

Like sticking your finger in a light socket.

"Do you feel other things? Hot? Cold?"

No, never have until the shocks. And they're bad. They go right through my soul.

"Are you the only one here?"

Yes. It was lonely—until the woman moved in.

"Like having company, right?"

Yes. Having another soul nearby helps.

"I'm sure. How about you? How did you pass? Is that something you'd like to talk about?"

I fell down the stairs. It was a stupid accident.

A long silence followed.

"Mildred?"

I'm sorry. I lied.

More silence. Natalie waited patiently.

I was pushed. My son, I think. I was old and came to live with them. I think he got tired of caring for me.

"I'm so sorry. I can't even imagine." Natalie tried to hide her shock and maintain a neutral tone. Mildred had been murdered by her own son? Then remained stuck here, alone? It sounded perfectly awful. The rotten bastard had probably gotten away with it too.

I'm sure you can't. It feels good to tell someone. Just to talk.

"I'm here for you, Mildred."

Thank you. I really want the shocks to go away. Can you talk to your friend, the scientist?

"I'll ask him. Whatever I can do to help. It may be a few days though." Natalie worked for the next three days.

Whenever you can. I appreciate your help.

Mildred was closing the conversation. The spirits tired easily but were also so desperate for company, they often cut the conversation short for fear of boring her, which couldn't be further from the truth. In time, she would explain that. She had so many questions but knew to proceed gently.

Please come back. I enjoy talking to you. I hope you find an answer.

She tried to sound conversational, but her tone was desperate.

Natalie signed off and reflected. She had learned little in her encounter with Mildred. The woman didn't know anything either. Instead, she had just befriended another desperate soul in the spirit world. She felt a little disappointed.

Then she thought about Kat. Should she say something? But she had promised to be invisible.

Silence was the best course for now.

★   ★   ★

Justin only heard half the conversation. She talked about him and the currents. It still wasn't amenable to analysis. She could fake everything. Maybe this was a waste of time.

Finally, she said, "I will, Mildred. As soon as I know something."

She emerged from the tent a few minutes later with her gear.

"What'd you find out?"

"She's being shocked as well. She doesn't know what to do."

"But is she—Mildred—willing to talk?"

"Yes. I talked about you a bit. She wants to know if there was anything she can do about the shocks."

"I haven't thought about that, but I will," he said. "Did she say what they feel like?"

"Like sticking her finger in a light socket."

"Hmm. I have some questions for her as well. Can I sit in?"

"No," she said tartly. "You can give me a list of questions."

With that, she up and left.

Justin watched her figure recede and imagined booting her in the ass, a fantasy that quickly escalated to strangling her with his bare hands.

Whoa!

That was freaky. He wasn't a violent man.

Where had that come from?

Twenty-Three

Standing on the porch, Kat dripped with sweat.

The day started hot and muggy and promised worse as the sun rose in the pale sky. The stagnant air clung like a damp blanket.

So far, the situation with Natalie had caused no problems. Justin's updates now included Natalie, and Kat found it all rather mundane. She had little faith that Natalie would be much help. Critically, no one else had ventured onto the property, and she relaxed a little.

A dozen days a year, she would miss electricity and air conditioning. This was one of them. The basement was musty and damp but also cool, a perfect excuse to clear the junk and scrub the floor. Maybe she would buy a cot and sleep down there on the worst nights. Her great-grandmother said they did that in the days before fans.

Max refused to go into the basement. He didn't growl or bare his teeth, he just stopped and balked. Was Mrs. Laskin's energy stronger down there? Something else? Kat felt nothing, but his refusal gave her pause.

She sprinkled water on his coat and he lay on the porch, content with her primitive but effective cooling method.

With a deep breath, she marched down the stairs, brushing aside the anxieties Max had raised. The basement was worse than she remembered, a veritable dumping ground for gardening tools, pots, wood trellises, and other junk. The tools were rusted and mostly useless. She opened the storm doors and hauled everything out to the dump behind the house until the basement was clear.

The concrete floor was covered with a murky layer of dirt, mud, and sludge. With a hand scraper, she scooped grunge into an old plastic five-gallon pail and hauled it outdoors. It was grimy, tedious work, but she had nothing but time and the air was deliciously cool. Tonight, after Justin left, she would take a cool bath.

Time for a break. Kat cracked a beer, hesitated, grabbed one for Justin, and wandered out to the encampment.

He was sitting, typing on a laptop, wearing shorts, a tee, and a ball cap, looking unfazed by the heat. He glanced up with an expression of gratitude when she handed him the beer.

"Where's Natalie?" Kat asked.

"Had to work, I guess."

"How's it going?"

"Pretty quiet today. There were two major voltage fluctuations and a minor quake overnight."

"I didn't feel anything." She glanced at his biceps. Hmm, he had nice guns. She flashed to her sex dream the other night and felt her face flush a little.

"You wouldn't. It was one-point-eight, but every time I get seismic activity with the strong voltage fluxes, I'm closer to proving the existence of microplumes."

Kat nodded and needled him in mock seriousness. "And what about the demons underground?"

"Evil, not demons. There are no monsters in my theory. But it's also a problem. I haven't yet determined what to measure. Is it some new value? Or simply the change in the telluric currents that influences people one way or another? Centuries ago, we knew about electricity and magnetism, but we didn't understand their nature or that they were a fundamental force. Now we do thanks to James Maxwell Clerk and others. We can't see dark matter, but we know it's there. I see this as the same sort of challenge."

"Fascinating," Kat said drolly.

"For now, I can only rely on anecdotal evidence, after the fact, like Jonestown."

She smirked. "Doesn't sound very scientific, Doc."

"Ah, you're mocking me."

"Guilty."

"Do you follow the news?"

"Not much. Internet service here is bad."

He laughed then turned serious. "Apparently, there's been an uptick in crime in the area. Theft. Vandalism. Especially vandalism at the schools in town. Not proof, but an interesting trend. Yesterday, a woman buried a hammer in her husband's head. The neighbors say she's the nicest person."

Kat recoiled a bit. "That's awful."

His phone rang. He checked the number, smiled a bit, and put a finger up as he took the call. He listened and said, "Sounds good. Your place or mine?"

With a nod, he tapped the screen and set the phone down.

"Girlfriend?"

"Nope. I have a friend with benefits situation. We get together when we feel like it."

"Sounds romantic."

"Um, you're living alone in an old farmhouse with a dog."

"Touche, Doc." Kat turned and started back to the house. "Have a good day."

Kat finished her beer, wet Max down again, and walked into the basement. She kept thinking about the woman killing her husband with a hammer. Spooky—but only because of Justin's plume theories. Otherwise, she wouldn't have given the story a second thought.

She realized she had been flirty with him. He was good looking, intelligent, and had no serious attachments. She felt some chemistry and a silly stab of jealousy when his friend called. It was hard to buck chemistry, even if a relationship wasn't an option. With her history, she couldn't imagine he would be interested. Knowing she was being pursued by ruthless people, she also worried about putting him in danger.

As she scraped and washed, clearing the corner where the debris had been piled, she uncovered something weird.

There was a square depression beneath the grunge—perfectly square, measuring about two feet on each side. It was filled with denser clay-like gunk. When she dug down an inch, she found a rusted metal surface. Further probing revealed two hinges along one edge.

It was a hatch of some sort.

Access to the septic system? That was usually outdoors. Some plumbing thing?

Curious, Kat dug the muck out and exposed the door. A small ring looped into the metal opposite the hinges served as a handle. She tugged hard but it refused to budge. Kat grabbed the broom, threaded the handle through the loop, and levered the door open an inch. Lifting the broom with both hands, the rusty hinges squealed in protest until the door rotated and lay open on the concrete.

Beneath was a square hole descending into darkness. It smelled musty and earthy, but not gross—so not the septic system. Nothing was visible but the top of an aluminum ladder. It was dark, mysterious, and creepy. Was this what Max was avoiding?

Kat was intrigued, regardless.

She trotted up to the kitchen, grabbed her camping lantern, and returned, holding the light up, eyeing the situation with caution. She could see a flat surface eight feet down at the base of the ladder, a landing. The walls were lined with random-width planking. Nothing else was visible. Should she tell Justin where she was going? While it sounded like a good idea, no guy would do that. Why should she?

Nope. She was her own person. She never used to be this fearless. Prison had hardened her in ways she only now recognized.

Just be careful.

Kat put a tentative foot on the ladder. It felt solid. Step by step, she tested each rung, then she noted that bolts secured the ladder to the wall.

At the landing, she found a narrow set of stone steps descending steeply into darkness. There was no handrail so Kat checked her descent by bracing her hand against the walls. Someone had carved the walls out of hard, dry clay that felt like concrete. Her anxiety rose with each step.

What was this place? Where did it lead to?

An old bootlegger's hideout?

The location was perfect. It was so well hidden. She wondered about the Underground Railroad, but didn't think they operated in

Wisconsin. Whatever it was, someone had invested significant time and effort to build it.

Was it something darker? A crypt? The secret den of a serial killer?

Kat pursed her lips nervously. She wasn't given to such musings. Was that the house? The ghost of Mrs. Laskin? Justin's plume? A drug or bootleg operation made more sense, a rationalization that failed to settle the twisty feeling in her gut. Almost every day, the house revealed some new mystery. What surprise awaited below?

Strangely, there were no cobwebs or spiders. No signs of mice either. The stairs were dusty but otherwise pristine. If need be, Justin was right outside, though she realized ruefully she should have told him first.

But no, she had to face her fear. That attitude had helped her survive prison.

As her mind boggled at the possibilities, she stepped down to a smaller dirt landing, a switchback where the stairs continued downward into pitch-black darkness. The light wobbled in her grip and cast unsettling shadows. It was dry and deathly quiet. So quiet, she heard nothing but her heartbeat, her breathing, and the shuffle of her bare feet on the cool stone.

Kat descended eight steps—she counted them nervously in her head—until she reached the bottom. No more stairs. Just a short, narrow hallway facing an oak door with an antique brass handle. With an arched inlay in the dark wood, it looked like a church door.

The moment of truth. What had she discovered?

With an intake of breath, she opened the door, leading with the lantern.

She jumped back and nearly dropped the light.

"Holy shit!"

From inside the room, the empty eye sockets of a skull gazed at her. Kat hardened her resolve and crept through the doorway, lantern first. Held her breath. Her eyes darted about the bedroom-sized space with rising horror. A small round table sat in the center of the room, Tarot cards strewn across the wooden top. Three chairs, tipped on their sides, were surrounded by an assortment of bones, skulls, and partial skeletons. A large wooden cross hung on the wall.

After one more visual sweep, Kat backed out, closed the door, and leaned against the dirt wall, her heart pounding in her chest.

Oh sweet Jesus.

It looked like an execution chamber.

Twenty-Four

Sam Koselek was weary.

Rolling into Walden, she felt bored, frustrated, and not the least bit optimistic.

Three weeks in on this job, it felt like a lost cause. A veritable needle in a haystack story. But it was the best paying work she'd had in a couple years. The client had deep pockets and seemed intent on paying her until the search yielded results.

On the surface, the assignment sounded straightforward. Find one missing person. Report her location to the client.

Except the woman had disappeared. Gone off the grid. A full background check revealed that Katrina Lundquist, nee Lambert, had no current driver's license or car registration, no known address, no credit cards, no friends, no family beyond parents who had disowned her. She had skipped on her parole officer and hadn't been seen since. The client was convinced Lundquist was holed up in a small town somewhere in east-central Wisconsin. It sounded plausible. Traveling created too many records and left trails behind. Going to ground in a familiar place had a certain appeal. The knowledge was based on a conversation years before, musings about where the woman would go if she ever fell into trouble with the law.

Sam wondered what kind of relationship led to that sort of revelation. Not her business, she decided. The woman was a druggie who had served nearly five years for dealing cocaine. Her sentence was light given the crime, and Lundquist had evidently struck a plea deal by turning snitch on her superiors, Tomas and Antonio Campo. After three months in a halfway house, she disappeared.

Kat Lundquist sounded like a waste of life. A loser.

Knowing all this, she questioned her client, Mr. Robert Smith, about his intentions when she found the Lundquist woman. She needed the work, but not the adverse fallout from a case gone bad if the woman turned up dead. That kind of publicity could damage her business and bring unwanted attention from the police. Until now, she had avoided ethically questionable cases. Was she pushing the envelope this time?

Smith, weaselly in appearance and demeanor, said Katrina Lundquist owed him money over a business deal gone bad. He claimed they were partners prior to her drug days and he was convinced she had blown the money on coke. There might be funds to recover though. Lundquist had received money from a divorce settlement. Sam assumed most of that had disappeared up the woman's nose. Addicts never changed.

Otherwise, the client intended to go to the police when she was found. If nothing else, he wanted her sent back to prison. Given his reasonably sincere presentation and the legitimate legal judgment he presented, Samantha believed him. He didn't look like the member of a drug cartel, nor the type to resolve an issue with violence.

Whatever the outcome, it wasn't her problem. If she didn't take the job, someone would. She needed the money. It was a matter of survival. Still, Sam made it clear she wouldn't be a party to violence, even by association. Mr. Smith understood and agreed.

Sam had visited thirty-four of these shitty little burgs at a rate of two to three per day. She wondered if the client was wrong. Maybe Lundquist had fled the state. But he seemed very sure of himself. And he continued paying her.

With a well-rehearsed routine, Sam approached people with a picture of Katrina and a story. The woman's father was dying. They were estranged but he wanted to see her one more time. Sam implied there was an inheritance. It was a feel-good story right off the Hallmark Channel that sold well with women. They wanted to help.

Being female had advantages anyway. Many of the people she dealt with were women and were more likely to confide in another woman. Male PIs were often viewed with suspicion. These days, men were effectively screwed. Not that they didn't deserve it. They had gotten away with murder for centuries and now the pendulum had swung the other way. A little too far, really. Sam liked men for the most part, despite two failed marriages.

Sam made similar stops in each town and she had four places to visit here: two convenience stores, a library, and the grocery store. Walden mirrored every other small town she had passed through: a fading Main Street, taverns, schools, churches, a small medical clinic, and a supper club that looked interesting. Sam loved dining out.

First stop was the BP Travel Mart on the west end of town. She spoke to a cashier. Nothing. No hesitation, not a flicker of recognition.

The other convenience store, the Quik Stop, sat on the east side. The girl at the checkout stared at the picture for too long. A mousy thing with blonde hair, she glanced at Sam, looked at the picture again, and bit her lip. "No. I haven't seen her. Sorry."

The girl made no actual eye contact. She was lying. Most people sucked at lying and couldn't tell a convincing lie if their lives depended on it. An irrational urge to grab the bitch by her cheap, shitty top and scare the truth out of her passed. Sam could not only recognize a liar, she could lie her ass off and fool almost anyone, even a well-trained detective. She also excelled at poker and worked as a jury consultant to detect dishonest potential jurors.

Verdict? Katrina Lundquist was somewhere in or near Walden.

She still made the other stops. The frumpy bag at Hanson's Super Value was a better liar, but Sam still caught her tells.

They were lying because they liked Lundquist more than they trusted Sam. The next time they saw her, they would confide in her. Good and bad, really. Lundquist would know she had been found and might run. But Sam would be ready and knew how to conduct a discreet tail.

She had no idea how the woman got around. She didn't own a car—not one that was registered anyway. An unregistered vehicle was possible—if she still had cash from the divorce. There was no public transportation anywhere in the area. Walking took too damned long. A bike maybe?

The librarian spilled the beans.

Yes, that woman comes in all the time.

But she had no name and no address for her. The librarian remembered that she always rode a bike. The revelation pleased Sam. Her instincts were still sharp—though the fact that two women hadn't trusted her suggested otherwise.

She opted to stake out the Quik Stop. It was the most likely place to catch Lundquist. The woman probably went there most often. The bank across the street had a convenient parking lot shaded by trees that would be perfect for surveillance.

Sam made a call to her client, Mr. Smith, reporting her location and a positive sighting. He sounded pleased and told her to keep up the good work.

She watched the Quik Stop until dark. Checking her phone, she searched for a place to stay. There were no motels or other accommodations in Walden. She found a Holiday Inn Express fifteen miles away. She booked a room and made tracks for Jake's Supper Club next to the BP for dinner.

Tomorrow morning at six, she would run a stakeout until she nabbed the woman.

Sam smiled.

Katrina Lundquist was going to jail.

Twenty-Five

Kat tried to collect her wits and calm her jumpy nerves.

She wasn't squeamish, just shocked. And frightened. She had expected beer kegs or drug sorting tables, not bodies. She couldn't comprehend that awful scene. Ghosts were one thing. Dead bodies under the basement? Much, much worse.

Staring straight ahead, she worked a relaxation routine with her hands and feet.

She learned the technique from her prison roomie, Jamie Dysart. The Hotel Anthony was a newer facility and quite civilized as prisons went, hence the moniker. Instead of cells or dorms, they housed inmates in basic rooms furnished with two beds, a shelf for their belongings, and a curtained-off area with a toilet. There were no bars anywhere. Just locked doors to prevent inmates from straying.

Her first roommate was difficult, bitchy, and antisocial. They seldom talked and mostly ignored each other. It seemed karmic given the life Kat had led. When they released the woman, Kat got a break and was paired with Jamie, who was serving fifteen to twenty for vehicular manslaughter.

Jamie drank. After a three-day binge, she hopped into a pickup and killed a family of four in a horrendous head-on collision. She had gone through the whole self-loathing, I-deserve-to-die phase and had somehow emerged intact. Jamie was the most composed, confident, and relaxed person Kat had ever met, and brutally honest about her situation. Entirely her fault. No one else to blame. She had a good upbringing, family, and husband. She just couldn't handle an addiction to tequila and her Margaritaville mentality. The experience had sharpened her focus on certain realities. Possessions, positions, and accolades were meaningless. She too had been disowned by her family, but was making inroads with her daughter.

Until then, Kat wasn't sure who to blame for her fall from grace. Her infertility? Her family? Life itself? Those or many situations she perceived as beyond her control, just like most prisoners who blamed the usual suspects: poor parents, bad breaks, an unfair world.

In their first long conversation, Jamie had been blunt. "You did the coke, you took the risks, you ruined your life. You did it. Nobody else. Just you. Want to blame someone? Look in the mirror."

It was startling and refreshing.

Jamie took Kat under her wing and they became close friends. She pushed Kat to understand that while she had done awful things, she wasn't a bad person. Further, through study, self-reflection, and serious effort, she could strive to be better. Interestingly, Jamie framed none of it with religion. No theology. No "come to Jesus" moments. It was a novel approach. Kat had little use for the higher power mantras of the twelve-step programs.

Jamie taught her mindfulness and, over time, Kat learned to dwell less in the past, or the future. Jaime also taught her a set of relaxation exercises for when she struggled and those were the techniques she used now.

When her heart rate slowed to near-normal, she steeled herself, crept back into the room with the light held high, and took stock.

There was no smell. No hint of decomposition. These people had been dead for years. Three of them—three skulls, one somewhat smaller than the others, a child perhaps. She wasn't a crime scene specialist, but the cause of death was apparent for each.

The smaller skull had a broken depression above the eye socket, the approximate shape of a hammerhead. A brown-stained hammer lay nearby. The second skull had a round hole in the temple about nine millimeters in diameter with a larger exit wound on the opposite side. A vague, dark splotch marred the wall above it. A gun lay two feet away amidst a jumble of small bones, a hand maybe. The last skull was intact. Nearby, she recognized a sternum or breastbone lying amidst a jumble of ribs. A neat bullet hole had pierced the lower quadrant—a fatal wound to the heart.

Murder. Murder. Suicide.

Tragic and far too common. What a horrible death, especially for the child. A hammer?

Ugh.

Why were they still here? While the discovery explained the state of the house as she found it—the abandoned dining settings and belongings—it failed to explain why no one had found them. Almost everyone had connections. Family, friends, a school for the child, neighbors. Yet these people had lain here for how long? Over forty years? How was that possible?

Then she pictured the state of the basement when she started cleaning this morning: the mountain of junk and tools piled over the trapdoor.

Holy shit!

At least one person knew about it. And they had covered it up!

Was it three murders?

She recalled the contents of the drawer. There were four members of the Laskin family. Three bodies.

Was the fourth Laskin a murderer who had buried their dreadful deed here? Was it Adam? The person paying the taxes? Is that why no one came looking? Had he taken the truck, shut off the utilities, called the school, and lied to everyone?

And what did the bizarre juxtaposition of the cross and Tarot cards mean? A cult thing? Witchcraft?

Mystery upon mystery—a story that may have died with these bodies.

How would she ever learn the truth?

No wonder Mrs. Laskin—or whoever she was—still wandered upstairs. Had she been trying to tell Kat something? Hoping Kat would find these bodies and give them peace? Or warning her to get out? The discovery gave her pause about the idea of ghosts, Mrs. Laskin in particular. Kat accepted her presence in an abstract sense. She felt infinitely more real now.

Suddenly, Justin's evil plume theory looked prescient and frightening.

Then Kat shook her head and told herself to get a grip. Seriously?

People did evil things without help from a mysterious force underground. They killed each other all the time out of love, greed, or jealousy. The dead people in the room proved nothing beyond the simple premise that people were base animals given to violence.

Kat knew one thing. Legally, she was required to report this to the police. Except she couldn't.

They had been dead for ages, over forty years. No reason to rush out and report it now. She could fill the hole with dirt and leave them buried right where they were. That might be best.

No.

Someone had gotten away with murder and they needed to be held accountable.

She couldn't close the door on it. These people deserved a decent burial—a rite that would have to wait. When she moved on, she would make an anonymous call to the police. Or send an email from a library somewhere.

Kat needed to think, but she couldn't spend another moment down here. She was sweating. It was warm in the room, unnaturally so. The basement had been so cool. Was this warmth a sign of the plume beneath her feet?

Better to consider the subject above ground. Kat closed the door, climbed out, and shut the hatch on that nightmare, craving sunlight and fresh air.

She returned to the documents in the kitchen drawer. Rifled through every slip of paper looking for notes or clues. There was nothing to cast any light on the awful scene below. No religious tracts. No occult symbols. No odd doodles or cryptic scribbles. She had missed nothing.

They were no crosses in the house. She hadn't found a Bible either. No evidence they were religious. The oddest note was the Tarot cards, a clue possibly, but an indecipherable one.

Kat felt certain Adam Laskin had covered up the murders. Had closed that door and purposely buried the evidence and paid the taxes to alleviate suspicion. A stab in the dark, but the only narrative that made sense. Whatever the story, Kat felt compelled to solve it.

She stepped out and paced on the porch.

Why? Why did she need to know? People had died badly in the basement forty years ago. Knowing what happened would change nothing—unless it had something to do with Justin's plume. She had trouble buying his theories, but the proof was stacking up around her. Disturbing proof. Now she felt trapped by it. But she wasn't stuck. The house was never hers. It was her fate to be rootless, the price for her sins. If things went south, it was simply time to move.

The realization hurt. She liked the house and had done considerable work to make it comfortable, to feel like home. Mostly, it was the absurdity of it all. If she were being chased off by a sheriff, or Harven appeared? That she could understand. No, she was being chased off by ghosts, dead bodies, and some malignant force underground.

A week ago, she would have laughed at such a bizarre story.

She needed to share this with Justin. The weight of it was too much. She couldn't fully manage the feelings she had.

How would he react? Would he be curious? Intrigued?

Absolutely. He would see it as further proof of his theories. Over dinner, they had developed some familiarity. It was an odd relationship—if you could call it that—and this business was freaking her out. But would he feel compelled to follow the law? Insist upon reporting it? She thought not. She had to risk it.

Kat thought about the pleasant woman in town who killed her husband.

She shivered despite the heat.

If the plume theory was true, were they safe here?

Twenty-Six

Kat grabbed two beers and walked out to the encampment.

The heat and humidity were oppressive, the sun a blast furnace. Cicadas sawed away in the trees. Dry soil crunched underfoot.

With his hat tipped forward, Justin looked unaffected by the heat under the canopy. He snored lightly. She bumped his chair and he startled.

"Hard at work, Professor?"

"Hmm. I must've dozed off."

She handed him a beer and sat in the other chair.

He regarded her curiously. "Here for an update?"

"Yes. I noticed things were getting pretty exciting out here."

He smirked. "No. Mostly quiet. A couple minor quakes overnight."

"Still on course to prove your theories?"

"The quakes are part of it. The ground temperature on the farm is rising too."

"Meaning what?"

"If there's magma rising underground, it would heat the crust and the soil above it."

Kat thought about how warm it was in that little room. She hadn't imagined it. At odds with her worries about the basement, she felt a sudden attraction to Justin. Found herself staring at him with sexual yearning.

Stop!

Where had that come from? She tried to push it away, swallowed, and said, "Tell me again how you plan to prove the second part?"

"Wait and see. I mentioned the uptick in crime locally including the homicide yesterday. I'll analyze that data statistically after this event."

"These events, how long do they last? Do you have any idea?"

"A little. The seismic evidence and the statistical analyses I've conducted on the second part of the theory—the rise in crime in places like Jonestown or Heaven's Gate, California—suggest a very short time frame of months to a year or two. That's completely at odds with the prevailing theories on mantle plumes, which persist for millions of years."

"Doesn't that contradiction disprove your central thesis?"

"You're very erudite for a homeless woman—"

"I'm not homeless." Occasionally, she forgot she was, in fact, homeless. And an ex-con. How differently would he treat her if he knew? She wasn't about to tell him.

"You're squatting here."

"Semantics." Despite her reservations, she liked him. Their conversations had an easy, relaxed feel. She was learning to trust him, which would make the next conversation easier.

"Can these microplumes reappear?"

"I don't know yet. That would be harder to prove. If they recurred frequently, I would have data to work with. If they recur over longer intervals, there would be no historical seismic data or crime statistics to analyze."

"What would proof look like?"

"Seismic data aligned with patterns of criminality going back through time."

Kat spoke softly. "I might have some proof for you."

Justin sat forward, eyes alert and bright. "What did you find?"

He was perceptive. She liked that.

"First, you have to promise me something."

"Sure. By now you should know my word's good."

"I'm getting there," Kat said. She inhaled and made full eye contact to monitor his expression. "I found something, but you have to promise you won't run to the police when you see it."

"Okay, I'm officially intrigued. And since we're both trespassing and breaking the law, I won't be running to the police. Promise." He crossed his heart. "What'd you find, an evil diary?"

"Worse."

He stopped mid-sip. "I can't wait to see it then."

"Let's finish our beers first."

Kat thought about the sketchbook in the attic. Wasn't that like a diary? She needed to share that with Justin and tell him about Mrs. Laskin too. They sat for five minutes, not saying much until they had each drained their bottles. She was leery about bringing him farther into the house, lest he judge her circumstances. Silly really. He didn't seem bothered by her unconventional lifestyle.

As they stepped into the kitchen, he looked around and said, "I can't get over how nice this looks. You'd never believe it from the outside."

"I know. Someone spent good money on this kitchen. I wondered why they'd just left it and now I think I know."

His eyes widened and he followed her down the stairs, ducking beneath a beam at the bottom. She pulled the hatch open and climbed down. He muttered something and followed her. She reached the lower door and waited as he moseyed down in a crouch, examining the walls and stairs.

"An old Prohibition cellar?"

"Possibly."

He looked at her expectantly. "Are there monsters beyond that door?"

"Might as well be."

Without dramatic pause, she opened the door and handed him the lantern. He took it and started into the room.

"Holy fuck!"

Kat had never heard him swear. It was rather shocking.

She stepped in and said, "What do you make of this?"

"I have no idea." His eyes darted around, taking it in. Various expressions crossed his face: shock, puzzlement, recognition. It was still jolting to Kat. Unsettling and repulsive. Human nature at its worst—the smaller skull, the worst aspect of the horror.

Finally, he said, "Murder by hammer. Murder and suicide by gun. A man, woman, and male child."

"How do you know that?"

"The skulls, the pelvises. Hidden down here? No wonder they were never found."

"I think somebody found them." She described the state of the basement when she arrived and the junk piled atop the hatch. "I think someone intentionally covered up the murders, probably Adam Laskin. I wonder if he killed them too."

"That's one interpretation. Murder-suicide also works. Maybe Adam found them and concealed the crime scene to protect his father's reputation."

"I hadn't thought of that."

Justin looked off into space. "This might be where Natalie steps in and proves her worth."

"What?"

"She's a medium. She's already sensed a disturbance here. It might be these people. It might be the plume. Maybe both. Fits my theory about disturbances near the plume. Obviously, this happened long ago. If I knew when, I could run a statistical analysis to look for evidence of the plume in that time frame."

"I think I know when it happened."

His eyebrows went up. "How?"

"Can we get out of here? This place is making my skin crawl."

They backed away, and Justin closed the door. They climbed out and Kat slammed the hatch shut. As they ascended the basement stairs, she told him about the junk drawer and led him to it when they reached the kitchen.

He rifled through the drawer and studied the checkbook. "This definitely helps."

"On a hunch, I did a missing persons search at the library. I didn't find anything."

"We might have more luck with Google."

"Worth a try," Kat said. "When Natalie shows up, what should we tell her?"

"I don't know yet. It might be better to hold off. See what she discovers without the foreknowledge."

"True. Good thinking."

Kat said, "One more thing."

"Something more? Wow! You've been holding out on me."

"I wasn't comfortable sharing this before now."

She led him up to the attic and handed him the sketchbook. "Page through that."

He raised his eyebrows, perused the cover, and studied the first drawing. "Good work, but—"

"Keep going."

She could read the progression in his face, first as curiosity, and then alarm. He closed it and said, "Wow! Can I keep this?"

"Yes, of course. Could the plume have that effect on someone?"

"I consider it likely."

As she pushed the attic stairs shut, Kat said, "Need another beer?"

"Yeah. Maybe two."

Twenty-Seven

Kat studied Justin as he drank his beer.

Sitting on the porch, languishing in the afternoon heat, her sexual desire had returned and she found it disconcerting. She struggled to concentrate on the gruesome situation in the basement. How could she think about sex right now? Maybe abstinence was to blame. With that thought, she had a sudden yearning for coke, the first in a year or more. A moment of weakness. She refocused on the present and the task at hand.

Justin had walked out to his camp and grabbed his laptop. Using his phone hot spot, he googled missing persons in Wisconsin. The Department of Justice maintained a missing persons page with over one hundred entries, but none were Laskins, so no official report had ever been filed.

"So murder-suicide? Or just plain murder. Hard to say," Justin said, closing his laptop.

"At first, I thought murder-suicide, but Adam Laskin could've murdered his family and covered it up by feeding people misinformation."

"That's a tall leap. The gun was positioned in a way that suggested suicide. Could've been staged, I suppose."

"We can hardly ask Adam, can we?"

"Nope."

"This helps prove your theory, right?" Kat said. "If you reveal the murder scene?"

"And you don't want that, I assume."

"Hmm. Let's say it's problematic."

"I promised I wouldn't go to the police."

"You did."

"Someday, we'll have to."

"I'm aware." Kat sipped her beer and turned her chair to face Justin. "There's a bigger issue. If your theory is correct—and until now, I've dismissed it because evil doesn't need a theory—are we in danger here?"

"Have you noticed any effects? Feel odd, see things...?" He tilted his head with a shrug.

It was cute.

"Other than Mrs. Laskin, no." She wasn't ready to open up about her nightmares. There was no good way to explain Harven.

His eyebrows furrowed. "Mrs. Laskin?"

"A nightly visitor, she—"

"The house is haunted too?"

Kat nodded.

"Wow. This gets better and better."

"Have you noticed anything?" Kat asked.

"No—other than my migraines, maybe. We know about the telluric currents. I'm hoping that remaining alert and being objective about any effects will help protect us."

"I hope you're right."

The beers went quickly. Kat offered him another and then said, "Want to stay for dinner?"

"Love to."

Dinner was a basic affair on the porch. Kat grilled a pork chop, baked potatoes, and tossed a salad of wild greens. She set a Thermacell repeller out to ward off mosquitoes. Max had taken a liking to Justin and lay at his feet.

Presenting the chop on a plate, Kat said, "How would you like to divide this?"

"Do you like the bone?"

She felt her face flush. When she didn't answer, he said, "I like to gnaw on the bone, caveman style. We'll split the meat if that's okay."

"That sounds good." She felt silly. He had to leave soon or she wouldn't be responsible for her actions. The sudden horniness was inexplicable and intense. She felt like a teen again.

They ate in peaceful silence for a few minutes and watched the sun slip away.

Justin sipped his beer and said, "Are you ever going to tell me why you live this way?"

"No."

"Okay." He nodded. "Nice job on the chop. How'd you get the potato skin so crispy?"

"Olive oil. And I wrapped them in foil. Thank you."

"Parents?"

"Huh?"

"Your parents. Alive or dead?"

"Alive."

"Where do they live?"

"Oshkosh. My turn."

He raised an eyebrow.

"A brief bio will do," Kat said.

"Born in Rockford, Illinois. My parents still live there. A brother in Denver who works in finance, and a sister in Chicago. She's an artist for an ad company. I live off a trust fund that allows me to pursue my wacky ideas—a fair assessment of how you feel about my work, I assume."

"I did. Before today."

"Thought so."

"Trust fund baby, huh?"

"Yep. Natalie thinks I'm the Antichrist."

"Natalie seems pretty cranky anyway."

"How do you support yourself?"

"That's it. No more questions." She smiled to cover her unease at the inability to talk about herself.

★   ★   ★

After dinner, Justin helped wash dishes and said goodnight.

He walked through the woods using a flashlight to follow a trail he'd marked with small daubs of paint. He checked the road. It was quiet and dark. He slipped sideways through the long grass of the ditch, trying to avoid leaving any evidence of his passage.

If those dead bodies weren't proof of his theories, what could be more convincing? He could wait though. The plume was still growing in intensity. When it peaked and he had documented the event, he could go back, look at the crime data, and bring the murders to light.

Kat was a strong, resilient woman. She had found three skeletons in her basement and was sleeping there tonight, regardless. He could do it, but women seemed more squeamish about such things. Then he recognized his sexist thinking. No wonder men had so much trouble getting things right. But she wasn't like any woman he'd met before.

Ha! He should have realized that when she first stepped out with the gun in her hands.

He was dying to know her background and story, but he didn't even know her last name. He liked her and thought she felt the same. There was that awkward moment over the pork chop. She blushed a little. What had she been thinking?

Play it cool, he decided. Pursuing her in any obvious way wouldn't work. He had blown it with the money question. He had hoped she would loosen up and reveal more about herself.

He drove home feeling pressure impinging behind his left eyeball like a knife probing the optic nerve. Another damned migraine. He had to remember to bring his pills so he could take one before things got this bad.

At home, he popped a migraine med, three Advil, and grabbed an ice pack. He lay back in his recliner, placed the pack on his temple, and napped for thirty minutes. When the alarm went off, the pain was fading.

The bodies in the basement were both horrifying and fascinating. They might never know what happened. Murder-suicides weren't uncommon, but the presentation was bizarre. It felt like a clue. He spent thirty minutes researching connections between the cross and Tarot cards but found nothing beyond a distant religious association. No mentions of occult symbolism, witchcraft, or murder scenes with a similar presentation.

The bodies raised another issue. He hadn't considered the plumes as being episodic, extending back in time and having a history that could be mapped. He still hadn't resolved their life cycle. Larger mantle plumes were episodic with periods of activity and inactivity. He had assumed that because microplumes were so small, they would be singular events, that insufficient heat would rise from the mantle to maintain them. Were the earlier deaths and the current uptick one ongoing event?

He had also imagined them being larger. This plume seemed little larger than the eighty-acre farm that lay atop it. Could the small size concentrate the effects? Or was he simply reading too much into it, a risk in any scientific observation? Was Kat right? Evil didn't need a theory? People were inherently evil and did awful things all the time. None of it required a demon—or electrical currents in the ground.

He didn't think she was. He believed in his theories and continued to gather evidence in their favor.

The discovery of the bodies beneath the basement wasn't enough. He needed more. Another historical event. He could check the news-paper archives to gather crime data from 1979, the date of the last canceled check. It would be more illuminating to go back further, to the era of the local Native Americans, but it would also be more difficult.

Native Americans had no written records. Knowledge was passed down as oral history and folklore. Little of it verifiable, though some of it was well known and seemed accurate, like the stories about the Porte de Mort passage in Door County, a place Native Americans called the Doorway of Death. The site of a fateful battle between the Ho-Chunk and Potawatomi tribes, it later became a graveyard for hundreds of ships lost to the treacherous waters in the strait.

Justin was no expert in Native American folklore, but he had a friend in the Weyauwega community, a tribe living in central Wis-consin prior to the European influx. Elliot Wolf was fluent in their folklore and history. They met in college while Elliot was working on his second doctorate.

He composed an email describing what he was looking for and sent it off, expecting little in return.

Justin sat back and thought about Kat's question. Were they safe atop the plume?

He didn't really know. No one did.

Tomorrow, he vowed to be more vigilant for potential dangers.

★   ★   ★

Kat was about to sit and read when she thought about the hatch in the basement. Until today, it had been covered with junk. Locked in effect. Now it was unsecured and she felt uneasy. Grabbing the lantern, she descended several steps and peeked. The hatch was closed.

Did she imagine it opening on its own?

A silly thought, but she wouldn't sleep until she acted to quell it. She opened the storm doors and carried in a dozen rocks and small boulders and set them on the door until about two hundred pounds of dead weight held it down. Kat shook her head at her superstitious worries. She had slept here for weeks. The bodies had been here for years. What had changed? Simple. She now knew they were there.

Feeling better, she read for an hour before climbing the stairs with Max.

She slept uneasily, her dreams a kaleidoscope of images: the skulls and bones, the cross, the Tarot cards. The moment she spotted the skull played over and over with cinematic clarity. Then the beast with the grotesque dinosaur hands clawed and gnawed its way into the bootleg cellar, ate the bones with loud chomping sounds, and slithered up the stairs calling her name—

Kat startled awake, rolled out of bed, and paced until the images faded. The bedroom seemed especially dark tonight. Max stood and dropped his head in her lap when she sat down, like he knew and understood.

When she fell back asleep, it was to a more pleasant place. She and Justin were locked in a passionate embrace, engaged in a bout of wild, delicious sex. She sat atop him, thrusting and grinding her hips against him until an orgasm swelled inside her. Maybe she just needed to do him in real life. Rip the bandage off—

A hard rap on the door ended the dream.

What?

When she opened the door, Harven stood there with a cordless drill in hand, leering.

"I'm going to screw you, Kat. Screw you good."

Kat awoke screaming.

Twenty-Eight

Kat awoke at sunrise, feeling uneasy about many things.

She let Max out, prepped the percolator, and set it on the side burner. The morning was warm and sunny but less humid than yesterday.

The dead people under the basement floor weren't as disturbing as they should be. What they implied bothered her far more. Until now, she had given Justin's second theory little credence. He was a nice guy. His microplume idea could be true. She wasn't a geologist, so she couldn't challenge the idea. But the idea of evil forces rising out of the ground sounded crazy. People were capable of evil and she saw no reason to dig deeper for a cause. It seemed like he was offering a free pass to people who committed dreadful acts.

See? It wasn't me, it was the plume.

More than most, she understood the importance of accepting personal responsibility for her failings.

Maybe deep down, she still framed evil like most people did: as a struggle between forces of good and evil. God versus Satan. But she had seen little evidence of a benevolent God in the world, and thus couldn't imagine evil personified as a demon or a fallen angel. She had given up on God years ago—or had he given up on her? She wasn't an atheist and considered herself an agnostic. She rarely thought about religion.

But the events in the basement struck a dissonant chord and had her thinking about nothing but. The hidden room, the Tarot cards, the cross, the gruesome nature of the murders. There was something perverse about them and nothing to suggest a cause. No evidence of religious zealotry. No donations to fringe groups. Best she could tell, the Laskins farmed, they paid bills, and they lived like everyone else— except they died in a strange, hidden room surrounded by symbols of faith and mysticism. She sensed a deeper meaning.

Hold it. Wasn't she doing the same as Justin? Looking for some greater cause? Still, his ideas no longer sounded quite so crazy. If she accepted his ideas, other disturbing questions arose. Would the plume affect her? Would she recognize it? Was everyone affected? Would individuals react differently? If Justin believed in his theory—which she assumed he must—why didn't he worry more about the effects?

Most of all, were they safe here?

And then there were her dreams. Her fears about Harven were un- derstandable. The man was a nightmare. But the monster was bizarre and inexplicable. A perverse type of nightmare she had never experi- enced before. Was that also the lava plume?

She needed to discuss all of it with Justin.

The last troubling issue was the man himself. She liked him and was growing comfortable around him. Their dinners were nice. She enjoyed his company. The conversations were relaxed, but she was experiencing a disturbing sensation: she felt perpetually horny. She hadn't had sex in a long time, but suddenly, it was all she could think about—either as sex dreams at night or irrational urges to proposition him during the day—which had never been her style.

Was it telluric currents? Or raging hormones after so many years going without? She didn't know.

That they wouldn't be discussing.

It was a bad idea to get comfortable with him. A relationship wasn't possible. Eventually, she would have to tell him about her past: her life as an addict, an ex-con, and a parole violator. How would he view her in that light?

And if Harven found her? Justin's life would be in danger. Best to keep her distance. This plume business would go away—as would Justin—and things would return to normal. While skeptical of Natalie's ghost whisperer claims, Kat was willing to entertain her process in the hope of shedding light on the mystery. Really, what did she have to lose?

★   ★   ★

Natalie emerged from the bushes just after ten o'clock.

Kat walked over to the encampment as Natalie set her things by the tent. The farm was unusually quiet today, lacking the normal chatter of birds and insects. Curious. Was that the plume as well?

Enough!

Natalie looked up as she approached. "Hey. It's Kat, right?"

She nodded. Natalie seemed cheerful in contrast to her usual dour self.

"Hi, Natalie. Isn't it hot working in the tent?"

"Yeah. But it's darker. It helps my process."

"I have a better idea. Why don't you set up in the house today?"

Justin gave her a questioning look. Kat responded with a light shrug.

Natalie's face lit up. "Really? I'd love to."

As she grabbed her stuff, Justin handed her a piece of paper. "A few questions for Mildred."

Natalie glanced at the list. "And your suggestion?"

"Tell her to find a metal building and go inside. It has to be all metal though," Justin said.

"A metal building? How would that work?"

"It acts like a Faraday cage—like the metal skin of a car protects people from lightning. The voltage should follow the path of least resistance through the metal on the outside of the building."

"I'll take your word for it."

Kat asked, "Can I carry something?"

Natalie handed her a wooden box, the Ouija board. As they walked toward the house, she said, "Why the change of heart? I thought the house was off-limits?"

Kat agreed with Justin to say nothing about the basement, but had to say something. Why not the truth? "It's Mrs. Laskin. I've seen her."

Natalie stopped and looked at Kat. "Awesome. How did she present?"

When Kat gaped quizzically, Natalie said, "How did she appear? What did she look like?"

"Like a reflection—if that makes any sense. I had an impression of a woman in a robe, but only her arm and torso were visible."

"Fascinating. Being in the house should be ideal."

"And you'll keep your promise not to talk about the farm?"

"Absolutely." Natalie gave her a side-glance. "You're running from a man, aren't you?"

Kat nodded and hoped she left it at that. It was true, just not for the reasons Natalie imagined.

As they walked into the kitchen, Natalie said, "Wow. This is really nice. You wouldn't know it from the outside."

It did look fabulous. The floor and quartz countertops shined. The cabinets, treated with oil, looked new. This remodel must have been the last thing they did before—

Yeah.

It was creepy any way she looked at it. Natalie didn't need the truth. Would she discover it on her own? Was that possible? Someone who could speak to the dead? If so, Kat felt it would fracture her world view. On the other hand, why not? Despite her skepticism and disbelief, anything was possible. Her friend Jamie had pushed Kat to entertain new ideas, and she already accepted the existence of ghosts and Mrs. Laskin.

With Natalie situated in the dining room, Kat said, "I'll leave you to it."

Kat went into the pantry, intending to eavesdrop discreetly. She continued oiling the woodwork, a quiet task that shouldn't distract Natalie.

For the longest time, it was quiet. Then Natalie spoke.

★   ★   ★

Natalie felt the odd vibration as they approached the house. A low frequency hum, faint but steady, like an electrical transformer. It grew stronger as she stepped indoors. It was like the sensation that drew her here, but stronger, deeper, more complex.

The dining room table was perfect. Working at an easy pace, Natalie placed the board and the mirror, her mind tuning into the space while she set the grounding stones in the corners of the room. She sat and waited, struggling to tame her excitement. To relax. Whatever was happening, this farmhouse had to be the center of it. She lit a candle and laid out a piece of fresh bread, inhaling and exhaling in slow, measured breaths.

She was still settling in when the planchette moved and straddled the H and I.

Clever. A spirit with a sense of humor.

"Is that you, Mildred?"

The planchette slid to YES.

"Would you like to talk?"

YES.

Natalie stared into the mirror and slipped into a trance. The old woman resolved out of the haze in the mirror with her permed brown hair and arthritic hands.

"How are you today?"

Unhappy. Feeling worse—if that's possible.

Her voice crackled but sounded close. Present.

"I'm sorry to hear that."

Have you spoken to your friend?

"I did. He has some questions and a suggestion that he feels will work."

Okay. What questions?

"Have you ever felt the shocks before?"

Once, long ago. Not this bad though.

"Besides the shocks, do you feel other things?"

I feel lonely sometimes. Otherwise, no. It makes this all the worse, to feel only one thing and for it to be awful.

"I understand. It sounds terrible."

Any other questions?

"Yes. What's it like there? What do you see?"

It's grey. Not much color. I don't mind, really. Besides that, the house looks the same. When the woman moved in, I could tell she was here, but she was almost invisible—almost ghostly, which seemed odd. I know I'm the one on the other side. Do you understand?

"I do. Other spirits have told me similar stories."

It's helpful to know that. Otherwise, nothing has changed. Except for the shocks.

"Okay, I'll let him know."

I've answered your questions. What was your friend's suggestion?

"He said you need to find a metal building and go inside. It should protect you from the currents. Somewhere in town, maybe?"

I'm not leaving.

"What? Why? I know you're probably reluctant to leave a familiar place—"

No. I can't.

"What if it works?"

I'm not leaving. Don't ask me again.

"I'm sorry. I won't bring it up again. I'll ask him if there's something else you can do."

Please. I can't leave my house.

And just like that, she was gone.

Natalie understood Mildred's reluctance to leave, but then realized she hadn't said, *I won't.*

She'd said, *I can't.*

What did that mean?

Twenty-Nine

Sam pulled into the bank parking lot at six a.m.

Across the street, the Quik Stop sat at the intersection of east-west oriented WI 196 and Kelly Road, which ran northeast out of town. She parked in a corner by landscaped bushes that provided partial concealment. Would the bank employees get curious? With the drive-through behind the bank, she thought not. Sam settled into the stakeout, sipped on hot coffee, and played a game on her phone.

Just after nine, a bike rider towing some sort of trailer pulled out from a side street onto Kelly Road, pedaling toward the Quik Stop.

A quick peek with the binoculars confirmed it. Katrina Lundquist in the flesh, looking older and rougher than her photo.

The woman rolled into the store parking lot and chained her bike to a lamppost. She spent five minutes inside.

Would the clerks tip her off?

If they had, it wasn't apparent in her casual demeanor when she walked out, grabbed a bag of ice, and hopped on the bike. Lundquist pedaled off with the same relaxed pace as her arrival, never looking back, continuing up Kelly Road past the side road where she emerged earlier. She must be staying somewhere out of town. But where? She had no known ties to Walden.

Time to find out.

When she had traveled two hundred yards, Sam pulled out and followed.

Lundquist continued biking at a steady speed, never once glancing over her shoulder.

Rolling at a snail's pace, Sam turned left and realized she hadn't thought this through. She had never tailed a bike rider. Who had? Following in the Explorer would be clumsy. If she puttered along, her intent would be obvious. Sam assumed the woman would be hyper-alert to any trouble or undue attention. She carried a bike in back for this possibility, but even that might be too obvious. Still, if she played this right, she wouldn't need it.

Sam pulled over and studied the GPS. Kelly Road ran northeast for four hundred yards, then curved to the north for two hundred yards before making a sharp right. Two hundred yards up, it curved back to the northeast and ran straight for three miles before another turn to the east.

As Lundquist disappeared around the curve, Sam eased forward and stopped as the roadway came into view, barely visible through the trees and foliage lining the shoulder. The SUV should be virtually invisible. Lundquist was approaching the sharp turn right.

Sam decided to let her bike through the next two curves to the longer straight stretch. Then she would speed up and pass. Drive to the curve three miles up, park out of sight, and observe. If Lundquist turned off, Sam would know where to look. If the woman passed her position, Sam would simply reposition. Really, how far could she travel on a bike hauling a trailer?

Sam sighed with relief. The search was nearing an end. The money had been good. She had built a nice financial cushion until the next job came along. Feeling bored, she was ready to wrap this up and take a little vacay. Maybe a week in the Maya Riviera.

As the biker turned to the right, Sam checked the time, allowed two minutes to elapse, and crept around the next bend. The road ahead was clear, as expected. She picked up speed, pulling through the longer left curve, expecting to see Lundquist and her trailer about a hundred yards ahead.

The road was empty.

How?

The woman didn't outrun her on a bike so she had turned off. Sam drove ahead two hundred yards, watching for driveways, made a Y-turn, and stopped.

She had a problem. If she crept along peering out the window, she would draw attention to herself. Too fast and she might miss something. She had a better idea. Sam drove back to town at the speed limit, videotaping the right side of the road with her phone.

Reaching the Quik Stop, she ran through the video at half-speed, looking for evidence of Lundquist, but found nothing promising. Six houses, garages closed, looking quiet as if the occupants were at work. No sign of life anywhere. No bike was visible. They were upscale places with nice lots. Lundquist wasn't living in any of them.

Sam turned and drove the other way, videotaping the other side of the road for two miles, then sped up to see if Lundquist had ducked out of sight and jumped back on the highway after Sam drove into town.

Had she spotted the tail?

Nah.

Five miles up, she stopped. No Lundquist. She checked the video. The terrain on that side of the road was more complex. A couple of houses, several farms, and two longer driveways where the houses weren't visible.

Either she lived along this stretch of road—unlikely, given her intention of staying off the grid—or she was squatting farther out. Or camping in the woods.

Sam returned to town and pulled the bike out of the Explorer. Maybe she should have tailed Kat that way. Too late. Besides, she felt confident she hadn't been spotted. Losing Lundquist was an inconvenience, not a disaster.

Sam pedaled up the road, watching for any evidence the woman had gone off-road: a break in the brush or trampled and crushed vegetation. She rode up the longer driveways, finding a couple of newer homes but no evidence of the woman.

Crap.

Maybe she did notice the tail. If so, would she run or hunker down?

Returning to the SUV, she drove the surrounding roads, running a grid search.

Nothing.

Sam stopped and hung out in town for a while in case she returned. It seemed unlikely. The woman had to be squatting somewhere: an abandoned house, a farm, an outbuilding. She drove the grid again and checked the few places she saw: a couple old farmhouses, one with a barn. Stopped and walked or drove into the woods in several places when she spotted trails or fire roads.

No Kat.

She then explored ever-widening grids in case she was attempting to flee, but Lundquist had vanished.

Shit!

Sam had found her and lost her. What a fricking pain in the ass.

When the sun set, Sam called it quits and called the client with an update. He would understand, wouldn't he?

Mr. Smith answered on the second ring. His voice, soft and mousy, developed an edge when she explained her efforts to tail Kat Lundquist, losing her, and the hours spent in an intense search. She reiterated her conviction that Lundquist was still in the area and finished by saying, "Another day or two and I'll have her."

His tone became pointed and angry. "I'm out of town. I'll be back tomorrow night. Until then, you will continue searching. I expect you to find her. Is that clear?"

"Yes, sir."

The call ended.

Shit.

Time for dinner and a martini at Jake's Supper Club.

Sam was now certain of one thing: she had been played.

Mr. Smith was no weasel.

Thirty

Kat biked to town after breakfast.

The day had dawned warm and thick, oppressive like a sauna, the trees and grass still, the sky opaque.

She stopped at Hanson's Super Mart for chicken and strip steaks, vegetables, coffee, and beer. After packing everything into the trailer, she pedaled three blocks to the Quik Stop. She wanted pizza on the grill tonight and they had appetizing take-and-bake pies in the deli case.

Kat felt an unnerving sensation the moment she walked into the store. A tickle at the back of her neck. A sense she developed while dealing drugs where situational awareness was a matter of life or death. Looking around, she noticed nothing amiss, no unusual attention. Or was the blonde checkout girl, Cassie, paying too much attention to her? Kat grabbed a pizza and walked to the checkout.

"Hi, Cassie. How are you?" The staff wore name tags, and Kat liked to address people by name when possible.

"Good, thanks."

"I'll need some ice too."

"Okay, got it." She glanced up and said, "There was a woman in here yesterday asking about you. Something about your dad. I didn't say anything. I didn't know if I should."

"Thank you. There's nothing going on with my dad. It's probably my ex trying to find me again."

"I'm glad I didn't say anything then."

"Thanks. I appreciate it."

Shit. The bad news just kept accumulating. Harven or the brothers must have someone looking for her. Why had they focused on Walden? She could be anywhere in the country, but they were searching here? Something she said to Harven? She couldn't imagine what, but they were looking in the right place. She must have. When she was high, who knew what she blurted out.

As Kat left the store, she did a casual scan of the area but noted nothing unusual or out of place. Cassie hadn't talked. Maybe they had moved on. But who else had they questioned and what was said? At this point, she could assume nothing. She certainly couldn't ask. It was unlikely everyone had lied for her.

She loaded the pizza and ice into the trailer, hopped on the bike, and pedaled away at her normal pace. She had small rearview mirrors on each side, on the handlebars, and kept a watchful eye on them. About two hundred yards back, a black SUV pulled out of the bank parking lot and turned onto Kelly Road.

Probably nothing. No—it was holding back, moving too slow. Then it pulled over and stopped.

Shit!

Did she have a tail? Had they found her?

Maybe, but they couldn't know about the farm. Not yet.

Was she overreacting to the news at the Quik Stop? The black SUV might be nothing, but Kat opted to react as though it was. If it wasn't, it would be an excellent rehearsal. If it was a tail, her life depended on how intelligently she acted in the next few minutes.

One thing was clear. Harven and the brothers hadn't forgotten, hadn't forgiven, and were closing in. She replayed the conversation with Cassie. A woman had come looking. So not Harven. Gina? No, she was just their accountant. A PI maybe? Made sense. Harven wouldn't take part in the drudgery of a search. That gave her a little time to plan.

Kat maintained a steady pace and considered the road ahead. In a few hundred yards, it curved to the left, followed by a sharp turn east. If she lost the tail now, it would leave her pursuer tail five miles short of the farm, a good buffer of safety. Kat knew this route like she knew her neighborhood growing up. She had studied and memorized every inch of the road for such an eventuality.

She was halfway to the curve right when the SUV edged into view and stopped. A glint of light off the black hood gave it away.

Definitely a tail. Hanging back, lurking in the vegetation along the road, thinking they were invisible.

Kat eased around the corner, pedaled hard for two hundred feet, and turned into the woods on an old fire road that was so overgrown, it was virtually invisible. She ran fifty feet to a hollow, hid the bike and trailer behind some dense brush, and scuttled back to the road.

The SUV crept by at fifteen miles an hour, the woman at the wheel staring straight ahead. She accelerated and had no clue Kat had made her. Once she went around the bend, the road was straight.

Then she'd know, but Kat would be gone.

The trail was thick with grass and bushes and a challenge to navigate on foot with a bike and trailer. She ran as fast as she dare to the south where she encountered a barbed wire fence running east to west. On the other side stood a field of sweet corn. The corn was tall—tasseling out—and would provide perfect cover. She struggled to lift the bike over the fence. Climbing up, holding the aluminum frame with one hand, she lifted it high and dropped it to the ground.

She debated over leaving the groceries behind, but couldn't. No more shopping in town. She would need them to hunker down. Unloading the groceries, she pushed everything through the fence, then performed the same lift and drop with the trailer. Thank God she'd spent the extra money for the light alloy frames.

Sweaty and exhausted, she lay back for five minutes, catching her breath.

To the east, a clear alley hidden from the road ran between the fence and the corn. Kat repacked the trailer and ran a brutal race alongside the cornrows to another fence and turned east, running until she came to Decker Road. Kat stopped, confirmed it was clear, and dashed across into another cornfield. Working the edges of the woods and fields, she pushed closer to the farm and—if she was lucky—leaving her pursuer far behind.

It took forty minutes to cover the distance, cross Townline Road, and plunge into the trees behind the farm. Feeling safe, she collapsed, wheezing, trying to catch her breath. Her legs were on fire, her side ached, her hands still clenched tight from the effort, her body drenched in sweat.

Kat flexed her fingers and tried to relax.

Instead, she panicked. Time to grab her stuff and run.

No. Too risky, too obvious on her bike. They expected her to flee and would patrol the roads. Harven was probably on his way. They might stop looking if she laid low long enough.

But how long was long enough?

Everything was coming unglued. Staying was risky. Leaving just as risky. Justin might be in danger. What to do? She couldn't outrun them on a bike hauling a trailer and a dog.

Working a calming exercise, consciously taking slower, deeper breaths, she forced herself to relax. Panic solved nothing.

There was only one option.

Go to ground. The farm was essentially invisible. Tell Justin the truth. Hope he was willing to help out. She shouldn't care, but even now, she couldn't imagine sharing her history with Justin. If she stayed low, would Harven move on?

After lying there forever, Kat got up and walked to the house, concealing her bike and trailer out of sight.

What the fuck was she going to do?

Thirty-One

Steve Dombrowski walked into work at two o'clock sharp.

He carried his lunch box and a long, gift-wrapped package. As he passed through the machine shop, Gary Ott said something and the others laughed. He ignored them and walked to the break room. It was empty.

Perfect.

Steve was a big man. Jack Reacher big. Six-four and well-muscled, he was nonetheless teased daily about his less than stellar IQ, which his coworkers judged to be about ninety on a good day. They did so because he took the abuse amiably. Played the role of the gentle giant. He had always been big, even as a kid, and his mother had taught him to be humble when dealing with others. If he complained about the names and other slights at school, Mom told him those were only words. He had never been in a fight, never used his size to intimidate, although he had thought about it once or twice.

He worked as a maintenance associate at Walden Stamping, a tool and die company. A glorified janitor, he cleaned and performed light repairs and tended to the plantings on the grounds. It was a decent job and paid okay, but in the past few weeks, the taunts had riled him. His sense of humor—and his tolerance for crap—had disappeared. Steve struggled to maintain a jovial veneer, but underneath, he seethed at the slights thrown at him from the front office to the shop floor. He thought about quitting, but what was the point? So he could go elsewhere and be mocked by different people?

Nope.

There were other things. Gary was especially mean with the comments and practical jokes. The shop guys swore a lot. He hated swearing. And the boss only gave him a crappy fifty cent raise in March.

Cheapskate.

Today, Steve decided enough was enough. He ate breakfast at six a.m. and packed a lunch—though he wasn't sure he would eat it.

He might be in jail. Or dead.

He spent an hour wrapping his AR-15 in a box with bright gift wrapping and a big bow. Then he grabbed his Springfield Hellcat Pro. Checked the magazine. Took a spare, just in case. Chambered a round. The gun fit nicely in his lunch box. Guns were the only thing he enjoyed in life. He had a safe full of them and practiced twice a week at the local gun club. They didn't tease him much there. He might be dumb, but he was a crack shot with a steady hand and 30-20 vision.

Usually, he left a note for Mom, but today, what could he say? He was about to disappoint her.

They lived almost five miles out of town on Kelly Road. The drive to work took ten minutes, so he left at a quarter to.

Whistling as he put his lunch box into his locker, Steve stuck the Springfield into a waist holster. Carrying the AR-15 at his side, he walked to the front office, pushed the door open, and fired six rounds before anyone moved or even registered the weapon in his hand. He targeted the boss and his wife, three rounds each, center mass. They were probably dead before they hit the floor.

Kalli, the front office girl, stared for a moment before erupting in screams. Steve let her be. She was the only person here who treated him decently.

The shop was loud and everyone wore ear protection, but they heard the shots and frantically rushed for the exit.

A few escaped.

Steve spotted Gary and fired a half-dozen rounds. As Gary fell, he sprayed the room with the rest of the magazine. Three more people went down, the shots echoing in the tall space.

Silence.

The screaming from the front office had stopped. Kalli was probably calling the police. A minute later, he heard sirens.

Was he hungry?

Nope. He didn't feel like lunch. Didn't feel like going to jail either.

He set the AR down, drew the Springfield, and waited until the police arrived. With a deep breath, he walked out the back door. When the cops screamed at him to drop the weapon, he pulled the pistol up with surprising speed and fired until a hail of bullets tore into his body and dropped him to the ground.

His final thought?

Sorry Mom.

Thirty-Two

Kat spent the afternoon on the porch.

The air shimmered with heat. Cicadas buzzed in the trees. The dog days were here.

Sitting, drinking beer, pacing occasionally, she tried to parse the options. Every action felt like an intolerable risk. Staying? Leaving? There were considerable dangers either way. Staying *felt* safer. The farmhouse was essentially invisible. Surely they would stop looking if she laid low long enough. But she felt trapped, akin to being back in prison. They weren't comparable, but Kat liked this place, the small town, her little freedoms, her life as it was.

Staying was easier, but when Harven made the same calculation about abandoned farmhouses Kat had, the search might lead here. Was that a risk she was willing to take? What about Justin?

She could stay for a bit, but ultimately, it was time to move on. No point in working on the house now, a thought that cut deeply.

Fuck it.

Nothing in her life would work out. She had squandered her karma and the universe was paying her back in spades. How she missed Jamie, her old roommate. She wished they could talk now. Jamie would know what to do.

She needed to tell Justin the truth. Hope he was willing to help. Hard to do though. They were becoming friends and she couldn't bear to see the look of disappointment in his eyes when she revealed her past. She considered lying, then weighed the ways doing so could backfire. Besides, wasn't she better than that now?

How would he react? She imagined he saw her as a woman of mystery. Not an addict, a drug dealer, and a rat. A felon who had done hard time. A common criminal.

There was a bigger issue. As a friend, Justin deserved to know the dangers he faced. While Harven wouldn't purposely target anyone besides her, he wouldn't hesitate to kill anyone who stood in his way.

So that was the plan. Hunker down for a while. Then move on.

First, the hard part.

Kat grabbed two beers and wandered out to the encampment. Justin was typing on his laptop, his hair disheveled, dressed in jean shorts and a tank top. He looked good. Hot. Manly, if a bit nerdy.

He looked up and said, "Sweet! Thank you."

"Busy? Mind if I sit?"

"No, go ahead." He motioned to a chair.

"How's it going?"

"Quiet today." He reached over and took a pill from a bottle and swallowed it with beer.

When she looked at him quizzically, he said, "Migraine med. I feel one coming on."

"Another one?"

"Yeah. I've had more than usual lately."

"The demons underground?"

He laughed. "Possibly."

"Have you considered *all* the risks?"

"Hard to say when I don't know what all the risks are. What's up?"

"I have a problem."

"Oh?"

She took a long draw from her bottle and made eye contact with difficulty. "As you surmised, I'm squatting here. Living off the grid. You haven't pushed the issue and I appreciate that, but now I need a favor. Before I ask, an explanation is necessary."

Kat gave him the short version of her addiction, the dealing, her prison stay, and the decision to jump parole.

He remained quiet with a thoughtful look even when she paused. Kat finally said, "The guys I ratted out, the Campo brothers, are not the forgiving kind. I'm certain they're looking for me and plan to kill me."

"I thought they went to prison?"

"They did. But the organization survived and their enforcer avoided prosecution." Kat sipped her beer, watching his reaction to the news. His face remained impassive. She added, "Yesterday, someone asked about me in town. Today, I think I was tailed on the way home. I lost them, but I can't risk going out on the bike again."

"I can drive you to town—"

"I can't even show my face. And it might be best for you to steer clear. These guys are dangerous. If you get in the way—I'm worried about you."

He didn't speak at first. She could see the wheels turning, assessing the revelations about her, weighing the hazards involved. She fully expected him to say no. Describing her circumstances aloud, she sounded like a loser, her situation dire, the risks unacceptable.

"You lost the tail just out of town?"

"I think so."

"So would they suspect the farm?"

"They might, if they do the same calculations I did—that you did, for that matter. It's obviously abandoned."

"Only if you look at a satellite image. Would they do that?"

"I don't know." And yet, the answer seemed obvious. Harven wasn't stupid.

"What can I do to help?"

"Do my shopping for awhile? Sorry, I know it's a lot to ask."

He sat, his face inscrutable. He took a long drink from the bottle. "I won't pretend I'm not shocked. I imagined you being pursued by a dangerous ex or something."

Uh oh, here it comes.

Kat steeled herself for the worst.

"You've been good to me. You act and sound like someone who's changed. You did your time and beat your addiction. You could've chased me off with your Glock, but you chose to help me. Just give me a list when you need something."

Kat nodded, feeling relieved and grateful—an emotion she hadn't felt in some time. She was just getting settled here, thinking it might work. Now this.

Figuring his answer would speak volumes, Kat quietly said, "Want to stay for dinner?"

"Love to."

"Walk over about six?"

He nodded.

Then she heard sirens in the distance. Lots of them.

★   ★   ★

Kat made a strip steak with fresh asparagus wrapped in swiss cheese and prosciutto. The fresh pizza hadn't survived the chase earlier. They sat at the table in the kitchen with more formal place settings and a bottle of wine, a cabernet Justin claimed was just sitting in his SUV. They small-talked for a bit before he said, "If you stay out of sight for a month or so, wouldn't they conclude you've moved on?"

"Logically, that makes sense, but these guys aren't necessarily logical. I still don't know how they found me—how they decided I was hiding out in small town Wisconsin. Most people would have run much farther."

"That's an interesting observation. Something you said to them, maybe?"

"That's what I think, but I can't remember anything. Of course, I was baked twenty-four-seven."

He glanced at her. "How did you beat it—the addiction?"

She told him the story and a little about her friend Jamie. "In the end, I simply decided I was done."

"That's amazing. Most addicts never make it out."

"Wasn't a choice really. I hated myself—"

"Still do from what I can see."

"I do. I've fucked up everything I've touched."

"I don't know. This dinner's awfully good."

She laughed, a release of tension after the big reveal. "You're a funny guy."

"Why did you stay in Wisconsin?"

"Familiarity. There's no place like home and all that? Maybe to be near my ex-husband? I don't know."

"Would someone know that about you?"

"Possibly. Harven and I talked enough over the years."

"Given your…profession, jail had to be a constant threat."

"I tried not to think about it."

"Where's your ex now?"

"Madison. He's remarried and probably living happily ever after."

A long silence hung between them as they sipped their wine.

He looked hot again. She struggled with the feeling. Needing to change tack, Kat said, "I have a concern. If you think this plume is an upwelling of bad energy—if your theory is true, are we safe here?"

"I've thought about it a great deal." He sipped on his wine. His teeth were tinged lightly red.

She ran her tongue over her teeth, concerned they looked red too.

"A lot of scientific exploration entails some risk. My hope is, being cognizant of that, I'll be more aware of any threats. I've carefully monitored my behavior and feelings and I'm keeping a log of any effects—just the migraines so far. Since I have no criminal leanings, I think it's reasonably safe for me to stay."

"What about me?"

"You're aware of the situation. I think you'll be okay. Have you noticed anything?"

"Other than Mrs. Laskin? I've had some bizarre and persistent nightmares." She told him about the monster in her dreams but left Harven out.

"That's interesting. Document it for me, please."

With the wine, his acceptance and understanding—feeling hopeful again, her hormones were raging. He needed to leave but she said nothing.

"You're right to worry about it, but you're intelligent and mentally tough—"

"You hardly know me."

"And—I hate to say it—very attractive. You try to hide it—"

Kat could no longer hold back. She leaned in and kissed him, tentative at first; more passionately when he kissed her back, deeply.

A part of her fought it. A tiny part.

Soon their hands were everywhere, and she pulled him up the stairs to the bedroom, yanking his pants off as she pushed him onto the bed.

Thirty-Three

Kat dreamt she was riding on a tilt-o-whirl when she was yanked from sleep and pulled toward the door.

What the—?

Justin tugged on her arm. "Move! Quickly!"

The house was dark and shaking. Things crashed and broke downstairs. Just as he pulled her into the doorway and she tugged Max in, the shuddering stopped.

"Quake?"

"Yep. Fairly big one. I've got to check my gear. Want to come?"

"Sure. Clothes would be good though."

She felt disoriented. By the earthquake, the man in her bedroom, the realization they'd had sex and it was amazing. They must have fallen asleep. Kat couldn't imagine willingly letting Justin stay over. Or could she? While the relationship was unsettling and not part of her plan, it wasn't a bad thing. Maybe it was time to revise the plan. Except Harven was out there somewhere. The man was a rabid Rottweiler that wouldn't quit. If she cared about Justin, she needed to stay away from him.

Suitably dressed for the night, they walked around the broken glasses in the kitchen and out to the encampment. The night was deathly quiet. Even the crickets were silent. The tremor?

Justin opened his laptop, whistled, and muttered, "Holy shit!"

"What?"

"Five-point-five, depth four kilometers."

He clacked away on the keys. Kat felt alert but was still pondering the change in their relationship.

"The ground temperature has risen four degrees in the last three hours. It's possible there's magma right under our feet. Impossible by everything I know and understand. Except I'm one step closer to proving my theory, the first part anyway. A lot closer."

"Magma under our feet sounds bad."

"With a bigger plume, yes. Here, I doubt it will reach the surface. That's a cornerstone of my theory. These are subterranean events."

"So the demons will stay underground too?"

He laughed. "Demons aren't part of the theory. It's the changes in electrical current that matter." He popped a pill and pointed to a graph with a tall, pointy spike that meant nothing to Kat. "That massive surge in voltage occurred during the quake."

"Another migraine?"

He nodded. "It's an effect, I guess."

Kat wondered what those currents were doing to her. "Breakfast?"

"Sure. Sounds great."

The sun broke the horizon as they walked back to the house. A wind shift overnight had swept away most of the humidity. These respites from Gulf moisture were a bonus of Wisconsin living. Sadly, there were few reprieves from the winter cold.

Kat swept up the broken glass in the kitchen and lit the grill. Put coffee in a percolator on the burner. Eggs and bacon, she decided. Justin hovered. She told him to sit.

Finally, he said, "About last night?"

"Am I having second thoughts?"

"Yeah."

"No." But she was. "You?"

"None. It was awesome."

It was. Why couldn't she just be mindful and live in the moment? Accept it at face value? Besides, she wanted to do it again. Now.

She set a mug of coffee in front of him.

"You don't want entanglements," he said.

"I'm leery of them."

"I'm not an entanglement. No commitment required."

"What about your friend—with benefits?"

"By definition, a friend. We're both free to see others."

"That's weird."

"More common than you think," he said, fiddling with his phone.

Kat concentrated on making breakfast, trying to convince herself this wasn't a bad idea.

When she set his plate down, he thanked her and said, "We'll take it slow."

"Got it."

She sat and felt like a teenager. They took surreptitious glances at each other. Something had changed. The silence between them was easy.

Suddenly, he blurted, "Holy shit! Look at this."

He pushed his phone at her. The headline blared:

SEVEN DEAD IN WISCONSIN SHOOTING

"It's national news. It happened here, in Walden."

"Oh no." Kat set her fork down slowly. "That's beyond spooky. Your theory suddenly looks…frightening."

Justin ran a hand through his hair. "This isn't how I wanted to prove it."

"Again, are we safe here?"

"Have you been feeling homicidal?"

"No, but I'm worried. I can't exactly run."

"I could sneak you to my place—or anywhere, for that matter—but I'm staying here. I hope you understand."

"No. I'm staying—for now. And Max and I are a package."

"This may work in your favor. This stronger quake will bring more scientists, media, and looky-loos, especially with the shooting. It may be hard for the drug guys to operate."

"True." Pointing to the headline, she said, "Likewise. That isn't how I wanted to find peace of mind."

After Justin walked over to his camp, she sat on the porch to finish her coffee. Suddenly, a wave of bitter self-loathing washed over her. She deserved no happiness, and Justin deserved better than the likes of her. An addict. A felon. A parole violator—though that gambit probably saved her life. Still, Harven and his minions could be closing in. Any involvement with Justin put him at risk. She had to nip this in the bud.

Natalie popped through the bushes. Instead of stopping at the encampment, she strode straight to the porch where Kat sat with her coffee.

"Did you hear about the shooting in town?"

"Yes. It's awful."

"Nice kid. I knew him. He lived out here somewhere with his mom."

Kat felt an arctic wind blow across her neck and down her spine.

Holy shit!

The shooter lived near the farm? She had to tell Justin.

"Did that earthquake happen near here?" Natalie asked.

"Justin seems to think so. Why didn't you ask him?"

"I'm not in the mood for Ritchie Rich today."

Despite her anxiety, Kat smiled inwardly at the friction between those two. Yes, Natalie was salty, but Justin had evidently never been challenged before. He took it personally. She might have to sit him down and explain mindfulness, though she should talk. She wasn't very mindful herself right now.

"Can I set up in the dining room again? The connection seemed perfect in there."

"Sure, go ahead."

Weird. Natalie implied her process was like a phone connection or cell signal. Maybe they were similar. What did Kat know? A lot of what she believed about the world had been upended in the past few weeks. She left Natalie and ran over to Justin's camp.

He looked up as she approached, eyebrows raised.

"Natalie said that guy, the shooter? He lived out here somewhere."

"Shit. That's bad." He mused out loud: "What can I do? It's hardly proof. If I issue some sort of warning, I'll be ridiculed, pilloried. I'm not anywhere near making a lucid case."

"Again, are we safe here?"

"I don't know. We'll revisit that question—hourly if need be. Right now, I think we're okay. Sorry, but I have some findings to post."

As she walked back, she opted to do some mindless work in the garden, but her effort devolved into a bout of recrimination and despair over her involvement with Justin. The need to up and move. She couldn't stay here with Harven chasing her. Was Natalie in danger too? Should she warn her? Her head was spinning. Between the sex, the quake, the shooting, and the dangers posed by the cartel, she didn't know what to do.

She sat on the edge of the porch, ruminating. Max moseyed over, leaned into her, and laid down. Had he sensed her mood? But his nose was dry, his eyes rheumy and dull. Was he falling ill? Or did he feel the telluric currents too?

"Not feeling well, buddy?"

He leaned into her touch. She stroked his back and tried to enjoy the quiet moment, regardless of the problems they faced.

Instead, she felt the powerful draw of cocaine calling her name, promising an end to her pain and worries. Right now, she would kill for a hit.

Was that how the plume spoke to her?

Thirty-Four

Natalie set the Ouija board on the dining room table. In measured steps, she placed the grounding stones in each corner of the room, intoning the Latin phrase to activate them. She lit a candle and a stick of incense, then gazed into the scrying mirror and began her relaxation routine. For some reason, she slipped into her optimal state of mind easily in the house. The atmosphere was soothing, the persistent low-level hum comforting, like stepping into the eye of the storm. While everyone in the spiritual world was in turmoil, she felt a preternatural calm.

Moments later, the planchette moved.

"Mildred, is that you?"

YES

"Would you like to talk?"

YES

Natalie tucked her hair behind her ears and stared into the mirror. The space within expanded in seconds and Mildred appeared, restless and trembling with a palsy like Parkinson's. Natalie felt empowered. Hyperaware. The connection that normally took ten to fifteen minutes was near instantaneous. Instead of merely touching the spiritual world, she had merged with it.

"Are things any better?"

No. It's terrible. Does your friend have another idea?

"I'm afraid not. I talked to a spirit in town. They moved to Timmer Welding behind the Episcopal church on Main. It worked. The shocks stopped."

I won't leave here. I can't.

"You said that. I don't understand. Why can't you? What's stopping you?"

A long silence followed. Natalie felt impatient. She didn't understand Mildred's inability to leave or reluctance to talk. If the shocks were so bad, wouldn't she welcome a solution that worked? Alice and the others were ecstatic with the outcome. Natalie was a hero in town even though the idea had been Justin's.

Finally, Mildred spoke in a muted voice.

The dead people.

Natalie felt her hackles rise. "The dead people? What do you mean? I thought you were alone."

I am. They're under the basement.

"There are bodies buried under the basement?"

They're not buried. That's the problem.

"I don't understand. Why aren't they buried?"

I'm not sure. I can't go down there.

"So how do you know they're there?"

I just do.

"Where exactly are they?"

I don't know. But I think the woman upstairs does.

Huh? What did the bike lady know? Certainly more than she let on. What were she and Ritchie Rich up to?

"Why are the dead people keeping you here?"

They need a proper burial.

"Who are they?"

I don't know. Family, I think.

Natalie pressed harder now, sensing something critical. "How did they die?"

They were murdered.

"How do you know that?"

I don't know.

Natalie wondered if Mildred had lost her mind. This was one of the most consequential yet irritating séances she had ever held. Was Mildred being disingenuous? Had she lied about being pushed down the stairs? Natalie didn't think so. Spirits were usually straightforward, emotionless. They simply existed and didn't emote or act out, except in anger or frustration. If anything, she sounded distraught. Believable. Maybe Mildred was simply addled by the shocks which prevented her from thinking or speaking clearly.

Natalie was beginning to feel the house was the problem, a negative node or vortex perhaps, a focal point of concentrated energy and a place where bad things happened with unnerving frequency.

"Have you ever met other spirits here?"

No.

"Have—"

I hear a voice sometimes.

"What? I don't understand."

A cry for help.

"Where does it come from?"

The basement.

Crap! Why hadn't Mildred offered that information first? What did it mean? She could hear someone but not see them? Natalie couldn't quite fathom the idea, but it was something to ponder. The house was a fascinating puzzle, revealing mystical secrets faster than she could absorb them. But Natalie suspected she had learned everything she could from this spirit and wanted to attempt contact with the other voice. Mildred had to leave first. It was in her best interest anyway.

"How can I convince you to go into town? I assure you, the spirits there are ecstatic that the metal building protects them."

Promise me you'll find the dead people and bury them. Then I'll feel free to go.

"I'll try."

Promise me!

"I promise. I'll do it. You leaving will help me find them. Maybe I can connect with the voice you heard.

Why should I trust you?

Good question. What should she say? "I came to help. And I came back with a solution. I live to help people like you."

You sound very sincere.

"I am. Now go find the others. You know where the Episcopal church is, right?"

Yes.

"Then go. I'll handle the rest."

Natalie felt her slip away with a sigh as the mirror went dark. Hopefully, Mildred would find peace and comfort in town and feel less alone.

As she slid the planchette to GOOD BYE, she wondered about the voice Mildred heard. Could spirits exist on different planes? That voice seemed to imply as much. Natalie always assumed the spirit world existed on one level, that the spirits she reached were simply the most talkative or the closest to her location. Were there other planes with spirits hidden within them? A question she desperately wanted to answer.

But where to start? And how would she make good on her promise to Mildred?

She had to grill the bike lady.

It was bright outdoors after the relative darkness of the dining room. Standing in the doorway, Natalie squinted and spotted Kat sitting on the edge of the porch. "What do you know about dead people under the basement?"

Kat jerked her head around, wide-eyed in shock. "How do you know about that?"

"Your Mrs. Laskin told me."

The bike lady pursed her lips, then said, "What'd she say?"

"She said it was murder. She wants them to have a proper burial."

The woman nodded reflectively. "Makes sense."

"Do you know where they are?"

"Yes. I found a room under the basement."

"I need to see it," Natalie said tersely, hands on hips. "Why didn't you tell me?"

"To see if you figured it out on your own."

Natalie humphed. "Satisfied?"

Kat nodded, looking suitably impressed, and said, "One condition—no, two. One, no police. We'll have to call them eventually, but not yet."

"Okay. And two?"

"You tell me what happened down there."

"Deal."

The woman got up as if burdened by a great weight. Natalie could barely contain herself, sensing the threshold of something monumental, beyond anything she could imagine. They went through the kitchen into the basement. Through a trapdoor and down a ladder and the steepest steps she had ever seen. The hum she noticed near the house was more intense. The sound of electrical currents flowing on a grand scale, like stepping into the engine room of a movie starship. She had never heard anything like it.

"Do you hear that?"

"What? It's deathly silent down here," Kat said. "No pun intended."

Despite approaching the brink of some magical destiny, her apprehension grew at the bottom of the stairs. She could almost hear the tortured souls crying out for help. Or was she simply swept up in the moment? But this secret staircase felt like the negative reflection of a stairway to heaven. Something evil had happened down here.

Despite those feelings and the growing sense of foreboding, nothing could prepare her for the scene beyond the door when Kat held up the lantern.

She startled and then saw everything with paranormal awareness. The bones. The people who once inhabited them. The room was a spiritual level unto itself. If she set up here, she could talk to those people. Natalie felt certain of it.

"I have to bring my stuff down here."

The bike lady started to shake her head, considered, and said, "Sure. If it'll help, go ahead."

"I need to work alone."

Kat nodded and walked up the stairs. Natalie followed and grabbed her things. The universe was speaking to her and was about to reveal deeper truths.

When she returned, she pushed the Tarot cards aside, uncertain what they represented. They felt like a distraction.

Natalie set the mirror down. The moment she opened the board and placed the planchette, a garbled voice spoke in her head.

Hello?

Crazy. This shouldn't even be working. She had never heard a voice before completing the full ritual. The usual rules didn't seem to apply here. Standing on uncharted ground, she was torn by a crazy quilt of emotions: excited, curious, nervous, and fearful, with no idea where this was going. Such moments seldom came without risk.

Natalie sat and stared into the mirror. "Who am I speaking with?"

Vera.

"Would you like to talk, Vera?"

Yes.

Natalie gazed into the mirror. The space was already fully three dimensional. A woman resolved out of the darkness. Barely visible, she was tall, wearing a nondescript tee and jeans. She looked about forty and world-weary. Beaten down. Her hair was a dull brown and shoulder-length. Haze or fog swirled around her in the dim light.

"How can I help you, Vera?"

Get me out of here.

Her voice sounded distorted and scratchy, wavering up and down in frequency, with an alien quality to it.

"Can't you just leave, like Mildred?"

Mildred? My mother-in-law? She's dead. I'm the only one here.

"You're alone?"

Yes. Always have been.

"Okay. Tell me your story. How did you end up here?"

I'm not sure. My husband, I think. He started acting strangely in the last month of my life and quoting nonsense from the Bible. Our son came home from school, we sat down to dinner, and then I was dead.

As Vera spoke, she saw the events play out in a mishmash of three-dimensional visions. No faces, just shadows. A man firing a gun. An explosion of brain matter. A hand tossing Tarot cards onto the table. A hammer swinging. More gunfire. She recoiled from the horror of it.

Vera closed with: *I've been stuck here ever since in this damn fog.*

"That's dreadful."

It's been horrid. A nightmare.

"Your son was never there with you?"

No. I assumed they went to Heaven.

They? Vera hoped her murdering husband went to Heaven?

After a brief pause, Vera said, *Can you get me out of here?*

"I don't know." And she didn't. She had never encountered anything like this. She sat there thinking, trying to make sense of it all, head swirling with questions and confusion. What was going on here? It felt like a tear in the fabric of the spirit world where anything was possible. Was that the hum she heard? Something like a spiritual vortex? Would her group have any answers?

"Are you getting shocked?"

Like electric shocks?

"Yes."

No. I feel nothing—other than fear.

"I don't have any experience with this. I don't understand it. As soon as I figure it out, I'll be back."

Vera spoke in a low, desperate tone. *Thanks for talking to me, but be careful. I can't tell you how dangerous it is here. Sometimes, I fear I'll be sucked into the center of the earth.*

A shudder went down Natalie's spine. The intense fear in Vera's voice was frightening. She had been trapped here for forty years? Surely a fate worse than death—if that was even possible.

Natalie sensed darkness and danger nearby. She closed the board, grabbed her things, ran up the stairs and ladder, and made for the door with a growing awareness she was woefully unprepared for this encounter.

Natalie shoved the screen door open and eyed the bike lady. "I need to do a little research. I'll be back in a few days."

Not waiting for an answer, Natalie stomped off to the tree line.

Thirty-Five

Justin settled in and rechecked the data from overnight. Besides the strong early morning temblor, there had been two minor quakes. The ground temperature had risen ten degrees in a day. Posting the data online, the sharp increase in temperature drew plenty of interest and speculation. Everyone wondered the same thing. Was magma rising beneath their feet? In Wisconsin?

The magnitude of the quake itself was shocking. There was simply no precedent for the event. Lava flowing to the surface would be biblical.

The shooting in Walden was a deeply disturbing escalation of violence in the area, beyond anything he'd imagined for this situation. Would it become a worst-case scenario like Jonestown? How could he prove they were related? The murder a few days back now resonated more clearly. It had looked like a simple crime of passion. Had telluric currents incited a supposedly placid housewife to murder?

Media outlets were losing their minds over the shooting and the quake, but only the conspiracy nuts and the religious zealots had connected the two. Talking about the end times, declaring the events to be a clear message from God: Repent or perish!

He didn't want to be lumped with that crowd, but discovered the worst possible association had already occurred: someone had found his papers on Jonestown and Heaven's Gate and posted them prominently alongside a list of batshit crazy theories about mass shootings.

Shit!

A warning from him would be pointless until he could present a coherent set of data about this event. The chances of being taken seriously were thin enough without the lunatic fringe trumpeting his ideas.

He also faced an almost unbelievable threat: the members of a drug cartel could show up at any moment to kill Kat and anyone who stood in their way. In normal circumstances, he would have bailed and left town, but things were anything but normal. Besides, they didn't know where she was, or they would be here. Maybe the circus erupting around Walden would hinder their search. Maybe they would simply stake out the town and wait.

Did it matter? Unless he saw gunmen in the bushes, he was staying. He might be the only person who realized the full import of what was happening in Walden. On the cusp of a major discovery, he sat at ground zero of a potentially cosmic shift in the geological understanding of the planet and age-old questions about evil. It could establish new paradigms in geology, seismology, and philosophy. Maybe even theology.

Curiosity, the scientific method, and professional ethics demanded he stay.

He would prepare to meet the risks. He had guns at home. Infrared gear. Tomorrow, he would come fully prepared to protect himself; and Kat, if need be. Knowing they were coming evened the odds somewhat.

Or was he being foolhardy or overconfident because of the telluric currents? He was a game hunter, not a soldier.

Too many questions. Too few answers.

While he fretted over those things, he also thought about the night before with Kat. She was wild in bed, her name fully apropos. But it was more than great sex. It had been a long time since he connected with another human so completely. First-time sex was usually awkward, but they hummed like a centrifuge in perfect balance. He wanted to do it again, but knew Kat needed time to process the change in their relationship. He would play it cool and wait for her to make the next move.

Justin swatted at an insect on his arm, then reached for the Off as another landed on his neck. Bugs and mosquitoes, a fact of summer life. As he settled back, he swatted two on his thigh. They seemed undeterred by the repellent. Then he noticed something odd. They only appeared in his peripheral vision. As he focused to brush them away, they grew blurry and disappeared.

He concentrated to confirm his suspicions: they weren't real. An effect of the telluric currents? The migraines were less clear. He suffered from them anyway. This was unique. An escalation. Would the symptoms be the same for everyone? Or would they be particular to each individual? An interesting question.

Kat was having regular visitations from a ghost and disturbing nightmares. Was that all? Had Kat seen bugs too?

He grabbed his hand recorder and noted the date and time. Deciding the insects were an illusion, he rationalized that, while unpleasant, they weren't awful. He would quantify his observations and reactions.

His phone rang. His friend Elliot Wolf, the Native American historian.

"Elliot. How are you?"

"Fabulous. I imagine you're sitting somewhere near Walden hoping to prove your microplume theories?"

"I am. Find something?"

"Yes, and you're going to love it."

"Do tell."

"Among our mythical figures, Na'ena, also known as Wapti Kokotni, is the Great Spirit or Earthmaker. His counterpart, Heregenina, is responsible for all the bad things in the world. He is often portrayed as an evil, demon-like spirit."

"Thanks for the lesson. How does that help me?"

"According to legend, the place in the world where his spirit dwells is called Heregenina Rock. The Weyauwega believed the rock was evil and gave it a wide berth."

"Interesting, but—"

"That place, marked by a limestone outcrop, is now called Heron Rock. It's nine miles northeast of Walden."

Justin almost dropped his phone. Justin did a search and found it less than a mile from the farm.

Holy shit.

"Justin?"

"Wow. That's unbelievable."

"You still trying to prove that evil lies beneath our feet?"

"More or less."

"My people could have told you that ages ago."

★   ★   ★

Kat walked over to the encampment just after six. Fair weather cumulus lazed overhead. The air smelled fresh. Justin typed busily on a laptop.

She put a hand on his shoulder. "Dinner? My place? Nothing fancy."

"Love to."

"How's it going?"

"The ground temp is still rising. Three minor quakes this afternoon. We're on the verge of something major here."

He stood, looking ready to kiss her, but held back. He grabbed his phone and they walked toward the house.

"So you're staying?" Kat asked. "Despite the risks?"

"Which risks?"

"All of them. The plume, the drug people."

"I have guns at home. I'll be armed tomorrow."

"Careful, don't underestimate them."

Kat marinated two chicken breasts and grilled them with a potato. They carried the breakfast table out and set up on the porch. Justin pulled two beers from the Yeti while Kat served dinner. A comfortable silence passed while they ate and watched a fiery reddish-orange sunset, an apparent consequence of forest fires in Canada.

Kat expected Justin to stay the night. He surprised her by saying, "Let's go to my place. I'll sneak you out under the cover of darkness."

"What about Max?"

"Max too. He's totally welcome."

Kat hesitated. There were a hundred reasons she shouldn't leave. Was it safe? What if someone saw her? But they wouldn't be looking for Justin or his vehicle. Maybe a night away was just what she needed. There were several good reasons to accept.

"Do you have a washing machine?"

"Of course."

"A shower?"

"No. No shower." He shook his head, his expression dead serious.

She stared for a moment.

He laughed. She followed suit. Whatever thoughts she had about avoiding Justin to protect him went out the window. He made her feel happy again.

Kat packed her clothing and food for Max.

They left once it was fully dark, following his trail through the woods. She realized they could drive around and assess the potential dangers. They drove several circuits around the farm. Other than the many observing stations, it was quiet. They checked the streets in Walden. Multiple media vehicles were parked on the main roads, but no black SUVs lurked anywhere. Several of the brick-faced buildings had significant damage. Hanson's Super Value was closed until further notice. The taverns were busy though. Their careful survey revealed no obvious risks.

It was a thirty-minute drive to his house, a lovingly restored Craftsman original just outside Sun Prairie. After the obligatory tour, Kat started her laundry and took a shower, luxuriating in the powerful stream of hot water.

Oh God, how she missed this simple pleasure.

When she strolled into the kitchen, hair dry, feeling marvelously clean, he stood and handed her a margarita. "Cheers."

It was perfect.

The evening was perfect. The shower, the electricity, the staples of life most people took for granted. She relaxed. The drink completed her descent into bliss. She remained mindful and ignored all the contrary thoughts harping on what a bad idea this was. Nope, not tonight. She pushed them away and reveled in the feeling of serenity. Had no second thoughts when he pulled her to him, kissed her, and led her down the hallway to his room.

Later, lying in bed, Kat felt truly safe for the first time in years.
Here, cocaine did not whisper to her.
Nor did the monster.

Thirty-Six

Gina Gallagher finished mixing a vodka tonic and turned to face Harven.

He looked unassuming. Five-foot-ten with mousy hair, a forgettable face, and average build—a man invisible in plain sight. He could be a math teacher or the manager of a fast-food restaurant. A nobody. Except that he was a martial arts expert in several disciplines and even more deadly with a multitude of weapons. He looked out of place in her lavish living room of white carpet, glass and steel furniture, and elegant artwork. She was an ardent fan of Picasso and owned several originals. Business had been very good.

She glanced down. Good. He remembered to leave his shoes at the door.

"Would you like something?"

"No, thank you." He maintained eye contact, never straying down to her black silk top or snug jeans. She knew he found her attractive but hid it well, unlike his lumbering associates.

"How did it go in Dallas?"

"Very well. Situation resolved. Discreetly."

"I never expect any less from you. Have you talked to the PI today?"

"Not yet. I was going to call her next."

"But you have a location?"

"Yes, a small area, about thirty or forty square miles, near a town called Walden. Positive ID, but Kat slipped the tail."

"Does she have friends or family there?"

"Neither. Her family disowned her. She has no friends, none that aren't in prison anyway."

"Where is she then?"

"Knowing Kat, she's probably hiding out in an old farmhouse. There are several empty farmsteads in the area."

"But if she thinks we're onto her, will she run?"

"I don't think so. She won't panic. And she has no vehicle that we know of, just a bike. I think she'll go to ground and hope the search moves on. If she runs, she'll wait a week or two first."

"The PI sounds incompetent. Call her for an update and terminate the contract."

"Now?"

"Please. I'd like to know how close we are."

Harven pulled out a phone and tapped the screen.

"Yes, it's Mr. Smith. I'd like a progress report."

He listened for a moment, nodded once, and shook his head.

"That's wonderful, but I'm no longer interested in your services. It sounds like you conducted a heavy-handed tail, lost the woman, and alerted her to your presence. Not my idea of good work at all. Send an invoice for the last week and cease and desist in any further efforts to track Katrina Lundquist. Understood?"

He tapped the screen and pocketed the phone.

"She had no luck today."

"That's unfortunate," Gina said. "What's your plan, Mr. Smith?"

Harven smirked. "Liam, Denny, and I will go up there in the morning with a drone and find her."

Gina lit a cigarette and eyed Harven. "I'm coming with you and running the operation. It's personal. I want to put the last nail in her coffin."

"Yes, ma'am."

"You're okay with that?"

"You know I am. Just so you know, there are some complications in the area. This morning's earthquake occurred there and there was a mass shooting yesterday."

Gina said, "That quake was something, huh?"

"Unbelievable," Harven said. "The first one I've experienced."

"Me as well. Will it affect the search?"

"I don't think so. Might even help, with everyone focused on other issues."

"Good. Thank you. I'll see you in the morning. Nine o'clock?"

"Yes."

With a curt nod, he walked out the door.

Harven was a little creepy, but loyal, even after her brothers had gone to prison. They had paid him well. She paid him even better. A bond of loyalty was usually stronger when people were well compensated.

When they went away, Tomas and Antonio demanded that everyone respect Gina as their heir, but she worried there might be a coup to oust her. Harven kept everyone in line, killing the few who objected. One murder had been in brutal cartel style: torture, decapitation, the body parts tossed in a ditch. All dissent ended after that.

Gina swallowed the rest of her drink and smiled. She had waited five years for this moment.

Kat Lundquist was all but dead.

Thanks to that bitch, her brothers were doing hard time. They had treated Kat well. Tomas had promised to pay her fines and insulate the husband from any fallout caused by a trial. They were working on the judge when Kat rolled on them. They couldn't get to her in prison, so Gina had been patient, waiting to exact revenge after she got out. Then the bitch skipped parole.

Ironically, the Feds claimed credit for taking down a major drug ring. In truth, it had been a hiccup. The Feds patted themselves on the back and walked away. With the scrutiny off their operations, business had flourished under her leadership.

Hiring the PI was Harven's idea. Gina assumed Lundquist had fled the state, but Harven offered a fascinating tidbit. Kat Lundquist had once told him she would never leave Wisconsin because it was home, cold weather and all. When Harven had asked what she'd do if the police pursued her, Kat said she would go to ground. Find some abandoned place and live off the grid. When he asked why, Kat said she felt it was safer. No need for a car. No trail of travel receipts and easier to stay below the radar.

Harven believed her and convinced Gina to spend the money on a PI. Now the effort was coming to fruition.

When Tomas and Antonio ran things, they kept their familial relationship quiet. She was the company CPA, nothing more. More than once, underlings had complained to her about the brothers, believing it safe to do so. It hadn't ended well for them.

Even now, she stayed in her wheelhouse, handling the books and the money laundering end of things. She wasn't opposed to the violence required in a business like theirs. After her brothers went away, Harven had encouraged her to perform a few "disciplinary actions" herself, as he called them. She had the stomach for the rough side of business and learned she could kill when necessary. She assumed that had been the point of having her taking part.

Now, she preferred to keep her hands clean. For Kat Lundquist, she would make an exception.

She went to the garage and packed a small tool kit. Essentials for the task at hand: duct tape, a drill with a quarter-inch bit, a box cutter with a pack of blades, a four-and-a-half-inch circular saw, and a plastic lab coat. She checked the batteries. They were fully charged.

All set.

Finding her in an abandoned farmhouse would be ideal. They would kill her and bury her there. Gina would insist on one thing: there would be no rape.

She couldn't abide the idea.

★   ★   ★

Sam was sitting at Jake's Supper club, sipping a martini, when the call came.

Fired.

It was a relief. The more she thought about Kat Lundquist's history and the enigmatic Mr. Smith, the more certain she became he was a narco and intended to kill the woman. She sat for a minute and turned her phone off. Such people were not to be taken lightly. In fact, she should disappear for a few weeks.

The revelation was disturbing. Her instincts had been faulty from the start. She had concerns about Mr. Smith. Made a subjective judgement about the Lundquist woman. Was heavy-handed in questioning the clerks and had evidently given herself away conducting the tail. There was a time when she was more skillful, more principled, and showed better judgement. She may have just gotten a woman killed.

She should feel worse, but even her empathy seemed jaded lately. Sam just hoped Kat Lundquist had run and kept running.

Thirty-Seven

Kat awoke with Max pressed against her back.

Justin's side of the bed was empty. She smelled coffee brewing.

Max had never jumped into bed before, and she didn't remember him doing so. She rolled over. He gave her an intense look before putting a paw on her shoulder.

Kat smooched his forehead and said, "I love you too, buddy."

She lazed, rubbing his flank and thinking about last night. The comfort of a shower, an actual bed, sheets, air conditioning. The sex. It had been wild. She hadn't imagined a man like him being so passionate. And vigorous. The first time had been a blur, but this experience was far more vivid.

Something else was clear. The plume *had* affected her and heightened her cravings for coke. She wouldn't give into them. Cocaine was how she ended up adrift in the world. Away from the farm, she felt better, more in the moment, her outlook more positive. No nightmares overnight either. Unless Harven or his PI found the farm, there was no reason she couldn't stay. If the cravings and dreams were the worst effects, she could handle them.

Was she deluding herself?

A life on the run usually involved running. There might be no end to it. She should have left the state, but she wanted to stay in Wisconsin. More so after prison. It was home and she was a homebody. Some people loved to travel. Not her. The seasons were bold, the summers heavenly. She had been to Florida once in July. It was like hell with palm trees. The Wisconsin landscapes weren't bold or mountainous, but they were green and familiar with their white farmhouses and red barns. Before her cocaine days, she tried to convince Josh to buy a hobby farm. They would have had horses, sheep, chickens—

Alas, a dream once. Unobtainable now.

Life as a fugitive had been acceptable—until taking Max in and meeting Justin. Apparently, she didn't want to be alone.

She rolled out of bed. Max followed.

Justin toiled in the kitchen, scrambling eggs, laying strips of bacon into a pan. He paused, poured a mug of coffee, and handed it to her.

"Good morning."

Kat let Max out and sat at the table, a small, round chunk of oak. The kitchen appeared mostly original with hickory cabinets and pine floorboards. The countertops were granite, the walls painted a similar sage green to the color of her bedroom. It looked tasteful and clean. Another thing to like about the man.

Kat said, "I assume we're going to the farm?"

"Yes."

"How do I sneak back in during the day?"

"We'll do a loop around the farm first. I have a hoodie you can wear. Camouflage you a bit. We'll be very careful."

He served her a plate of eggs, bacon, potatoes, and toast, sat down, and dug into his food.

Kat noticed gun cases in the hallway.

"What's with the guns? Going hunting?"

"I'm a hunter, but no. As I said, I'm taking them in case someone does show up."

"I didn't ask you to fight my battle."

He gave her a look of high dudgeon. "I should just let them kill you? And if they come, I'm in danger too."

"Fair enough," she said defensively. He was putting on a good show, but she wondered how nervous he felt beneath that veneer. The breakfast was hot and delicious. She couldn't do a spread like this at the farm.

Between bites, Justin said, "I'm still impressed that Natalie learned about the murders by herself."

"It freaks me out. I didn't believe in any of this a month ago."

"But I'm still not convinced she's genuinely psychic."

"Huh? How don't you believe after that?"

"I accept the possibility of paranormal phenomena, but I'm con-flicted scientifically by the lack of tangible evidence."

"Says the guy who believes in evil plumes."

"I don't believe in them. I've theorized they exist. And *evil* is an emotionally charged word. If people do bad things in the vicinity of the microplume, that's an effect of the telluric currents. The plume is neither good nor evil in the religious sense. A natural evil, yes. Possessed by demons? No."

She smirked. "I was just needling you."

"Whatever." He smiled sheepishly. "Her discovery, as impressive as it was, is proof of nothing. Mrs. Laskin told her? It's a little thin.

She wasn't operating in a controlled environment. And she won't let me participate."

"You might be a distraction."

He flexed his biceps in a bodybuilder pose. "That's a given."

"Yes, Natalie is in awe of your manliness." Kat rolled her eyes. "How soon do you want to leave?"

"Twenty minutes?"

"I'll be ready." Kat really wanted to drag him back to the bedroom and fuck him silly—though the urge wasn't as strong as on the farm.

Justin loaded the weapons into the Land Rover while Kat folded her laundry. They avoided Walden and approached the farm on back roads, driving a lap around the property first. The area was becoming a circus. Besides the seismic stations, the media was everywhere, the roads busy with steady streams of traffic. Most looked like gawkers. Kat wore a hoodie and a ball cap and sat low. She didn't see Harven or the black SUV.

Otherwise, it looked like just another quiet summer day.

Justin let them out where he normally slipped into the woods. She and Max were only visible for seconds as they plunged into the foliage and disappeared. When they broke into the open, the farm looked peaceful, inviting. Her home—for what it was worth.

She had been stressing over the negatives. Engaging in catastrophic thinking. Assuming the worst. She took a deep breath. Then another. She let the stress and worries slide away. Listened to a cardinal call to his mate. Closed her eyes and let the sun warm her face.

In that moment, she was mindful, focused only on the present.

Everything would be all right.

Thirty-Eight

Brett Donovan was late for a meeting.

Worse, the client was a prick and traffic was slow, the roads populated with morons. His anger neared the boiling point.

How had these idiots passed a driver's test?

He lived on Kelly Road and, almost overnight, his quiet country neighborhood had turned into a three-ring circus. There were cars, vans, and media trucks parked everywhere. People setting up tents. A wing-nut church group with their bus. Cars pulled in and out without warning.

He understood the brouhaha over the quake. That was something. A kitchen cabinet had fallen, spewing shattered glass and dishware everywhere. His garage was also a mess.

Now some people were linking the quake to the shooting at Walden Stamping. Nut jobs. The world was full of them. Lately, they irritated him more than usual. He worked on his temper with a therapist, but he had control issues, especially while driving. It didn't help that he drove a big, beastly Silverado High Country.

And he had a raging headache. Too much scotch last night. So far, the Ibuprofen hadn't touched it.

Things went downhill in Walden, the traffic heavier. There were road and lane closures because of the quake. He crawled through town. Then the light at the intersection of Main and Oak turned yellow. The car ahead tapped the brakes.

"Don't stop, asshole!"

He didn't, but Brett ran the red light and got the finger from some jackass on a motorcycle.

Clear of Walden, he took a deep breath. Ten minutes on the highway, he might make it yet.

Traffic slowed.

What the hell?

Cars had backed up behind a woman on a bike and people were having difficulty passing into oncoming traffic.

Jesus! These fucking bike people!

One by one, cars passed her, but time ticked by. His chance to make the nine o'clock appointment evaporated.

Then he was behind her. She sported a green tee with a bold inscription:

3 FEET

IT'S THE LAW

Beneath the lettering, an arrow pointed left. The bitch peddled along without a care in the world, eager to prove her point. He faced a long line of oncoming traffic.

Brett honked.

She flipped him off.

Fuck!

That finger was the very last straw in a morning filled with annoyances, morons, and final straws.

He focused on her bony ass and sped up. The Silverado leapt forward and her eyes snapped back in fear as the big chrome grille closed in and knocked her down. The truck jolted twice as the big tires crushed her into the pavement. Brett laughed.

He glanced in the rearview mirror and laughed harder at the sight of her mangled bloody body lying in the road.

God, that felt good.

For a while.

As he drove, he recognized the insanity of that rash act. Someone had his plate number. Or a video. He would be arrested, sent to jail, and his life would be over. His temper had always been a problem, but what in the hell just possessed him?

Cascading images of imminent ruin played in his mind. Losing his truck, the business, his hot new girlfriend. His house. God, he loved that house.

He turned right when he saw a farm track disappearing into a grove of trees.

In the woods, it was cool and dark and smelled of damp black dirt.

Brett stopped and pulled a Beretta from the center console. Twisted it in his hands and stared at the open end of the barrel.

So much faster than a trial.

Less painful too.

He chambered a round, flipped the safety, and held the barrel to the notch in the center of his chest.

Just tense the finger.

A little squeeze.

No more pain—

Thirty-Nine

Gina was waiting when Harven arrived.

With him were Liam and Denny, his right-hand men and body-guards. They looked like thugs. Tall, with broad shoulders and big biceps, they were stocky, but neither man carried an ounce of fat on them. Liam was personable, but she had the feeling Denny didn't like her, especially in a position of power. A streak of misogyny he had difficulty concealing. Harven had confirmed as much. Gina didn't care so long as Denny did his job and stayed out of her way.

Liam had gone to school with Tomas and they were still tight, so he was fully invested in the hunt for Katrina Lundquist. Antonio had hired Denny, a casual acquaintance. Gina never understood it. Denny was tough but also a bumbler in her estimation. Harven had chosen him and that was acceptable, even if she had reservations.

They were a small but highly skilled crew and perfect for the situation.

Gina hopped in her Escalade and followed Harven in a Navigator down the driveway. She lived in Germantown, near Milwaukee, about an hour from Walden. She tapped into the entertainment system and chose a Mozart piano sonata to relax her. To set the mood. When she took Kat Lundquist apart, it would be with a cool head. Methodical and measured. Torture was about pain, but also about time and apprehension. There would be no rush to finish.

Harven had trained Gina in weapons and self-defense. Tomas and Antonio had insisted, given the business they were in. But she suspected it was personal: they wanted to ensure no one ever took advantage of their baby sister. She was proficient in Krav Maga and practiced shooting weekly at a range. Beside the tool kit in back, she carried two legal concealed pistols: a Kimber Micro 9 and a Sig Sauer P365, small guns but deadly at close quarters.

When they resolved this issue, she was taking time off. She had done little but work since Tomas and Antonio went away. No trips or adventures, no relationships, and little time to enjoy the flood of cash flowing in. She worked hard to make her brothers proud. They had entrusted her with the business and she hadn't let them down.

When they reached Walden, they pulled into the Quik Stop for drinks and snacks and plotted their next moves.

Liam and Denny drove off to scout discreet locations to put the drone into the air. Liam was the drone expert, and once the craft was airborne, he would fly over wooded areas looking for tents and other signs of a camp in case Kat was hiding in the rough.

Harven hopped into the Escalade with a list of addresses to check. He had narrowed it down to seven properties. Gina drove while Harven surveyed the terrain, alert for any sign of Katrina Lundquist. Harven looked like a farmhand himself, wearing nondescript jeans and a tan tee, all in keeping with his bland appearance. He was more dangerous precisely because he looked so inoffensive. Gina never dressed down that much, wearing Guess jeans and a Fendi tee. With her black hair and fine features, she was too attractive to blend in anywhere.

He punched the first address into the GPS. Ten minutes later they approached a small farmhouse, painted brown. The yard was overgrown and dotted with rusty farm machinery and a broken swing set.

Harven pointed. "Pull in there."

"Looks like shit."

"Yes, it does. Exactly what we're looking for."

Gina stayed in the Escalade, gun at the ready, while Harven stepped out to inspect the property, carrying a Glock low in his right hand. He disappeared behind the house. She was happy to sit in the air conditioning while Harven did the dirty work, but grew concerned after five minutes. Then he reappeared, shaking his head, face red with the heat.

"Empty. Rotting. Dangerous. She hasn't been here. Next place is seven miles over."

He wiped his brow and punched the address into the GPS. Gina nodded and followed the directions to the property.

It was a wreck with a big hole in the roof. Slats of siding had fallen off. Most of the windows were broken.

"Do we bother?"

"Absolutely. No stone unturned. We're finding her today. We should make no assumptions about any property."

"Okay. I trust your judgement."

Harven disappeared around the back. Gina assumed he was breaking in and checking the interior. He reappeared five minutes later and shook his head.

He hopped in and tapped in the next address, a twenty-minute ride. Gina enjoyed the beauty of the countryside but couldn't understand how anyone lived or worked out here. The houses were mostly small and shitty. The air smelled of manure. She felt isolated, a million miles from real civilization. She could never be a farm girl.

The next property was almost invisible, hidden by trees at the end of an overgrown driveway. An old American Foursquare, it had once been an attractive house. The roof was old and weathered but otherwise intact. The paint on the wood siding had peeled, leaving a rough grey surface flecked with white paint. The windows looked sound.

"This looks interesting," Harven said. He stepped out and started his loop around the front.

A gun popped out the front door.

"Ay! Alto!" The accent sounded Hispanic.

Harven stopped and raised his hands. There was an exchange of conversation. Gina couldn't make out the words, but they were speaking Spanish. With her Sig drawn, she slipped out the door and crept around the back end until she spotted Harven. She raised her weapon, prepared to react.

The pointed gun went down and a short Hispanic man stepped out wearing only shorts. They talked and then Harven pulled his phone out and showed it to the man. A picture of Kat Lundquist, she was sure.

The man shook his head. They talked a bit more, then Harven walked over and slipped into the Escalade.

"That looked scary."

"A little. I could have disarmed him but he was willing to talk."

"And?"

"They haven't seen her. It's just a couple of beaners squatting and doing day labor around here."

"You sure?"

"Kat wouldn't stay with them."

The next property was also empty. The situation became clear after visiting four of the seven properties. A large industrial farming operation had moved in and was gobbling up farmland in the area. The farmhouses were abandoned, but the fields were alive and thriving, planted with hay, peas, soybeans, and corn.

Checking in with Liam, he reported that the many tents and canopies set up by the geologists in the area had complicated the search for a hidden camp. So far? Nothing.

Gina was growing weary, her frustration level rising.

"I'm thirsty," Gina said. "Let's stop for a drink in town and then eliminate the last three."

"Call Liam back?"

"No, they can keep looking."

Forty

Natalie awoke from a nightmare in a cold sweat.

In it, she became lost in a foggy abyss while trying to free Vera Laskin from that strange murder room and couldn't find her way out.

Understandable. Since learning Vera was a prisoner and lived in fear, she had thought of little else. The nightmare captured the horror perfectly. Too perfectly.

Last night, she discussed the issue with her group, gathering a variety of answers and solutions. There was consensus on one thing: spirits violently dispatched into the next life could become dislocated from the spirit world and lost in a separate plane or dimension.

If Natalie found that place, could she lead Vera out and back to the larger spiritual realm? Many of them thought it was possible. They also warned her about the dangers of pursuing such a solution. The risk of becoming lost herself. Encountering evil spirits or wraiths who might do her harm.

Worst-case scenario? An encounter with evil forces too powerful to resist. Losing her soul. That risk seemed enhanced by the troubling events in Walden, like the shooting. Some noted the recent earthquakes and suggested the farm represented an energy vortex or portal. The warnings had played into her nightmare.

She stared at the ceiling, a mess of conflicted feelings.

Whatever problems existed at the farm, she was the most qualified to meet them. She sensed a strong, disturbing aura around it, and the bike lady and Richie Rich knew something about it. What were they up to? In her mind, they had placed her soul in harm's way by withholding vital information.

Her anger rose, but then she pictured poor Vera trapped in limbo. She had to do something. She had promised Mildred the bodies would receive a proper burial. And they would. Her promise to the bike lady was out the window after she freed Vera. She was going straight to the cops.

Natalie looked at her phone.

Shit!

It was after 10 o'clock. She had to work at noon.

She jumped out of bed, put a kettle on to boil, and flicked the TV on, curious to see what new mayhem had occurred overnight. The anchorwoman was talking about a case of road rage turned deadly in Walden, then noted the other recent events. Suddenly, the town was front and center in the national spotlight. The backdrop to the story blared:

WHAT'S HAPPENING IN WALDEN WISCONSIN?

Holy crap.

Natalie turned the TV off. She couldn't stand to listen anymore. Bad things were happening here and making people crazy.

A few days ago, a woman bashed her husband's head in with a hammer, the town's first murder in twenty-seven years. Yesterday, the shooting occurred. Now, this road rage business.

Was it coming from the farm?

Between the disturbing news and the warnings from her group, Natalie felt deeply uneasy. She was entering uncharted ground and recognized her limitations, especially after the weird and unnerving session yesterday.

Then she remembered Vera.

Pushing her negative feelings aside, she tried to imagine the psychic magic that would free her. Natalie wasn't waiting for two more days to act. She called into work, complaining of a stomach bug.

Vera's situation presented unique possibilities. Discovering a space in the spiritual realm beyond her knowledge was exhilarating. Was the spirit world made up of multiple levels? Were the dimensions she could explore limitless? It might explain an inconsistency—why only certain people seemed to transition to a spirit existence.

She assumed—as many did—that spirits existed in an earthly purgatory. Why hadn't she questioned that belief?

It felt like a serious oversight.

Was the spirit of every person who ever lived lurking in the ether somewhere?

Hoping to reveal those larger truths and help Vera, a deep sense of responsibility and curiosity compelled her to act and return to the farm. Natalie felt ready to meet the challenge.

She dressed in a pair of mom jeans and a plain grey tee and fried an egg for a breakfast sandwich. She worried the woman would say no to further indoor sessions. But Richie Rich was interested, even if the woman was a cold fish. If need be, she would charm her way in.

Ha! That was funny. Even Natalie knew she lacked charm.

She arrived at noon and pulled off into the designated parking spot, grabbed her stuff, and walked to the house, breaking into a sweat in the heat. Kat was sitting on the porch with her dog.

She stood, cross-armed, and said, "Hi, Natalie. I thought you were done for a few days?"

"I got the day off. Is it a problem?"

Kat hesitated, maybe just to annoy her. "I suppose not. The dining room again?"

"No. Down in that room—if that's okay?"

A frown. Again with the hesitation. "Only if you tell me what happened down there."

Natalie nodded. "I know a little already. Mildred Laskin said it was murder."

"Did she say who did it?"

"No. She seemed confused, addled. Hopefully, I'll learn more today."

"What's it like, talking to spirits?"

Fine day for the bike lady to get gabby. Natalie didn't feel like talking. "Hard to explain. I see them. I hear them, though the voice often sounds scratchy. It's like we're on opposite sides of a curtain—or a confessional screen."

Kat looked thoughtful. Skeptical? She merely said, "I expect you to keep me updated."

"I will."

She walked Natalie into the basement and opened the trapdoor. "Help yourself."

The basement was cool and damp, the walls glistening with condensation, but the air smelled fresh. Natalie went through the trapdoor and struggled down the stairs with the mirror case, the Ouija board, and a lantern. At the bottom, she stopped at the door and took a deep breath, feeling her anxiety rise. Reminded herself she was doing a good thing and opened the door.

Natalie placed the four reddish-brown hematite stones in the corners of the room, muttering *"Salvum Iter"* over each. She sat, setting her mirror and Ouija board on the rickety table. There was no condensation on these walls. In fact, it felt much warmer than the basement. She placed the lantern on the floor and lit a candle.

She fell easily into a trance, feeling particularly in tune with the spirit world. Natalie gazed into the mirror and cleared her mind. As she did so, the view morphed into a three-dimensional space, like a cavern. As she opened the board, the planchette lurched.

"Vera?"

Yes.

Vera resolved out of the darkness, vague and indistinct with her shoulder-length brown hair, wrinkled tee, and old jeans. Haze or fog swirled around her.

Natalie spoke. "Vera, I've been thinking. Maybe I can lead you out of there."

That would be wonderful. Are there others like me?

The distortion and warping in her voice was especially pronounced today.

"I don't know. I've never tried this."

I appreciate you trying.

"Okay. We'll do this as a mind exercise, but I have to explain a few things first."

Natalie went on to explain the situation with Mildred and the spirits in town. Then she said, "Imagine me there with you, but I'm blind. What do you see?"

Nothing. Just haze. Fog.

Oh no.

Vera was so lost, she couldn't see? How could she follow if she was blind? She hadn't come prepared for this possibility. It sounded like her dream last night and just as awful.

Vera called out. *Are you still there?*

"Sorry, yes. Just thinking." Natalie had a flash of insight. Maybe the universe was speaking to her. She felt extraordinarily connected. A mind exercise might help lead Vera out. The technique unfolded in her head.

Natalie closed her eyes and imagined extending her hand through the mirror. A tingly sensation traversed her skin as it entered the glass.

With her arm extended, she said, "What do you see?"

A hand.

It was working! Amazing! An experience more profound than anything she imagined. Natalie was thrilled.

"It's mine. Take a hold of it."

Vera did. The sensation was otherworldly. The touch was delicate, like a feather, but colder than January snow. She shivered. It was amazing and creepy all at once. She was touching the spirit of a dead woman. Would the people in her group believe the story later?

Natalie imagined tugging her closer with a flick of the wrist. "What do you see now?"

A door.

"Go through the door."

Now I see stairs.

"Climb the stairs, Vera."

A ladder.

"Follow it up."

A long silence followed. Then she said, *I'm in my old house—ouch!*

"What?"

I just got a terrible shock.

"You're almost free. Run. Go to town, to the metal building behind the Episcopal church. Do you know where that is?"

Yes! Thank you!

Vera's last words faded into the distance.

Natalie smiled. She had performed a good deed. Vera was free.

Were there others like her?

What incredible experiences awaited?

Forty-One

Justin parked and walked through the brush, alert for intruders or watchful eyes. He scanned the farm before stepping into the open.

All quiet.

The humidity was back, the morning muggy, cicadas buzzing loudly in the trees. A steady southerly wind helped moderate the heat. In two more trips, he transferred the weapons, his cooler, and a fresh power pack.

He laid out the guns. A Sig Sauer P320 with two boxes of ammo, and his rifle, a Browning Mark II Safari with a Nikon scope he used to hunt elk in Colorado. The rifle would give him greater range than the weapons the drug guys would bring, assuming they carried pistols. The night vision gear he left in his satchel.

How real were the dangers he faced?

If assassins were coming for Kat, the answer was obvious. But the likelihood they would find Kat or the farm seemed small if she laid low. He was no hero, but he possessed a male sense of chivalry and felt a growing attachment to Kat despite his promise of no commitments.

The real issue? He didn't want to lose his prime location atop the microplume, which helped temper the anxiety he felt. He could imagine himself as a knight, but his motivations included a healthy dose of self-interest.

He still hadn't processed the idea of sleeping with a former drug kingpin. Other than her tough, flinty nature, he simply couldn't picture her in that world. Or was that the attraction? Kat as a bad girl? But she wasn't. She seemed wise and reflective. A kind soul. He was impressed she beat her addiction, paid the piper, and was now determined to live a quiet life on her own terms. He liked her a lot. Or was it all just hormones?

Justin sat and opened his laptop.

Five minor quakes overnight. Several sharp voltage spikes. The ground temperature was up four degrees as well. Events were peaking. He noticed an audible low-level hum for the first time. Checking his gear, he found nothing amiss.

It seemed to be coming from the ground, but when he put his ear to the dirt, he heard nothing. Another sensory disruption because of telluric currents? He pulled out his recorder and noted the observation.

Justin had a feeling today was the day. He didn't normally prognosticate by gut feeling, but he couldn't resist.

Today, something profound would happen.

★   ★   ★

Kat walked to the house, trying to plan her day.

She spent time in the garden, weeding and harvesting wild greens, but couldn't concentrate. Her earlier calm had evaporated. Nervous and edgy, she continually scanned the perimeter of the farm, looking for a hint of movement or a sign she had been found. The sun was a furnace, the air thick and muggy and not conducive to yard work. Adding to the muddle, she could think of little but sex, especially after their wild session the night before. Her craving for cocaine had returned in force.

Kat grabbed a Coke Zero from the cooler and sat at the edge of the porch with Max.

She nearly had a heart attack when Natalie burst from the bushes and marched to the house. She had been relieved when Natalie left for a few days. One less thing to worry about. But if Natalie was here, she wasn't in town gabbing about the farm. Still, Kat had to consider her safety if Harven showed up. When Natalie left today, Kat would tell her the farm was off limits for a while. Did it matter if she talked now? Maybe she already had.

Resist the idea as she might, Kat knew it was time to leave.

She was curious about Natalie's experience with Mrs. Laskin, but when she asked, the description about a veil sounded implausible, like a cliché, not an actual interaction. Kat then understood Justin's skepticism.

Still, how did she know about the bodies? It was mind-boggling.

Kat guided Natalie down the stairs to the trapdoor.

Her anxiety was stronger in the basement. So were the cravings.

Walking to the porch, the conviction grew. This place was no longer safe. She struggled to accept Justin's theories, but the effects of the plume grew ever more obvious. There was no other way to explain her feelings. Even Max seemed off. Moody and aloof, wandering from spot to spot, unable to find comfort anywhere. His nose remained dry, his eyes red and puffy.

As the day wore on, the effects worsened. No rationalization or awareness of the problem reduced the cravings, which felt as strong as her first few weeks of detox. The violent events in town couldn't be ignored either. Knowing Harven was out there, searching, further fueled the feelings of stress and anxiety.

But she had options and a safe place to go, away from the farm. She didn't think Justin would object. Or was she assuming too much? What if he didn't want the hassle or the commitment? But he was safer if she wasn't here when they came looking. They hadn't actually discussed the idea, but she planned to over dinner.

She grabbed a beer. In several long draws, she emptied half the bottle. She sat cross-legged on the porch, working a relaxation exercise while the calming effects of the alcohol soothed her worried mind. She had to get a grip. Just a few more hours until dark.

When her anxiety eased, she stood and arranged her things in the kitchen. Just the essentials. Her clean clothing still sat on the counter, folded. She added her shoes, boots, winter gear, and the bedroll. The Glock and the ammo. She hoped they could get her bike out. Beyond that, there wasn't much she could do to erase the evidence of her presence.

She pumped and boiled water, then washed the greens, planning chicken and a salad for dinner. Simple but healthy. She felt a pang of sadness, knowing it might be her last meal here.

The shadows grew longer. They would leave after sunset, like last night.

When she glanced toward the encampment, Justin was strolling to the house carrying the rifle and a satchel, looking around with an unnatural attentiveness to his surroundings. Was he worried about gunmen bursting out of the bushes? An even better reason to leave and stay away. She felt guilty drawing him into her problems, but also had a powerful urge to push him down and rip his clothes off. He looked so damned hot carrying the rifle like some rugged frontiersman.

The familiar wave of self-loathing swept over her. Everything she touched turned to crap. Why would this be different? This wasn't the way to embark on a relationship nor the basis for a lasting one. She was essentially twisting his arm to save her ass even if he was safer with her gone. On the verge of a major breakthrough, he wasn't staying away.

No, this wouldn't end well either.

Forty-Two

Gina and Harven stopped at Alex's Pub.

Bearing little resemblance to a pub, it looked quaint and more inviting than the other taverns in town. It was very dark inside. Everything was made of wood: the bar, the chairs and tables, the walls, the floor—everything except the brown embossed-tin ceiling.

Gina ordered a vodka tonic, Harven an IPA on tap.

"Three more places," Gina said. "It's not looking good."

"Oh, but it is," he said. "I saved the best for last."

"What? Why?"

"I wanted to make no assumptions and eliminate the less likely candidates first. I also considered the possibility that she had moved from one farm to another after losing the tail. To a less obvious location like the dumps we looked at. You'll see what I mean when we get to the last farm."

Gina didn't care for Harven when he got like this. Holding details back, then presenting them like some Zen master.

"Besides, it makes more sense to go in after dark."

That much was true.

After finishing their drinks, they drove to the next address fifteen minutes out of town.

The farm looked abandoned, the lot and fields wild with long grass and saplings. The house was clearly visible and decaying. Harven walked around the house and returned a few minutes later.

"Terrible mold problem inside. Next." He punched the address in.

He didn't get out at the next stop. A huge oak had fallen through the house, cutting it in half. The corners still standing had crumpled inward toward the fallen trunk.

"Hmm, didn't look like that on the satellite image." He tapped the last address in and said, "Okay, the moment of truth. The next place is called Laskin's farm based on the county plat map. It looks perfect."

Gina bit her tongue. If they found Kat at the next place, she might have to shoot the smug bastard. They could have wrapped this up hours ago.

When the GPS announced they had arrived, Gina saw a long wall of green foliage. No mailbox. No rural route marker. No driveway.

"There's nothing here." Gina said.

"Oh, but there is." Harven brought up a satellite image on his iPad. Once he enlarged it, he pointed to a house behind the wall of trees. It didn't look bad on the screen, but the previous farm had only proven that Google Maps was outdated and unreliable. The land looked wild, a patchwork of trees, brush, and prairie grass.

They drove a circuit around the farm but at no point was the house visible from the road.

"It has to be the place," Gina said.

"I think so."

"Should we take a closer look?"

"No. I'd hate to tip her off. Let's maintain the element of surprise and wait until dark. We'll use the drone to confirm it."

Harven phoned Liam and told him to land the drone, change batteries, and be ready to fly.

It was a short ride. Liam had located a field access road with reasonable privacy within a wooded grove three farms over. He and Denny were waiting in the shade with the drone when they pulled up.

Liam was six-two with sandy hair, a snake tat on his neck, and a flattened nose that looked like it had been broken.

He flashed a genuine smile. "Good afternoon, Ms. Gallagher."

Denny just nodded. He was a little shorter with black hair and puggish features. He wasn't a handsome man and his shoulders seemed perpetually stiff.

Gina laid the iPad on the hood of her vehicle and motioned for Liam to step over.

She pointed to the Laskin farm. "This looks the most promising. Will she see or hear the drone fly over?"

Liam shook his head. "Probably not. The drone operates at 60dB, about the volume of our conversation. The cicadas should cover the sound. I'll be flying at about five hundred feet, a bit above the legal limit. She'd have to be looking for it."

"Okay, let's go."

Liam grabbed a hand controller and turned his laptop toward Gina and Harven.

"You'll see everything here on the screen."

After studying the map for a moment, Liam set the drone on the ground and maneuvered it skyward until it was just a speck. He flew southeast over to the Laskin farm. Gina recognized it from the satellite picture. Everything looked so small.

"Is that the best view we can get?"

"No." Liam fiddled with the remote control to focus and enlarge the feed. Working on his laptop, he improved the image further. The level of detail was amazing. He turned the drone and looped around the periphery of the farm.

Gina pointed to the tent and canopy. It looked like a man was lying beneath the canopy, but their view was limited. "Is somebody underneath that?"

"Hard to say. I think so," Liam said. "Those geology people are all over the place."

"Yeah, I noticed."

Liam navigated a second loop, closer to the house. Gina saw chairs on the porch. Part of the yard behind the house had been cleared. Somebody was living there. Gina spotted a bike lying in the grass and pointed. "That bike. That looks like the bike the PI photographed."

Harven said, "Yes it is. Good eye. I think we've got her."

Denny clapped his hands together. "Okay, let's nab her."

"No," Harven said. "We wait. Too many media people around, and I think somebody's under that canopy. They'll probably leave before sunset. For their sake, I hope they do."

"Harven's right," Gina said. "We passed a supper club in town. Let's have some dinner, plan an approach, and return in a few hours, nearer dark."

Liam turned the drone around and brought it in.

As Gina climbed into the Escalade, she looked over and said, "Denny, don't get any ideas. She's mine."

He chafed visibly at the command.

Tough.

She was the boss.

Katrina Lundquist was hers.

Forty-Three

Justin sprawled out on the tarp to nap.

When he awoke, his vision was tinged a faint red. It was freaky, like an LSD trip, something he had done only once but remembered vividly. His skin, the trees, the sky, his gear. He grabbed the recorder and noted the time and observations. His temperature was normal. He felt fine—other than the occasional sensation of insects on his skin. He was used to that and had tamed the reflexive urge to swat them.

Two minor quakes had occurred while he dozed. The ground temperature had risen another two degrees. Soon, Kat would have hot water coming out of the pump. The water was already warm and he had warned her to boil it. Warm water was a good breeding ground for bacteria and dangerous amoebae, especially the brain-eating kind.

He went to Twitter. There was considerable chatter about the quake and the violence in Walden. Several people suggested that the Sommerfeld microplume theories warranted further study and consideration. Posters were arguing both sides of the issue, so he jumped in with his latest observations in support of his work. He sparred with a few people in contentious exchanges and announced that he would soon release updated papers on both theories.

He logged off, feeling gratified. Vindicated. He had been largely ignored or ridiculed—until now. People were now openly debating the merits or shortcomings of his ideas. Some of his previously rejected papers were being reconsidered for publication.

Following the local news, he continued to catalogue events that might be plume related: the mass shooting, the woman who murdered her husband, the deadly case of road rage. Those events had pushed Walden far beyond the normal murder rate, which was effectively zero with exactly three murders in the past one hundred years. The police blotter also reported an increase in lesser crimes: domestic violence, suspected arsons, and incidents of breaking and entering. People were snapping for no apparent reason. Justin expected more death and mayhem in the next few days and felt powerless to stop it. Really, they should evacuate the town. He only hoped his work would prevent similar violence in the future.

His primary theory about microplumes now had strong evidentiary support. Dozens of stations were collecting data to further confirm the theories. The proof lay beneath their feet. More stations were adding temperature sensors and emulating his equipment to measure telluric currents. He still doubted magma would reach the surface, but it would be dramatic as hell if it did. A smoking fumarole or two would be a nice touch though.

Acceptance of the second theory would follow in due course. He collected his own observations and gathered data, but it wasn't yet sufficient to frame an unimpeachable case. But once the seismic activity settled down, he would complete analysis of the crime data and encourage others to do the same, and then start writing formal papers and presenting them for publication.

The Sommerfeld microplume theories. He liked the sound of it.

With everything in hand, he grabbed his rifle and satchel and wandered over to chat with Kat, continuing to marvel at his strange tinted vision. Even tinged red, Kat looked smoking hot. He hoped she would agree to go home with him again. He wanted to suggest she hide out for a few weeks. It would be better for both of them, but he was hesitant. She was very protective of her little fief.

★　★　★

Kat watched Justin meander toward her, his mouth agape, his head swiveling about.

As he reached the porch, she said, "What's up? Are you worried about the drug people?"

"No. I'm seeing red."

"Huh? What are you angry about?"

"Not angry. My vision is literally tinted red. An effect of the plume."

Kat said, "I'm craving coke quite badly. Also the plume?"

"I think so, but you have a history. I wouldn't know how to separate the two."

"It's much worse than normal. I hardly thought about it when I got here."

"You don't have any, right?"

"No!"

"Sorry. I had to ask."

"No, you didn't!" Kat glared at him, fuming, feeling an irrational urge to punch him. "Why would you do that? Do I look high?"

He put his hands up. "Sorry. I think the currents are getting to me. We should leave again for the night."

Kat took a deep breath and tried to relax.

"I agree. I was thinking the same thing. Let's make dinner and eat. We can go after dark."

"Sounds good to me."

"Start the grill, please?" Kat asked. She remained on edge, feeling volatile.

"On it."

She thought about Natalie. "I never saw Natalie leave. Did you?"

"No. But I napped for a bit."

Kat yelled down the stairs, "Natalie?"

Silence.

She yelled louder. Still no answer.

"I guess she left. She promised to keep me informed." Kat felt her anger rise again. "She's done here."

"I'll tell her tomorrow—if she shows."

As she stepped out the door, Max tried to squeeze through and knocked her off balance.

"Damn it, Max!" She raised a hand to smack his butt and stopped. She glanced at Justin, who couldn't conceal his shock.

"I think you're right about the currents. I would never hit Max—"

"We both need to take a deep breath and have a glass of wine." He produced an Australian shiraz from his satchel.

He poured two glasses and they sat. Kat felt mortified by her anger toward Max. The plume was real and dangerous, perhaps more so than Harven.

The wine had the desired effect and they mellowed into their version of domestic bliss. He prepped the greens and diced peppers while she seared and cooked the marinated chicken. They snatched glances at each other. They sat at the breakfast table on the porch, a candle burning while they ate and chatted. In his presence, she felt more relaxed. Safer—though she hated to feel beholden to anyone.

Finally, she said, "Do you mind if I stay at your place for a while? A couple weeks, maybe?"

"No. I think it's a great idea. I was going to suggest it."

"It's not an imposition?"

Justin shook his head.

Max growled slightly.

"You too, buddy," he said.

But Max was looking toward the encampment. Kat followed his gaze and saw movement in the long grass behind it, like an animal passing through.

Only it was black, the disturbance too purposeful to be anything but human.

Shit.

Forty-Four

Natalie moved the planchette to GOOD BYE and severed her connection to the spirit world.

She considered going outside for a breather, but given the bike lady's reluctance earlier, Natalie wasn't risking an encounter and being sent packing. She wanted to meditate for twenty minutes to clear her mind, but the session with Vera had been intense. Fatigue set in and she lay down for a quick catnap. The floor felt cozy. Almost heated.

Sometime later, she awoke, refreshed. She closed the door, sat, and refocused on the board, lifting the planchette and placing it in the starting position on the word OUIJA.

Clearing her mind of every stray thought, she waited, tingling with excitement. Vera had been uncharted ground. This was a step beyond. Had anyone ever gone this far? She doubted she was the first, but Natalie felt like an intrepid explorer. Mildred had lived above. Vera had been trapped in this room. Were there other levels above or below? Did spirits inhabit them? Would they talk to her?

Thirty minutes later, the planchette moved.

"Who do I have the pleasure of speaking with today?"

Silence.

When Natalie repeated the question, the silence felt more profound. Her vision dimmed at the edges. She waited for the board to spell out a name. Instead, the planchette drifted to NO and stayed there.

"Can I persuade you to talk?"

No way was she giving up now. The room grew darker yet warmer as heat radiated from the floor. She lit a second candle and laid out a dinner roll. Natalie Schaal was many things, but she was no quitter.

She sensed a subtle presence. Just a little hum or shimmer. The board remained mute.

Patience was key and Natalie felt like she had superpowers. At one with the universe and more in the spirit realm than the real world. She aspired to reach and touch every level. Already, in the little time spent on the farm, Natalie felt like a master psychic. She was grateful Kat hadn't come down and kicked her out. Soon, they would have to drag her out of here. Maybe she would stay all night.

Her mind free and clear, she settled into a meditative state where she felt truly at peace. Natalie gazed into the mirror, hoping for a glimpse of what? Visions? Revelations? Feeling certain she had reached some new territory, she felt like a traveler on a vast new continent. The mirror grew darker and became impossibly black, like the foggiest, darkest winter night.

Would a curtain open? Would angels burst forth?

Something lurked just out of reach, the silence absolute.

Then Natalie smelled something bad. A sulfurous stink.

Icy dread replaced bravado and certainty. Her friends had warned her of the dangers and now some menace had crept in.

Time to run—only she couldn't move.

The planchette bumped slightly. The mirror became a bleak and cold wasteland.

Had she gone too far?

Natalie tried to regain control of the board and spoke nervously. "Who do I have the pleasure of speaking with today?"

The planchette scratched out an answer.

SATAN

The room grew warmer. Her anxiety threatened to overwhelm her. Were the spirits angry with her for pushing the envelope?

"Not funny. Who is this really?"

BEELZEBUB

"Seriously! Knock it off!"

At the edge of terror, she tried to rationalize, to find a way out. The spirits she dealt with never engaged in pranks or trickery. Clearly, things were different on the other levels. The feeling of peril was persistent and growing. She needed to end the session and walk away. Or run. But she had to close the Ouija board first.

Natalie reached for the planchette but jerked her hand back when a spider crawled on top of it.

God, she hated spiders.

She reached for the dinner roll to shoo it away when another spider appeared.

Where were they coming from? Natalie had the sudden and frightening suspicion they were coming from the board itself.

Sure enough, another spider appeared. And another. Soon the board would crawl with them! She couldn't let that happen. Somehow, she had opened a conduit to a dark place through the Ouija board. She had to slam it shut before things got worse. She tried to swallow her fear and brush the awful creatures away, but they were multiplying too fast.

As she grabbed the planchette, icky spiders and all, a creature appeared in the scrying mirror, a large black snake.

The only thing she hated worse than spiders were snakes.

Natalie screamed and jumped back as the reptile emerged from the glass. She tried to tell herself it was an illusion, that it wasn't real, but the thing had horrendous breath, like the stench of a dead animal. The mirror rocked as the beast slithered out and across the board. Then the frame split in two. For a moment, she sat rigid, paralyzed by fear until she screamed and threw herself backward off the chair and away from the hideous creature.

The table collapsed under the weight of the snake. Dozens of spiders spilled onto the floor. They scrambled toward her as she tried to scuttle away from it all until she bumped up against the wall.

The snake coiled around her ankle and gripped her as it slid up her leg to her chest in a convoluted spiral. Spiders assailed her body—crawling in her hair, over her face, down her neck, up her sleeves.

Natalie clawed them away but more arrived to torment her.

"No no no no no—"

With spiders on her face and the snake wrapped around her body, her mind rushed to a sensory overload that erupted in a terrified, braying scream as her body locked rigid like a slab of oak. Spiders fell into her mouth and nibbled at her eyelids as the reptile ran its slippery, slimy tongue up her neck in a repulsive streak.

The snake twisted and squeezed along its length, stealing her ability to breathe, to scream, to make any sounds beyond tortured squeaks.

A rib snapped.

Then another, each break sharp like a stabbing knife. Intense pain kept her conscious until the oxygen in her brain ran out.

The room faded to black. Natalie fell limp.

Her eyes wide open and fixed.

Sightless.

Dead.

Forty-Five

Harven pointed to a small turnoff and Gina slowed down.

"There. According to the GPS, we're right behind the farm. About a half-mile walk to the house."

"Perfect." The house wasn't visible but the GPS never lied. They were on a narrow country road without shoulders and lined with trees. The turnoff was the only place to park safely. They had seen no other traffic. After dinner, they stopped and changed at the Quik Stop, dressing in black from head to toe. They looked like special forces operatives and were too conspicuous for Gina's liking. Harven, Liam, and Denny were armed with AR-15s while Gina carried her pistols. She didn't care for the bigger guns. The others could handle any dirty work with the ARs if needed before they took Kat.

She pulled in, stopped, and spoke into her headset. "Liam, are you in position?"

"Yes, ma'am."

"Okay. When Harven and I locate a good vantage point, I'll let you know."

"Roger."

It was about an hour before sunset, the evening languid and sticky. Not ideal weather, and uncomfortable in their gear, but Gina didn't care. This was happening tonight. The bitch who sent her brothers to prison was about to die. Painfully. She was still irked with Harven for drawing this out. Instead of luxuriating at home, she was out in the heat, playing commando.

Gina applied black camo paint to her nose and cheeks. Harven did the same. He donned a black hat. She pulled her hair into a pony-tail, then sprayed herself with Off. Even though she had no military background, she was well trained in weapons, close combat, and self-defense.

Harven led the way, doing the grunt work as they maneuvered through the brush. He was ex-military and made almost no noise as he slipped through the trees. Every so often, he sprayed a small paint dot on the tree bark. He gestured, pointing out hazards, holding branches so they didn't snap back at her—something of a gentleman even if he was a killer. He never leered at her or made inappropriate comments. So unlike Denny, who could barely hide his piggishness and misogyny. That was one man she never wanted to meet in a dark alley.

Working through the trees quietly took time as the sun fell low in the sky. Crickets chirped in the dim light of the woods and birds flitted overhead. The air was dead and Gina was sweating everywhere: her forehead, between her breasts, down her back.

Ugh.

About three hundred yards in, they found a break in the dense foliage with a view of the house, their position obscured by long grass and brush. Harven signaled her to a crouch. They had a partial view of the tent area, but not enough to call it clear.

She pulled out her binoculars and scoped the porch.

A woman sat in a deck chair at a small table. Kat Lundquist. She looked older, rougher. The five years in prison hadn't been kind. A tall dude sat next to her. They were eating dinner with a romantic element, a candle burning between them. It wasn't her ex-husband. They had monitored him—just in case—but he had remarried and cut ties with Kat.

Gina assumed the guy went with the tent and was one of the geological people monitoring the quakes in the area. Unfortunately, he was about to become collateral damage. A large dog, a mutt, sat next to the woman, looking alert and staring at the approximate area where Liam and Denny were sitting in the dense brush on the other side of the farm.

"Liam, position?"

"About ten feet left of the drive, hidden in the brush. We're ready to roll when we get the word."

Now they just had to wait for the night to settle in. Gina checked her phone. It was 7:09. Sunset was 7:44.

Once they were in the house, they would slip in and grab Kat before she had any clue to their presence. Duct tape her to a chair and get to work. Hopefully, the man would leave first. The dog was a wild card they hadn't counted on. He might alert Kat to their approach.

"Hold your position." Gina and Harven moved a bit left and farther forward to catch a better view of the house. "If the man leaves, let him go."

"Will do."

Gina turned to Harven. "What do you think?"

"I hope the dude leaves. Otherwise, it should be dark enough in one hour to move in—as soon as they go into the house. We should make sure that camp over there is clear too."

"Agreed."

Gina spoke into her mic. "Denny, check the tent area when it gets a little darker."

"I'm checking it now. I'm well covered."

"No! Wait!"

She saw the brush rustle and a flash of black.

Gina hissed, "Jesus! I saw you, you fucking idiot!"

Shit!

There was every chance the Lundquist bitch had seen him too.

Forty-Six

With a low, calm voice, Kat said, "Look at me and keep looking at me."

He turned and peered quizzically at her. "What?"

"Eyes on me. Make like we're having dinner conversation. I think I saw someone near your equipment. We need to assume the worst. Give me your plate. I'm going to get up and walk indoors. Call Max and follow me in. Pick up your rifle casually and bring it along. If someone is there, I want them to see it but not feel threatened."

"Uh, that seems counterintuitive."

"Maybe. I'm hoping it says that while we haven't seen them, we're ready if and when they show up."

He looked less worried than he should have. Maybe he didn't believe her. Maybe he thought it was a drill. Regardless, she had to think hard and fast. Like the tail, it was best to prepare for trouble first, ask questions later. With the movement earlier, she had seen a flash of black fabric, the favored color for nighttime guerrillas the world over.

Who would come for her? Harven, Liam, and Denny for sure. One or two more for good measure. Would it be better to slip away or stay and fight? The farmhouse was no fortress. Wood frame with wood siding, they could open fire on the building and kill them with sheer firepower. Harven liked AR-15s and she assumed they were all similarly armed. Unlike shootouts on TV, the AR rounds would shred the house and anyone in it. If they sheltered in the basement, Harven would burn the house down. A little gasoline on this dry old structure? They would be incinerated. Harven would enjoy that too.

She hoped they saw Justin's long gun. It might give them pause. A warning they were facing a rifle with a scope and couldn't just charge in, guns blazing.

Still, they had to run. It was the only way. Harven wouldn't be deterred, just more careful. Other than the rifle and the dark of night, they had no advantages. None.

If she ended up dead, it would be a fitting end to her wretched life. Getting Justin killed made her feel awful in ways she could scarcely comprehend. When did she get a soul? When did she start caring? And what about Max? They wouldn't shoot a dog, would they? She feared they would. There was no time for recrimination now. They had to flee, and she had to get them out alive.

Justin resisted the urge to look toward the woods.

Good.

Kat stood casually, took their plates, and walked into the house. She heard Justin get up a moment later. Nothing happened. No shots rang out.

Whew.

Either they were caught off-guard or planning an approach after dark—which seemed more likely. That gave them a little time to plot an escape.

Any pretense of coolness evaporated as Justin stepped through the door with Max. Wide eyed and animated, he said, "They're here?"

"I think so."

The look on his face belied all the bravado he'd expressed earlier. "Fuck! How many?"

"I'd guess four. Maybe five."

"What should we do? Run for my SUV?"

"The path to your vehicle is probably blocked. It's too dangerous to assume otherwise."

He ran a hand through his hair. "How about calling the cops?"

Kat spoke in a whisper. "Too late for cops now."

"What? Why?"

"We'll be dead by the time they get here."

"Hunker down here?"

"No. We're sitting ducks. This house offers zero protection."

"The basement?"

"They'll just burn the place down."

Judging by the horrified look on his face, he hadn't considered the possibility. "What then?"

Kat felt like she was calculating at the speed of light. "I'm hoping they'll wait until dark. Then we'll slip out and go south. There's better cover that way. The field to the north is too open. They're probably sitting on either side of us."

Justin rubbed a hand across his face. He looked scared. Freaked out. "How do you know that?"

"I don't, but I know Harven, and that's what he'd do."

"Harven?"

"Their enforcer. He'll be in charge and I know how he thinks."

He looked at her with equal parts horror and suspicion, apparently unnerved by a side of her he had never seen.

She touched his arm. "I'm sorry I got you involved."

"I'm here now. Let's figure this out."

"What do you have here besides the rifle?"

"My night vision gear. I left the pistol in my tent."

Kat felt a rising dread. "How much ammo for the rifle?"

He looked stricken. "One magazine in the gun, one in my pocket. Eight rounds."

Fuck!

They weren't shooting it out. Kat nervously wandered the first floor, checking windows, but saw no movement.

Harven was waiting—for now.

They were too lightly armed for a shootout with her Glock and the rifle. Kat had a knife if it came to that. If it did, they were probably dead. She had no chance against Harven in hand-to-hand combat.

"We've got to run," Kat said. "They'll be armed with assault rifles. We won't survive a gunfight. There's a big cornfield three hundred yards south of here. If we can reach it without being seen, we can get lost in the corn. We'll have a chance."

"Agreed."

Forty-Seven

Gina sat and stewed, sweating profusely.

The heat was hideous in this garb. How the hell did combat soldiers do this for months in places like Iraq where it was five million degrees? Only her determination to nail Kat Lundquist kept her from throwing in the towel.

One thing was certain. Denny was done when this was over. That might lead to trouble with Harven. The three of them were tightly knit and loyal to her brothers. Harven had her back, but the other two? Who knew? A problem to consider later. Harven looked at her expectantly.

"I don't think they saw him," Gina said. "You?"

"No way to know. Kat's a cool customer, but I'd say no. But the guy has a rifle with a scope. It looks like a Browning."

"I saw that. Just being careful?"

"We can hope. But it means they know we're coming eventually."

"So she spotted the PI."

Harven nodded and said, "Denny's got to go."

"Yep." Gina was relieved. Harven was on her side. Finally, she said, "I think we sit tight and lull them into complacency. Move at dark, take the guy out—unless he leaves—and deal with Ms. Lundquist at our leisure."

"We'll have to. We're dressed in the wrong gear for daylight ops," Harven said. "Maybe I should go sit with Denny and send Liam this way."

"Excellent idea. Send him back in the Escalade."

"Yes, ma'am." Harven disappeared silently into the foliage.

She spoke into her headset. "Liam, Harven is on his way over. Meet him on the road in five minutes."

Gina sat and continued to stew in the heat, binoculars locked on the farmhouse. She really wanted a cigarette. And a drink.

Ten minutes later, Liam slithered into position and looked at her expectantly.

"No movement. Sit tight and watch. Give me the key fob, please."

She spoke into her headset. "Harven, I'll be gone for five to ten minutes. Keep me posted."

She slipped back to the road quietly but not with the stealth Harven demonstrated. Hopping into the big SUV, she turned it on and blasted the air conditioning, then put her face in front of the vent, soaking up the cold.

God, that feels good.

She lit a cigarette and reached into the center console. A pint bottle of Grey Goose sat inside a small cooler. She took a long swig and let the burning sensation sink to her core, soothing and relaxing her. She took another. A perk of her position. She answered to no one.

Gina wasn't cut out for this kind of detail. Nor was she a trained assassin. Add in the heat, the bugs, the skulking through the forest, it was almost too much. But she dare not show weakness. She had insisted on coming and leading the operation, so she had to deal with the discomforts. And for the chance to take Kat Lundquist herself, she would.

She felt confident. They had Kat and would soon close an ugly chapter in the business. She noted one of her nails had chipped. Damn. She needed to schedule an appointment for a mani-pedi. And a trip. Bali? Kind of cliché, but why not? Find herself a handsome island man and fuck his brains out.

Yes, definitely.

Harven reported all quiet from the woods on the other side of the farm. Liam followed with the same.

"I'm coming," Gina said. "Be ready. We're going soon."

She took another stiff draw from the vodka bottle. Between the nicotine, the alcohol, and the AC, she was half-tempted to stay put and let them handle the dirty work. Casually stroll in afterward and finish the bitch off. But no, that would set a bad precedent. Besides, she never had to do this again.

Gina grabbed her pistols and stepped into the woods, following the dabs of luminescent paint Harven used to mark the way. The sky was darkening and there were no lights in or around the farm.

Now she felt a little anxiety. She wanted adequate time with Kat Lundquist, but if she ran, they would have to shoot her. Better than letting her escape, but less satisfying.

Then what? Bury her and hide the evidence? Leave her and let her rot? Either way, they would never find her.

No, Gina liked Harven's idea. He brought ten gallons of gas to burn the place down and draw attention to the house after they left. All that would remain was the skeleton and a skull. Dental records would identify the body as Katrina Lundquist. That would send a message to anyone who doubted her control of the organization. Actually, fire would be a great way to kill Kat when she was done with her.

Gina moved silently and slipped into the small clearing next to Liam, and announced, "I'm ready. Still quiet?"

"Yes. No movement at all," Harven said into the headset. "We need to go in slow and keep our heads down. We don't want to draw fire from the rifle. If we surprise them, the rifle will be virtually useless."

"If do they see us and run, kill the man and take Kat down," Gina said. "Don't kill her. Just wound her. I want her alive."

"Understood. When?"

Gina looked at the sky, which had faded to a deep blue.

"About fifteen minutes."

Forty-Eight

Kat stared out the back door into the decreasing light. She whispered, "Justin. We need to go soon."

Justin glanced out the front door and walked into the kitchen. "How are we getting out of the house? They probably have a clear view of the front and back doors."

Yes, they would. Harven had night vision gear. They probably all did. Out a window? Also risky. Basement window? Too small. If they just ran, they would be gunned down. Stealth was best, but even then, Kat felt their chances of escaping were slim.

Justin didn't need to know that. Her nerves were jangling and he looked worse. She couldn't blame him. This was her fault. She had messed up and landed him in terrible danger.

Then she had a flash. The storm doors!

Facing south at ground level, they could slip out and crawl away undetected. Even if they were ultimately spotted, they should have the lead.

"There are storm doors in the basement. We'll go out that way.

Less chance they'll see us leave. Like I said, three hundred yards out, there's a fence and a cornfield. The corn is tall."

"When?"

"Soon, when it's a little darker. Let's watch for ten or fifteen minutes yet." She pointed to the rifle. "How good are you?"

"Very. I probably could have been a sniper."

"If they come sooner, we might be better off here."

"But you said—"

"There are no correct answers," she said, trying to hide her anxiety and fear. "I'm winging it. You watch the front, I'll watch the back. An escape will be safer when it's darker—if they wait. If they come sooner, choose your shots very carefully."

She wanted to think Justin could kill them but he would only get one. Harven would change tack and find a way to spray the house with gunfire. Was she wrong about Harven and the crew coming? She didn't think so. It was a feeling, one she had learned to trust. Assume the worst, always. If they ran and nothing happened, it would be a funny anecdote later.

Justin watched out the front door with his night vision gear. Standing by the kitchen door, Kat peeked again and saw nothing. Slipping her money belt on, she checked her magazines. Both were full. She clipped a combat knife to her belt and put a box of ammo in her pocket. If they needed more, they were probably dead.

As dusk settled in, Kat moved from window to window, keeping an anxious eye out for any movement. The darkness favored them, and tonight it would be especially dark after the sliver of moon just above the western skyline set. Time ticked by and the farm remained quiet as the light faded. They would come soon.

Kat called Max and walked to the front door by Justin.

"Anything?"

"No."

"Almost time. Let's go into the basement and open the doors so we're ready to move out."

They dashed down the basement stairs, using her lantern. The trapdoor was open. That bothered her. She never saw Natalie leave. Kat had to make sure she was gone—though it would be a terrible complication if the woman was still down there.

"Wait a second."

She hustled down the ladder and stairs to the bottom landing. The door was closed. Natalie was probably gone, but she had to be sure.

Opening the door with the lantern held high, Kat glanced in and shrieked.

Natalie lay on the floor, eyes wide, her face locked in a rictus of terror. The nails of one hand had dug into the flesh of her cheek, the other hand was outstretched in supplication. Kat couldn't stop staring into the dead woman's eyes. The expression was worse than any horror movie fright mask she had ever seen.

Jason stepped in next to her. "Jesus Christ!"

His words broke the spell. She looked around. The room otherwise looked unchanged, the mirror and Ouija board undisturbed on the table, the skulls on the floor bearing mute testimony to some unknown horror.

"It looks like she died of fright," he said.

It did. And it felt like an omen.

"Yeah. We have to get out of here. Now!" Kat could barely contain her panic.

Justin pulled out his phone and snapped several photographs.

"What are you doing?" Kat asked, incredulous.

"We're not coming back. No one will believe we saw this otherwise."

He wasn't wrong, but it was a horribly ghoulish thing to do.

"Enough!" She pushed him ahead and they ran up the stairs. Kat slammed the hatch shut—as if that might stop whatever evil lurked below. She threw the bolt to unlock the storm doors and pushed them open. Flanked by arborvitaes, she hoped the opening was hidden from their pursuers.

Kat looked out and listened.

Stars were visible in the dark grey sky. Crickets chirped loudly. She heard nothing else.

Justin stared into space. "It had to be the plume and the currents. That sort of outcome is something I never even imagined—though I never imagined dealing with a medium either."

"What do you think she saw?"

"I'm not sure I want to know."

Kat shuddered at the thought, as afraid of the house and the plume as she was of Harven.

As her eyes adjusted to the night, she nudged Justin and whispered, "Time to go."

Kat slithered out onto the dry earth and scrambled forward on her elbows, dragging her body. Justin followed and Max moseyed alongside.

Three hundred yards to a big cornfield. If they made it that far.

She prayed they were invisible.

Their lives depended on it.

Forty-Nine

Gina wasn't wearing night vision gear.

It was a stupid oversight. No hat either. She didn't like her head covered and she was sweaty enough without it. Too late now.

To the west, a thin wedge of moon slid behind the trees on the horizon. Time to go.

She nudged Liam and whispered, "Any movement?"

"Nothing yet. I don't think they suspect—"

Harven broke in. "Heads up. Movement south of the house. One person for sure. And the dog. They're running."

Gina couldn't see anything, but Liam said, "Got them."

She followed his finger and saw vague movement low in the grass. Possibly people, slithering like snakes. Then she saw a dim outline of the dog emerge from behind a bush. As Gina shifted to get more comfortable, they stopped. Had she given their position away? That would be ironic after bitching at Denny. Naw. Had to be a coincidence.

"They're moving south," Harven said. "Two people and a dog."

"Remember, I want Kat alive."

"Understood."

Then Harven said, "Kat has night vision optics. Looks like a hunting rig. Keep your heads down."

"Harven? What's your suggestion?" Gina asked.

"I think they're heading toward the heavier brush and grass where they'll be harder to follow. We should move south parallel to them. Now we're playing catch up."

"Thanks to someone blowing our element of surprise, Denny," Gina said tartly.

Denny wisely said nothing.

Harven continued, "Liam, move a little faster than Ms. Gallagher. I'll do the same until we box them into a square. Denny, hang back a bit. Keep our positions staggered to avoid the danger of crossfire. We'll close in on each side of them like jaws snapping shut. Acceptable?"

Remembering that she was in charge, Gina took a deep breath and said, "Yes. Perfect! Let's go."

She felt a little edgy. Hyped up. Unusual for her.

Liam moved out as she crept forward at a slight angle. The crickets were noisy enough to mask the sounds of their movements. Gina had no idea crickets could be so fricking loud. In town, they were always in the background. Here, they sounded like a screeching cacophony of violins that she couldn't tune out.

With a rush of excitement, her pulse racing, she fell into the chase. It was the ultimate game hunt. And she was close to fulfilling a promise to her brothers. To catch and settle the score with Kat Lundquist. In a couple of hours, that bitch would be screaming to die.

Liam's dark silhouette slowly receded into the deepening night. The soil was dry and hard. Thank God. She couldn't imagine doing this in mud during a rainstorm. Even so, it was harder than she imagined.

Crouching and crawling to keep her head down took serious effort even though she was in great shape. With the dirt and the bugs, it was close to hell on earth. Add the threat of gunfire? A little spooky.

She wished now she had worn night vision gear. Instead, she relied on a poor visual of Liam's back to keep her positioned.

They called out their locations as they moved. She caught a brief glimpse of Denny about sixty feet over. They were moving almost level with each other. She needed to move faster.

"I've pulled even with them," Harven said. "Denny, stay down more. I caught a glimpse of you."

"So did I," Gina said. She stopped and looked up. A clear night, the stars were growing brighter. Seldom visible in town, they were a dazzling sight out here and a surreal contrast to the drama playing out on the ground.

"Actually, that might work to our advantage," Harven said. "If Liam and I can wrap in front of them without being detected, they'll think they're ahead of us and walk right into the trap."

That suited Gina fine. A less strenuous workout for her. She could hang back while Liam and Harven flanked and trapped Lundquist, shot the dude, and brought Kat to her. If Kat was smart, she'd kill herself first, but she wasn't suicidal. She had gone to great lengths to live. Gina would change her mind.

A moment she relished.

Fifty

Kat and Justin low-crawled through the brush.

The cover of foliage and field grass was mostly solid but spotty in places. Twenty feet in, Kat turned to Justin. "Give me the rifle and the night vision goggles. I'll take the lead because I know the terrain and the shortest path to the fence."

They swapped weapons and Kat stroked Max under the chin. "Stay with me, buddy."

Max was more visible, but he was just an animal wandering at night and less likely to draw attention. Or was that wishful thinking?

Kat led the way, struggling a little with the long gun. They spread out as they moved, opening five feet between them. Max stayed close, kept his head down, and seemed to sense the danger in the situation. She hoped she didn't get him killed tonight.

It was almost dark with little residual light in the western sky. The moon had set. A clear night, the stagnant air was uncomfortably warm and sticky. The crickets were loud, the only sound she could hear besides the occasional hoot of an owl.

Justin watched the fields over his shoulder, occasionally muttering, "All clear."

She felt virtually invisible, like a ghost in a fog. They communicated in whispers, but spoke as little as possible. The ground was dry and hard like concrete, facilitating their movements. If they made it to the cornfield farther south, they might survive this. And yet, she wondered if Harven was even the biggest threat. Kat couldn't get the look of terror on Natalie's face out of her mind. An expression of unrelenting fear.

What terrifying vision could kill someone by sight alone? Would such things appear to them?

They continued south in a combo of low-crawl and crouched run. Using the night vision gear was awkward in the grass. The nearer vegetation appeared bright and interfered with her ability to see the bigger picture. Maybe she was using it wrong. No time to learn now.

She stopped occasionally to look on each side of their position. As yet, she had seen no one. No evidence of a pursuit.

Could they pull this off?

Every yard covered gave her a little more confidence.

Then she caught movement to the west.

Fuck!

Kat whispered, "Someone on my right side. Forty yards out."

"How many?"

Kat stopped to assess. With the night vision, she spotted two people. A woman perhaps, one she didn't recognize, and a taller man, almost certainly Liam. That was surprising. What woman? The PI who had tailed her?

"Looks like two on the right."

On the left, she saw only one. Denny maybe. They were slowly closing in. The only advantage they had was the distance to the fence. Their exit was a straight line. The others had to move diagonally to catch them, a slightly longer distance. Would it be enough?

"One on the left."

They brought only three people? Were they that confident? Three would be a relief—

No. She hadn't seen Harven. There had to be at least four. And if she saw them, they must see her, Justin, and Max. Or had they expected the move to the south? Harven would.

The terrain was uneven. She and Justin were following a depression in the field. Better cover, she thought, but their pursuers were on slightly higher ground. Inadvertently, she was helping them.

Damn it!

Knowing Harven, they would pursue and position for a closing pincer move. He had stories of pursuits and gunfights like that in the desert. That would put Harven on her left, ahead of Denny. He was the least likely to slip up and be seen. He would maneuver to outflank them.

They were trapped. Almost. Even so, they dare not flat-out run and risk a hail of bullets in the back.

She tried to contain her anxiety.

"What do we do?" Justin whispered.

"Keep our heads down and keep pushing south as fast as we can. Right now, we have a slight edge, but we can't panic and run. They'll mow us down."

Then she realized they could do the same in the cornfield. It felt like a lose-lose situation. But they could have opened fire if they wanted. Clearly, the order was to take her alive at all costs.

How could she parley that to her advantage? She didn't know. It felt impossible to make life and death decisions under pressure like this.

One mistake...

They had to maintain their lead. Reach that fence and cornfield before Harven closed the trap.

Kat pushed herself to scramble faster and whispered, "Hurry!"

Fifty-One

Battlefields at night were dangerous places.

Yet Harven felt fully in his element, armed with his favorite weapon and crawling through the field tinted green by the night vision optics. Hot and sweaty, he loved the thrill of combat, the pursuit, the risks. It was the ultimate game. There were no trophies for second place. This differed from war, but he had trained Kat and knew how capable she was. He expected a fierce fight.

He was surprised Gina hadn't complained. A city girl, she rarely roughed it and whined if she did. But she wasn't the worst person to work for. Gina paid him very well and often deferred to his judgement. He effectively ran his end of the business with little interference.

When the brothers went to prison, he could have seized control of the operation. It would have been risky and dangerous with little assurance the rank and file would follow him. Liam and Denny expected him to, but it wasn't a job he wanted. Harven didn't want to be stuck behind the scenes and out of the action, consigned to schmoozing with morons in restaurants, the mob equivalent of a desk job. He already had plenty of money. He craved action, not power.

If he looked out for Gina, his life and position were secure.

Harven hustled forward in low-crawl using his elbows, stomach flat to the ground. When cover allowed, he ran in a crouch, certain he remained invisible.

If only he could say the same for Denny and Gina. He then realized their visibility could work in his favor. Kat might think she was ahead and had a chance.

He felt no need to hurry, no urgency. The snare was closing. They were in the trap. He had never felt more confident. Surprising, since he had spent less time training in the past year.

He spoke into his mic. "I'm ahead of them and closing in. Liam?"

"Same."

Kat was doing a fair job of moving stealthily, but must have seen them on their flanks because she and the man looked harried and rushed. The frequent glances over their shoulders gave it away.

The guy was struggling and Harven felt a little unhappy about killing him. Poor schlep was simply in the wrong place at the wrong time. He didn't hate Kat either. He had liked her, found her tough and unflinching in business, but he couldn't believe she dimed him out. For that alone, she had to go.

Gina's hatred of the woman was pathological. Harven shuddered to think what horrors Gina planned to inflict upon her. He might step outside for that session. Harven had no problem with torture to suit a specific need, but not when it involved women. He could kill them if need be, but torture? Nope. Some soft streak in his nature toward females, he assumed. If they ended up in a firefight, he might just aim a head shot at Kat and perform a mercy killing. Gina would be mad. She would also get over it. He was too valuable to the operation.

As he moved forward, musing, he saw success within his grasp. The field was like a chessboard and his knights were closing in for the kill.

Then Gina broke silence and yelled, "Kat! You're surrounded! Give it up!"

What in the fuck was she doing?

Harven stopped dead and dropped to the ground to assess and regroup.

Had she lost her mind?

⋆   ⋆   ⋆

With her eyes fully acclimatized to the dark, Gina caught glimpses of the plan playing out.

Denny was the most obvious, about seventy feet to her left. She couldn't see Harven but spotted Liam, about fifty feet ahead, swinging slowly east. She imagined Harven on the other side, in roughly the same position, pushing west.

Then she saw Kat and the geology dude. Just for a second. The dog gave their position away.

As Harven and Liam announced they had outflanked their position, her excitement level rose.

Just a matter of minutes now. They fucking had her!

Harven's plan was working. Kat was trapped.

After a five-year wait, she could barely contain herself. In the thrill of the moment she shouted, "Kat! You're surrounded! Give it up!"

Kat and the man dropped from sight.

Gina followed suit, stunned by her outburst. By her lack of control. What the fuck was she thinking? Harven would be pissed.

Worse, Kat might escape.

Fifty-Two

Kat dropped and froze.

The voice came from behind and to the right. They weren't boxed in—yet. Liam was just forward of due east. Was it a bluff? Were they hoping to end this without gunfire?

Not a chance.

The voice sounded familiar, like Gina Gallagher, the company accountant. Why was she here?

Then a light bulb lit up. Gallagher was her married name. Kat always thought Gina bore a resemblance to Antonio Campo even though they denied a familial relationship. Gina had come to court every day of the trial and stared daggers at Kat. Being the sister made sense and explained her presence. Kat now understood the plan. They wanted her alive so they could rape her. Drill holes in her kneecaps. Cut and torment her before killing her. She knew how these people treated their enemies. She glanced at Justin, who looked less freaked out than he should be. Good thing he didn't know the ugly truth.

This wouldn't end well for him either. She wanted to vomit with guilt. She had gotten him into this mess by thinking she could outsmart Harven and the cartel and live quietly off the grid. Like everything in her life, it would end in failure. She wasn't meant to be happy. Ever. But she didn't want to take Justin and Max down with her. Maybe they would let them go?

She barked a bitter, "Ha!"

Never happen.

Justin gave her a quizzical look. She put a finger up and thought hard. Ran through all the tricks Harven had taught her to use in conflict exercises. The principal theme? Exploit the weakest link.

Meanwhile, their pursuers had stopped moving. Why? Waiting for an answer? Regrouping?

Parsing the options in fast-forward, Kat saw a path out. A slim chance—a sliver, like the crescent moon earlier.

If they could punch through Liam's position, it was a straight shot to the fence and cornfield. He was less dangerous than Harven. Gina was probably the weakest link, but falling back accomplished nothing. Nowhere to go after that. The fence was the goal. She felt a sudden confidence in her thinking and actions, and a streak of ferocity that gave her strength.

She put a reassuring hand on Justin's shoulder and said, "I have an idea, but we have to move fast."

Spoken aloud, the plan sounded foolhardy, but given the situation, they had nothing to lose. Kat explained it quickly. Justin asked no questions and nodded in agreement. The plan seemed to give him hope. His posture firmed up. He looked more resolute and aggressive. Justin was ready to fight back.

In her head, she pictured the four pursuers arrayed in a staggered pattern around them. Harven in the field to her left. Liam just ahead to the right, about forty feet out, moving forward and inward to close the trap. Gina Gallagher lay behind on the right, holding her position. Denny was behind on her left, also stationary, as best as she could tell.

If they were waiting for an answer, she had one.

Kat told Max to lie down and stay, then made eye contact with Justin. He nodded, showing his readiness. With a finger, Kat pointed toward Liam's position to give him a target and whispered, "Go!"

Justin jumped to a squat, fired twice, lunged forward into a straddle stance, and fired twice more. He dropped and scuttled backward on his ass, spun and crouched, poised to shoot anyone trying to sneak in from behind.

Just a few seconds had elapsed.

As Liam eased in, adjusting to the right, he returned fire twice, slightly forward of Justin's second position, angled low into empty ground.

Kat eyed the muzzle flashes and tracked his movement, then ran forward in a crouch and fired four quick rounds with the rifle in a splayed pattern. Liam reared up and fell back. A disturbance in the brush followed as he went down. Certain a bullet hit him, Kat still needed to confirm the kill.

The field was deathly quiet. The gunfire had stilled everything, including the crickets.

Why? Confusion? Surprise? Kat didn't trust it.

They had to keep moving.

Kat rushed forward into thicker cover, ejecting the magazine from the Browning and popping the other in on the fly. She raised the barrel, ready to respond.

She saw Liam's prone body as she approached. He was gone. The round caught him just above the eye.

As Justin and Max closed in from behind, Kat grabbed Liam's AR-15 and passed it to Justin, feeling safer having him guarding the rear with an assault rifle. It evened out the firepower a bit.

Glancing back, she saw movement to the southwest as a man broke from cover with an assault rifle. Had to be Denny. Justin hadn't seen him. All Denny had to do was open up and they were dead.

"Justin! Down!"

Kat drew a bead on the dark form and fired four fast rounds in a slight spread before turning and running forward. She felt certain at least one round hit home. Denny dropped from sight, but it looked like a controlled move to avoid her gunfire. He would be wearing a flak jacket and probably wasn't seriously wounded. She had gotten super lucky with Liam.

Two shots rang out from the left. Gina?

Kat heard them rip through the grass far too close to them.

As Justin caught up, she tossed the empty rifle aside and said, "Give me the Glock! Keep moving!"

She grabbed it and thought about returning fire—

No. Too risky. It would give away their position. She yanked on Justin's arm, gave Max's collar a tug, and scrambled toward the southwest as she whispered, "Hurry! Fast as we can!"

Harven would come fast and hard with Liam down. Did he know yet?

She stumbled and fell, then rolled back to her feet, feeling the tiniest bit of optimism.

They had just a slim chance to survive.

But it felt like victory.

Fifty-Three

Harven seethed at his team's incompetence.

In seconds, his carefully considered plan fell to pieces.

In yelling out, Gina revealed her position and warned Kat of the impending danger. Then Liam made a boneheaded mistake. With stunning bravado, Kat and her friend pulled a classic feint on Liam and the idiot fell for it. The man fired, jumped forward, fired again, and fell out of view. Liam returned fire, revealing his position. Kat shot at him with the rifle and Harven thought he saw Liam go down. Then Denny tried to rush them and Kat hit him with a round to the torso. Hopefully, his vest stopped it. Gina completed the insanity by firing toward him!

Harven couldn't understand it.

He had trained these people, but in seconds they had degenerated into an unruly mob of gangbangers. Gina, he could understand. Liam and Denny? Not so much.

While that went down, his night vision gear freaked out and flipped from a green hue to a luminescent blue and blew his concentration.

He tried to draw a bead on Kat or the man, but they disappeared into heavier foliage and he lost sight of them. Now he couldn't even find the dog.

What the fuck was Liam thinking? And where was he?

Swallowing the aggravation of a plan ruined by idiots, Harven whispered into his mic, "Liam? Sit rep."

No response.

Finally, Gina said, "Liam?"

Silence.

Was he dead?

Torn between the desire to strangle Gina and the need to answer that question, Harven said, "I'll check his position."

For a moment, he set all other concerns aside and scrambled through the brush to the spot where Liam went down. He was still there, lying on his back, a bullet wound through his left temple, his eyes agape in surprise.

Jesus!

Harven was stunned. He could hardly fathom the loss of his friend in an operation where superior weapons and numbers should have ruled.

Other than himself, Harven realized Kat was the coolest, smartest player on the field. She knew where Liam was, lured him out, and killed him. As her trainer, if he wasn't so focused on eliminating her, he might be proud of her savvy.

Harven refocused on the task at hand, formulating a plan to regain the upper hand while keeping Gina and Denny in line.

He spoke into his headset. "Liam is out. Denny, were you hit?"

"One to the vest. Hurt like fuck."

"Are you good to go?"

"Yep. Ready and able."

"I've lost my visual fix on them. They have to be heading southwest. Ms. Gallagher, move straight south as fast as you can. Denny, move southwest. Close in behind Ms. Gallagher and watch her six."

He could see their trail in the brush, but the quirky blue optics made it hard to follow. His depth perception was off.

No pretenses now. Harven was taking charge. The dangers of letting Gina run this operation were clear, and he suspected that applied to the organization as well.

They had no choice but to kill Kat and her friend and cut their losses. Gina wouldn't like it.

Tough.

What if he accidentally shot Gina on purpose?

Bad idea. He liked the current status quo. And with Liam out, he had one less reliable accomplice in a hostile takeover.

Harven added, "Shoot the man on sight. Attempt to wound Kat, but if it looks like she'll break out, shoot her."

Gina yelled, "No!"

"If she gets away, we'll never see her again."

"Let's just kill these assholes and be done with it!" Denny snarled.

"Shut up! I want the woman alive! Track them down and take her. Kill the dude and the dog."

Whatever.

Harven shook his head. Fuck Gina. For now, he was in charge. Killing Kat was the only goal.

He checked his gear and crept southwest, trying to spot Kat and the dog. As he did, his optics flipped from blue to bright orange and a voice spoke into his headset.

"Jake, I'm hit. Help!"

Harven stopped and dropped. He recognized the voice at once. It was Fitzweiler, a kid he served with in Afghanistan. Only nineteen, Fitzweiler was hit by a sniper round and had died in his arms. It had been one of the most wrenching KIAs on his watch. A nice kid, smart and good looking, he was destined for better things.

What the fuck?

Why was he hearing that voice now?

The optics were a malfunction. This was—?

A problem with his perception. Then he recalled a story they heard on the radio earlier. The area had been affected by lots of crazy events in the past few days. An earthquake. A mass shooting. A couple of murders. The conspiracy nuts were blaming the government, jet contrails, and something in the ground. Was that possible? He was a sane, sensible man, but inexplicable things were happening. Three of his people had just acted like morons. His optics went nuts. A dead kid was talking to him through his headset.

All the more reason to finish the mission and get the fuck out of here.

He hustled forward. Moving into deeper brush, he could jog ahead in a crouch and cover ground more quickly.

But so could Kat.

Harven felt their advantage slipping away.

Then Fitzweiler called out again. "Jake, I'm hit. Help!"

For the first time in years, Harven felt a frisson of fear.

Fifty-Four

Gina bristled at Harven's incompetence.

His handpicked team had blown a simple clean-up operation.

While she may have erred in taunting Kat, that shouldn't have changed the outcome. They had her surrounded! She had also erred in firing toward Harven. Fortunately, hitting him at that range with her pistols was almost impossible.

Then came word that Liam was dead.

That was on Harven, who had clearly underestimated the threat Kat posed.

Trying to deflect blame, Harven took control of the operation, as if he no longer trusted her to run things. She knew he would ignore her order to keep Kat alive, though he was right about one thing. If Kat escaped, she was gone forever.

Shit.

She had to concentrate and regain command of the situation. Harven might be out of a job after this—though thinking about firing him and actually terminating the psychopath were two very different things.

Gina spent a minute in meditation, a technique Harven had taught her to push extraneous problems aside and focus on the immediate task. Gina drew resolve and strength from the exercise. Feeling renewed, she hiked through the brush, anxious to catch Kat Lundquist before Harven found her.

The thought of stalking her down and shooting her in the face spurred her on.

★   ★   ★

Denny didn't like the odds in this battle.

The field was murky, hot, and buggy. Triple whammy. They should just open up with the AR-15s and spray the field. Kill the bitch, her friend, and their stupid dog. Gina was consumed with nabbing the woman alive and killing her slowly, only increasing the odds one of them would be killed instead.

He moved slowly, plodding through the grass, grumbling, when Gina yelled out to Kat.

Denny froze.

What the fuck was she doing?

Silence followed. No one was moving. He waited for Harven to react.

A minute later, several shots rang out. Then Liam returned fire. Was he fucking nuts? Denny was about to bitch through the headset when four rapid shots rang out from a heavier gun, a 30-06 maybe. He didn't see any muzzle flashes, so the gun was facing away from him. Had to be one of the people they were chasing.

More silence.

It was unnerving and confusing.

Then he glimpsed the tall dude's back, moving away. Denny rushed forward in a crouched position to follow and take him out, but ran out of cover. As he tried to scramble back, Kat bobbed up slightly and fired four quick rounds at him with the rifle.

Oof!

He took a round to the vest on his right side, a blow like an iron fist, stealing his breath. Denny dropped out of the firing line. His chest hurt like hell. He lay for a minute in crazy pain. Then he took a couple of deep breaths, shook off the pain, and rolled into a crouch. He was insanely angry. Angry that Kat nailed him and angrier that Gina had nearly gotten him killed.

Then Harven announced Liam was dead.

Had they really killed Liam? He couldn't believe it. For a moment, he couldn't catch his breath. He and Liam were a team. They had worked together for years. Denny couldn't get his head around the idea. The kid part of him wanted to cry, but he turned the feeling into rage, as he always did. Liam's death was on Gina. And the bitch who pulled the trigger. He wanted to rip Kat's arms off. Given the chance, he would.

Harven took charge. About time.

They had lost sight of Kat, so Harven ordered them forward. Denny was to slide over and watch Gina's back. He saw her about forty feet to the southwest while Harven and Gina argued about killing Kat.

Denny threw in his two cents but Gina shouted him down. "I want the woman alive!"

Harven didn't answer. So Gina got her way.

Again.

God, he was sick of her shit. He fumed at taking orders from her. Right now, the feeling was especially intense, part of the rage building over Liam's death. Women served only two functions in the world, and running an operation like this was not one of them. Gina was a fucking accountant and he couldn't believe Harven had bowed to her instead of whacking her and taking the business for himself. But Liam liked her and had sided with Harven.

Something had to change.

And suddenly, Denny saw with utter clarity what he had to do.

He needed to kill Gina. Personally finish this mission and take the operation for himself. The brothers were gone for twenty years. Fuck 'em. He felt clearheaded and empowered, his inner vision like a hi-res video game.

Harven had to go too. But he was a veritable terminator, and one of the few people Denny feared. Now was the time to do it.

The plan was clear. Take Gina quietly and kill her with a knife or his bare hands, then sneak up behind Harven and mow him down with the AR. He would never see it coming. Never suspect it. He should have. He had no idea how angry Denny was that he sided with Gina.

Then he would kill Kat after he raped her and fucked her up good with a knife.

Denny would spin a bold story to the brothers about Harven underestimating Kat Lundquist and getting Liam, Gina, and himself killed. Fortunately, he had operated more carefully and nailed the bitch.

He felt certain they would put him in charge of the organization as a thank you.

Gina first.

"Ms. Gallagher, I'm coming in from your left." She might not like it, but he couldn't risk sneaking up and getting shot if she mistook him for a target.

"Why? Just go forward now."

"I'm moving over to cover your flank, like Harven said."

"Denny, I'm running this show—!"

"Trust me."

"Go forward. That's an order!"

"Yes, ma'am."

She was moving too. That was good. She was less likely to hear his approach. He imagined he was moving silently, like an Indian guide.

Anger consumed him. He felt indestructible, a veritable warrior. Not even bullets could stop him.

Fifty-Five

Kat, Justin, and Max scrambled through a confusing jumble of bushes, saplings, and prairie grass.

In a skirmish with a young hawthorn tree, Kat gashed her arms in several places. Her emotions ran a confusing gamut from elation and fear to a stone-cold craving for coke that muddled her efforts to stay focused on finding and crossing the fence. The night vision gear was almost useless in dense brush, though it did help her avoid blundering into tree trunks.

The fence was nowhere in sight and Kat hoped they were running in the right direction. She didn't know how to read the stars and feared veering off course into the arms of their pursuers.

When Liam's body lay a decent distance behind them, maybe a hundred yards back, Kat stopped, grabbed Justin's hand, and pulled him into a crouch. Huffing from exertion, she couldn't speak at first.

Sweaty and weary looking, he gave her a questioning look. "What?"

She slipped the night vision gear off, took a deep breath, and whispered, "I've lost my bearings. Can you navigate by the stars?"

He nodded. "Absolutely."

"We need to go southwest. Are we heading the right way?"

He looked up at the sky, swiveled his head back and forth, and pointed his hand in the direction they were running. "That's southwest. We're good."

The cricket noise had ramped up again and a breeze had kicked in, making it difficult to hear any movements. Replaying the encounter with Denny, she saw him go down. She was less certain he was out.

Kat eased her head up and scanned the field to the north and west. Somewhere out there, one or two people were still in pursuit. She saw a little movement almost a hundred yards away, a good buffer. Looking to the east, she saw nothing. Whoever was out there gave nothing away. It had to be Harven.

She pulled Max in for a hug as she prepared to run again.

Justin, who seemed revitalized, said, "We just kicked their asses. We should stay and make a stand. Take the rest of them out."

His change in tack alarmed Kat. He didn't know Harven, who was as dangerous as they came and lurking somewhere nearby, an invisible ghost stalking them like a pit bull.

"No! It's too risky. We need to keep running!" She pulled him up and continued fumbling across the field.

Movement quickly grew tougher. The cover was better, but the trade-off was pushing through tangles of bushes over uneven ground. Kat could see with the night vision, but Justin was almost blind. She had to hike at a slower pace and guide him. Occasionally, she opened a hole for Max by kicking through the underbrush.

The dense cover also meant they could see nothing farther afield. They had no clue where their pursuers were. Between the racket of their movements, the crickets, tree frogs, and other night creatures,

Kat could hear nothing. Harven could break through at any moment and ambush them.

Her anxiety was through the roof.

It shouldn't be more than two hundred yards, but it felt like they had walked miles. Still no fence in sight. She kept nudging Justin to check the sky to ensure they weren't walking in circles. He reassured her they were fine.

At times, the cravings, the fear, and the uncertainty weighed her down until she grew convinced they would die tonight. She was fit and tough but maybe not enough to keep them safe. Whatever she did, Harven was better at it.

And now, she felt dizzy too.

Kat just needed to see the fence to feel a little hope. Hopefully, just a little farther—

Her foot snagged on a root and she went down hard.

Something dug painfully into her ribs as her head smacked against a rock.

The world spun away into darkness.

★   ★   ★

Justin watched Kat go down and reacted too slowly to catch her. When she didn't jump up immediately, he knelt and spotted a bloody gash on her forehead. Her eyes were closed, her mouth slack. She was out cold.

Jesus! What next?

He shook her but she remained unresponsive. Seeing her lying there, injured, helpless, he felt an ineffable rage. He wanted to rise up and kill them all. Seriously, how bad could this Harven dude be? Armed with an assault rifle, Justin felt righteous and ready to mow them all down. Just spray the field with lead until they were all dead and then stomp on their faces until the anger was gone.

Ready to leap up and hunt them down, his rational brain suddenly kicked in.

The microplume. The currents.

He had to remember where he was and what was happening beneath their feet. Every thought was suspect. No feeling, no reaction could be trusted. He wasn't a soldier nor a superhero. Kat seemed to know much more than he did and he trusted her.

Looking at her unconscious face, a dread crept up and seeped out of his pores.

If she didn't wake up soon, they were dead.

Fifty-Six

Denny spotted her twenty feet ahead.

Gina was striding toward the thicker cover and making too much noise. She was no soldier. Between her rustling through the long grass and the damned crickets, Gina hadn't heard him approaching. Hadn't faltered or glanced over her shoulder even once. She really was clueless in this arena. He felt superior in every way.

Harven had taught her self-defense, but given their difference in weight and size, Denny considered her skills little threat. She was hot though. If he only had time to throw her down and rape her—but taking Harven out was far more important. Besides, if this night worked out as planned, his future would be filled with hot women.

When he was five feet away, she sensed him closing in. Her head snapped back in alarm. He half-expected her to scream. Instead, she swiveled, set her feet, and punched straight for his throat with lightning speed, evidently reading his murderous intent and using one of Harven's signature moves. He managed a slight deflection with a right-hand block, but caught unaware, the blow still struck hard enough to catch the side of his larynx and make him cough violently.

As he recoiled, he grabbed and ripped her headset away before she could summon Harven. But that left him vulnerable for an instant and she swooped in and kneed him in the nut sack.

Hard.

Pain shot through him like a spear. He sucked in his breath and held it. Gritting his teeth, fighting the pain and nausea, he punched her in the face.

Denny expected her to fold, but she went down on one hand and kicked out, knocking him on his ass.

Wow!

Way tougher than he expected. He thought she might run, but she showed zero fear and seemed to have a tolerance to pain equal to his own. She radiated determination as blood oozed out of a gash on her cheek.

Denny relished the challenge.

As Gina pulled one of her shitty little pistols, Denny kicked it out of her hand. Knowing she carried two, he leapt at her before she could pull the other. She kicked out and checked his progress as she fumbled about, looking for the gun. He lurched right and regained his footing. Anticipating the next kick, he shoved it aside with a forearm block and knocked her off balance.

As the gun came up, he grabbed it and flung it over his shoulder. He, too, had been trained by Harven and he was feeling pretty good right now after a rough start.

In the microsecond she stared in shock, he pushed off his back foot and brought his weight to bear, shoving her onto her back. He smirked and shifted stance, ready to drop and wrap his hands around her delicate little neck. She was defenseless now.

Instead, with crazy agility, she rolled over and jumped to her feet, brandishing a knife.

The little bitch!

Where had that come from?

Harven had trained her well and Denny continued to underestimate her. He could shoot her, but he wanted the satisfaction of throttling the life out of her. And he couldn't risk gunfire and alerting Harven to his intended treachery.

They jockeyed for a few seconds while he focused on her knife hand, preparing to grab it and break her wrist. His right hand shot out to snatch the knife, but she anticipated the move. With startling quickness, she sidestepped and lunged, raising the knife and plunging it into his neck.

★   ★   ★

Gina shoved him away as he choked and gagged and blood spurted from the wound. The look of shock and horror in his eyes was priceless. Denny yanked the knife out, increasing the gush of blood pumping from his neck. He staggered and toppled face first.

Dead.

She fell back gasping, exhausted from the fight, shaking from adrenaline and the near-death experience. But she also felt a strange exhilaration at engaging in close combat and prevailing against a larger, stronger opponent. Harven's program was excellent, and she trained for an hour every day. As a smaller woman in a tough business, Gina knew she might someday need it. She just hadn't imagined using it against one of her own people.

Denny? What the fuck was he thinking?

An attempted takeover? Did Harven know about it? She doubted it. He had proven his loyalty, but a seed of mistrust had been sewn. More likely, Denny imagined himself as the new boss. Did he really think he could take Harven too?

Idiot.

Replaying the fight in her head, she saw Denny's last move coming and responded with a preternatural clarity of mind. Now she felt turbocharged, like a ninja assassin.

Gina let her breathing settle and rolled to her feet. Ready to kick some ass, she grabbed her Kimber and Denny's AR. She spotted her headset, but it had been stepped on and crushed. Denny's headset was covered in blood.

Yuck.

She hoped Harven would wait to kill Kat. Her tool kit was sitting in the SUV, but shooting Kat in the kneecaps and the elbows would suffice to inflict pain. Maybe a couple in the belly too. Harven had told her with gut wounds, acid leaked out of the stomach and caused an agonizing death.

Gina regained her bearings and set off due south, creeping through the brush.

She felt empowered. Strong and invincible. Even without the night vision.

A vague figure like a ghost lurked in the shadows ahead.

Kat Lundquist?

She was so dead.

Fifty-Seven

Harven crept forward with consummate skill, trying to locate Kat and her companions.

The optics had flipped back to green and Fitzweiler had stopped calling to him. He felt in control again. The pressures of combat and night ops sometimes rattled the most experienced of veterans. Between the malfunctioning optics and Liam's death, he understood. The dead kid talking had been a memory, not a voice.

The operation had devolved into a clusterfuck. After Gina gave her position away, they should have killed Kat and fled. Instead, Kat killed Liam and chaos ensued. Now they were taking at least two unnecessary risks: the threat of being shot by the people they were tracking, and the danger of drawing unwanted attention if they stayed too long. With the gunfire, someone would call the police sooner or later. But Gina wanted the woman captured and Harven would try to entertain her wishes for now.

Any further problems? He would kill Kat and deal with the fallout later.

His confidence in the team was shaken. Liam was dead. Denny was bumbling through the operation, and Gina had acted with reckless disregard and endangered the entire team. Regardless, he was certain that if this went badly and Kat escaped, he would be blamed. For the first time, he seriously questioned his allegiance to Gina.

The terrain grew increasingly challenging, the foliage denser, with thickets of brush, bramble, and hawthorn. The wind had picked up, moving the grass, making it difficult to see any purposeful movement. Gina and Denny hadn't checked in. He wondered where they were.

"Ms. Gallagher, what's your position?"

No reply.

"Denny?"

Silence. Were they trying to reposition and unable to talk? Seemed unlikely. He waited a moment and called again but his headset remained ominously silent.

Harven had a worrisome thought. Denny hated Gina, especially after she took control of the operation. With Liam gone, was he using the fog of battle to take matters into his own hands? Denny could take Gina from behind and kill her, then sneak up and shoot him in the back. If Denny then killed Kat, he could present himself as a hero to the brothers. Stupid fuck was dumb enough to think that might work. If so, Harven realized he had to watch his back carefully. But the fool lacked the skills and the smarts to pull off a coup. If Denny came for him, the stupid bastard would rue the day. Harven had no problem torturing a dude.

He stopped to regroup and knelt, eased his head up, and peered over the sea of grass. Held perfectly still. Observing. Listening. Trying to reorient himself given the changed circumstances.

The field was a mishmash of tall grass, bushes, and trees. The wind sent greenish waves of motion across the grass in the night vision optics and smelled of compost, an ambivalent scent of decay and renewal.

He saw no movement to the northwest where Gina and Denny should be, further raising his concerns about Denny and his intentions. He hoped the problem was just faulty headsets.

Then he saw quirky movement in the grass to the southwest as an animal or human moved through it. The gunfire would have scared off any animals. It had to be them. Kat had been in that general area.

He saw the top of a head.

Kat. Gotcha!

Harven gauged their direction and speed and worked silently through the grass on an intercepting course, working an arc to the left, keeping eyes and ears alert for Denny.

Several ways this might end. He could just shoot them and be done with it. But it was more personal now. They had killed Liam, the closest thing he had to a brother after Antonio and Tomas went to prison. They had treated him like the family he never had, and Liam had been a steadfast friend since.

Harven was primed to kill and had no compunction about wasting Kat. He looked forward to it. Better if he could kill her with his bare hands. Strangle her and watch the light and life leave her body. The dog and the dude were dead too. Collateral damage.

The perils of combat.

★   ★   ★

"Kat!"

She opened her eyes, feeling groggy and disoriented. Justin gazed at her with concern, looking green through her night vision gear.

"You conscious? Feel okay?"

"Not great." Her head throbbed. Oh well. They had to keep moving.

She rolled to her knees, looked up, and spotted the fence thirty feet away. Kat felt her heart jump. Freedom was at hand. They just might escape. Maybe she wouldn't end up being the death of Justin and Max.

Kat scanned the horizon. No movement was evident anywhere. The area was quiet. Was everyone waiting for someone to make the next move? Max snugged in next to her. He looked concerned and exhausted. Kat rubbed his big head, rolled to her feet, and pointed toward the fence. "Let's go."

Sprinting forward, motion to the north in the foliage caught her eye. She stopped. Some disturbance in the field grass. Someone walking?

It didn't matter. She was wasting time when they should be moving. Kat tugged on Justin's sleeve and pulled him forward, trying to thread a narrow path between the trees, stands of grass, and pockets of open ground. She knew one thing. A big cornfield lay on the other side of that fence. The corn was head-high and tasseling out. They would disappear in that field. Become invisible.

First, they had to scale that hurdle. It was a serious obstacle, almost head-high with seven shiny strands of taut barbed wire. The neighboring farm operation must have put it up this spring. She and Justin could climb over it, but getting Max across would be tough.

As Kat approached the fence, she eyed the wire and decided she would go over and have Justin hand Max to her.

She smiled.

They were almost free.

Fifty-Eight

Harven kept an ear to the north.

Denny was incapable of stealth and would be audible moving through the foliage, but Harven heard nothing.

He was closing in on Kat silently, using skills honed from years of training and a tour in Afghanistan. They had no clue he was behind them. He was just waiting for the right moment to pounce. He could shoot them and end it quickly, and he would if need be. But if an opportunity presented itself, he would shoot the dude and kill Kat with his bare hands. He wanted to look into her eyes as he snuffed her life out, a favor given the horrors Gina intended to inflict on her. He no longer cared that she would be pissed. Maybe he would kill her too.

Approaching at an angle, he saw the fence and understood their plan. The corn to the south was tall. They would disappear and he would never find them.

At least five feet tall, the fence looked new. A tough barrier especially with the dog. Harven stopped and lurked. A shadow within the shadows.

They stopped to climb the fence. The dude was tall but seemed little threat otherwise. The dog was big. Some weird retriever mix. A harmless breed that had failed to sense his presence.

Kat was the only serious threat.

She had a Glock in her hand. The dude was carrying an AR-15. Probably Liam's. That pissed him off and would make throttling Kat even more rewarding.

Without warning, the night vision gear morphed to red. What the hell? Worthless fucking shit. The company was getting a call when this was over. But the malfunction wouldn't interfere with the immediate task.

He could shoot the dude as he moved in, but that would alert Kat. A bad idea. He knew how fast and resourceful she was. As he considered various approaches, an opportunity presented itself, gift-wrapped.

Kat shoved the AR under the fence. Harven holstered his gun at his belly and waited until she slid the handgun under the fence and started to climb. They were unarmed. Throwing all caution to the wind, he charged the last fifteen feet.

The man, who was closer, turned to face him, clueless to the danger. Harven nailed him with a powerful right hook to the jaw, the force and momentum of the punch enhanced by his forward motion. The dude fell like a domino. Out cold.

Kat was only five feet away.

★　★　★

Too late, Kat saw the figure emerge from the shadows and run toward them.

Harven!

As he knocked Justin to the ground, she dropped to her knees and scrambled for the Glock.

Harven rushed the last few feet, grabbed her by the shoulders, and threw her to the ground. Kat rolled aside as he twisted and fell to his knee to pin her, landing on the spot she had occupied a microsecond before. With a half turn, she kicked him with a heel, nailing him in the ribs and knocking him on his side. She crabbed forward trying to reach a weapon when Harven kicked out and knocked her flat.

She rolled with the jolt and grabbed a rock as she flipped over and jumped to her feet. She had no chance to reach the Glock and didn't like her chances in hand-to-hand combat against Harven. On her right, Max paced in the dim grey of the night, looking confused.

She flung the rock hard and low, anticipating his bob and weave, and nailed his forehead, opening a gash and dislodging his night vision gear. The blow and loss of the optics stopped him in his tracks for a moment.

Running was the only option. Maybe she could circle back for Justin and Max.

She ran straight away from the fence but saw she was trapped. Someone was approaching from the north, about fifty yards out. A smaller person. Gina? And where was Denny?

She had to get out of this field. Too open, too many threats.

Kat swerved ninety degrees left with a plan to loop around Harven, scramble over the fence, and get lost in the corn. She was leaving Justin and Max behind, but logically, fleeing was in their best interest too. Harven and Gina wanted her and would abandon the others in that pursuit. She might even be able to loop back to the guns and ambush them.

She just had to get over the fence.

But Harven ran faster. Kat had forgotten how quick he was.

No matter how far she skewed away from him, he continued closing on her like a machine. She wouldn't make the fence, but she wasn't quitting either.

As Harven reached out for her, she dropped, folded up, and turned herself into a stumbling block. Unable to correct, Harven tripped and went sprawling.

Kat scrambled away but Harven lunged with crazy speed and agility, grabbed her ankle, and jerked her onto her stomach, sending her night vision goggles flying.

The move startled her and sent a spear of dread through her heart. Harven was lethal at close quarters. Where was Max? Maybe he didn't know what to do. Maybe he wasn't aggressive enough to attack Harven. Or hadn't been trained to protect his owner, but she had nothing to lose.

"Max! Help!"

Harven flipped her over by her legs and leapt, straddling her hips, pinning her and delivering a stunning punch to her cheekbone. Stars blazed in her vision. He leered and clasped his hands around her neck. She tried to wiggle loose as she pummeled him with her fists, but her body was firmly pinned and he seemed oblivious to the blows.

"Goodbye, bitch. Consider yourself lucky that I found you first."

His hands tightened around her neck until she could no longer breathe. As her consciousness fluttered, she heard a chilling snarl. Harven cried out, let go, and tumbled sideways.

Kat coughed and struggled to sit, her vision blurred, her head woozy.

Max had bitten into the back of his left thigh and held fast, shaking his head, trying to rip the leg off. Harven fought and lashed out and tried to pull away from those jaws, but Max held firm, teeth locked into the tough, sinewy meat of the hamstring muscles, growling deep in his throat.

Max tried dodging the punches, but Harven finally landed a solid blow and Max relented, allowing Harven to yank the leg loose. He rolled away and jumped to a wobbly stance as he reached for something at his waist—his gun, probably.

But Max charged too quickly. Harven fell backward as he tried to fend off the attack. Kat had never seen such fierce devotion but feared it would get him killed.

As Harven felt along his pant leg where Kat knew he stowed his knife, she scrabbled for the Glock, hoping to shoot him before he killed Max.

With a primal scream, Justin burst through a wall of brush wielding a big rock and leapt, smashing Harven on the head. Harven reeled from the blow and fell back.

In anger, or in a crazed adrenaline moment, Justin lifted the rock high and smashed it down on Harven's forehead with a sickening crunch of bone.

He went limp.

Dead.

Somehow, impossibly, the three of them had killed Harven.

Just as she felt herself relax, she heard thrashing in the dark brush nearby.

Denny or Gina.

Coming fast.

Fifty-Nine

Her eyes attuned to the dark, Kat quick-glanced both ways.

Harven's pistol jutted from a sticky holster on his waist. Her Glock lay on the far side of the fence. Both were about six feet away when someone opened fire with an assault rifle.

Gina broke through the brush with an AR-15 in her hands, her face locked in a grimace as she blasted the bejesus out of a Colorado spruce.

What the hell?

The woman was shooting at a tree! At nothing. She didn't even seem aware that Kat and Justin were staring at her, mouths agape. Had the plume gotten to Gina too?

That might be true, but sooner or later, she would see them and mow them down.

And she did.

Kat leapt as Gina spotted them and turned, swinging the rifle around. Kat rolled and yanked the Sig from the holster on Harven's waist. She aimed with a two-handed grip and fired five or six times, hitting Gina with several rounds, including one to the forehead.

Gina fired a few wild shots before she dropped and fell face first into a tangled sprawl, the back of her head a bloody mass of brain tissue and bone fragments. She was gone.

Kat slumped to the ground.

Was it over?

She couldn't believe it. Where was Denny?

Gina attacking them only made sense if Denny was dead or disabled. Otherwise, he would have come first.

Hypervigilant, the Sig ready in her taut hand, Kat waited for several minutes before falling back, dazed and exhausted. She stroked Max's head. Justin sat mute. He appeared shell-shocked. And something else. She couldn't put a finger on it.

He spoke in a hush. "I've never killed anyone."

"You saved my life. And Max's. Yours too."

He held his head and massaged his temple with his fingers. "Ugh. Terrible migraine."

She took two deep breaths and sat up. "We have to leave. We'll get you some meds and then go. I can't believe the police aren't here already."

Indeed, the night was dark, starry, and tranquil. Even the Milky Way was faintly visible.

Kat stood, found the night vision goggles, and turned to the north, scanning the horizon, listening. A fresh breeze blew out of the south. The relative silence was an odd contrast to the violence that had just taken place. She couldn't tell if the crickets were quiet or she simply couldn't hear them. Her ears were ringing after firing so many rounds. But she saw no sign of Denny or anyone else.

"Grab the AR. We need to watch for Denny—though he may be dead." She wondered how that might have happened. She didn't think her shot killed him, but there was still no sign of movement anywhere.

Kat took her Glock and the Sig, already thinking about fingerprints. They walked slowly, Kat exhausted and horrified by the awful chain of events tonight. She had seen violence before, but never so close and personal. No training could have prepared her for this. She had never killed anyone either.

Scanning the terrain, maintaining a wary eye, Kat parsed what had to be done next.

There were dead bodies in the fields. Once discovered, all hell would break loose. They would find her prints all over the house and would identify her in no time. A manhunt would ensue.

Burn it down? But fire would only draw attention to the bodies sooner.

No matter.

She had to risk it to destroy the evidence of her presence lest she be blamed for the deaths here.

Kat knew nothing about setting a controlled fire. Could she create some type of delay fuse? Maybe Justin knew how to do it. There might be no escaping this mess.

She retraced their steps, following damaged vegetation and the occasional footprint. She picked up the rifle and the empty magazine and handed them to Justin.

He looked at her blankly.

"Take it!"

He jumped and complied.

She had worn gloves when she loaded her magazines. Her brass wasn't an issue, but they spent ten minutes collecting the spent rifle shells with Justin's prints on them.

Right now, she felt stunned and irascible, angry to be pushed out by events beyond her control, and yet, a consequence of her stupidity and hubris. She felt no guilt over the deaths of Harven or the others. They had tried to kill her. But now she was adrift and on the run again. And the Campo brothers would surely come after her, especially after killing so many of their people. Or would they? She had effectively destroyed their leadership. Something to worry about later—if she lived that long.

She had to run, but what about Justin? He had come and tried to do the right thing. She may have ruined his life. Was there some way to insulate him from the legal fallout?

As they approached the dark house, she worried about the threat posed by the house itself. It seemed to have a life and mind of its own. Would the house resist and fight back? Anything was possible in this crazy place. She had no stomach for another fight.

Then Justin said, "Everything's still red; the stars, Max, even you. I hate red."

What an odd thing to say.

Sixty

Stepping onto the back porch, the night remained dark and quiet. Kat couldn't believe that sirens and scads of red and blue flashing lights weren't descending upon the farm. Unbelievable that no one had called the police.

Maybe they had time to plan an effective retreat from this nightmare.

Justin might not be much help. He was restless and fidgety and looked catatonic, staring into space with a dazed expression. His behavior was unnerving. Was it a consequence of the last few hours or an effect of the plume? Likely both. No matter. She had to motivate him to act.

Kat was shaking and struggling to focus herself as the adrenaline bled out of her system, the fallout from killing two or three people and nearly dying herself. But she felt little affected by the telluric currents other than her cravings for coke. Maybe mindfulness and her rough life experiences made her tougher and less susceptible to the effects. Or better able to resist them.

Or was that an illusion created by the plume?

Did it matter? Right now, they had to move fast.

"Justin."

His face remained a blank slate.

"Justin!"

He looked up. "Sorry. I'm having trouble focusing. Everything is still red."

"It's the plume. We need to get away from here. Now!"

"Makes sense."

They had to split up. Was he fit to drive? His best chance of avoiding legal entanglements lay with putting plenty of distance between the two of them.

"Go dismantle your gear and get it out of here. Leave no trace, if possible."

He stared at her blankly.

"Now!"

"Why?"

His intransigence was super annoying. She had no time for this. She imagined police converging on the farm any minute. And with the fight behind them, the memory of Natalie's face returned—that expression of pure terror. Kat desperately wanted to put the house in the rearview mirror.

"Your best move is to go home. If the police question you, you can say you packed up your gear and left earlier in the day. Disavow any knowledge of me or events at the farm."

"Makes sense."

He nodded but she wasn't sure he understood. She pushed him out the door. "Go! Hurry!"

She lit a candle to see better. Her mind was racing, calculating and recalculating every angle. As she did so, Kat inventoried her belongings on the kitchen counter. The cooler. Her clothes and shoes. Enough food for a few days. The lantern and her Glock. A bedroll and small pillow. Max's kibble. It was about all she could manage. They would have to walk since she couldn't expect Max to keep up with her on a bike, not for any distance anyway—

Holy shit!

What was she thinking? Harven or Gina must have a vehicle parked somewhere around the farm. Surely she could use it for at least twenty-four hours before the police started looking for it.

The house rattled for a moment. A minor tremor. Footsteps landed on the porch, followed by a knock on the door.

"Justin? I told you to pack and leave. I'm leaving in a minute."

"Can I say something quick before you leave?"

Kat vacillated. Leaving was hard enough without him behaving like a lost puppy. She liked him a lot, but he wasn't himself. The currents were affecting him with peculiar intensity and he seemed unaware of it. But she could talk for a minute. Say goodbye. When this was over, maybe they could reconnect—though why would he want anything to do with her after tonight?

"Come in."

He stepped in, wringing his hands, and stared at her. It was creepy. Finally, he said, "Still intent on going your own way?"

Trying to sound patient and conciliatory, she said, "Yes, it's best for now, especially for you."

"If you say so."

"You also need a suitable lie to explain the blossoming bruise on your head. Go to the ER and say you fell at home, lost consciousness, and want to be checked out. Might work as a partial alibi anyway."

He nodded. "Probably a good idea."

Kat said, "You've got my number. Call me when things settle down. We can meet somewhere. Look on the bright side. Seems like your theory is on the money. I, for one, am a firm believer."

He gripped his head with his fingers. Still suffering with the migraine, probably.

"Go take your meds first. Try to get on top of it."

The ground and house shuddered with a stronger tremor. Kat thought she smelled sulfur and felt a spasm of fear.

Justin stared at his hands, tipping his head like Max often did when she spoke to him. Raising his head slowly, his face turned from little boy lost to demented psycho in a millisecond.

With a lunge, he grabbed her by the throat with a powerful grip and spoke with sheer menace.

"I'm going to choke the fucking life out of you!"

Sixty-One

Kat was stunned by the force of the grip around her throat.

Was he serious? Then he brought the other hand to bear and squeezed harder.

Shock and paralysis hobbled her as she tried to recover her wits and process his sudden shift in affect. He shoved her back into the hard edge of the quartz countertop, knocking stuff to the floor in a clatter. What had Harven taught her to do? If she didn't act now she was dead. Justin's height and surprising strength scared and intimidated her. As he closed in a bit, she lashed out and punched upward at his throat.

It wasn't hard enough to disable him, but he choked and coughed and loosened his grip with a look of surprise. She swung and slammed her forearm down, breaking his hold.

Spinning away, desperately seeking a weapon, Kat saw the dirty dishes and began flinging them at him in a barrage that was noisier than effective. One plate glanced off the side of his head but proved no deterrent.

As he came at her, she tried to kick him in the crotch, but it was awkward given his height. Most of the energy went into his inner thigh. Justin swooped in and slammed her to the ground with a vicious two-handed shove. He lunged to fall on her, but she rolled aside as he landed on one knee.

Max, circling the melee, turned and glared at Justin with fangs bared and hackles raised.

Their eyes met and Max lurched in to attack. With improbable timing, Justin swung a roundhouse punch and drilled Max on the side of his head. The force of the blow knocked him sideways. Max dropped and fell still, unconscious, or worse. Justin stared at his fist in apparent disbelief he had landed that blow.

Kat kicked out, missed, and screamed, "Leave him alone!"

She rolled to her feet and grabbed the nearest object in reach. A baking pan. She bashed Justin on the side of the head and pulled back to swing again.

He grabbed the pan from her, tossed it aside, and threw a quick right. She arched back, but the blow glanced off her cheek, her vision erupting in a blaze of stars. It hurt like hell but focused her resolve. She had to move and stay out of reach.

Kat ran headlong into the dining room and scuttled around the table to put something solid between them. She needed the Glock. Where was it?

Spying her stuff on the kitchen counter, she remembered setting it down there—

Justin barged into the room. She shifted away from him to the right, then left, as they jockeyed from side to side around the table. Kat saw little chance of reaching the gun and prayed he didn't realize it was right behind him. But given the crazed look on his face, he was thinking of nothing but barehanded murder.

He leapt onto the table without warning in a near superhuman move. Vulnerable for a microsecond, she punched him in the face, but he kept coming, seemingly immune to the pain. She blocked his thrusting arm and skipped past him into the kitchen, looking for the gun.

Where was it? She scanned the countertop.

Shit!

It was gone.

Justin shoved her toward the sink. She grabbed the bottle of Dawn and squirted a blast at his face.

Most of it missed, but a glob shot into his left eye. He blinked wildly but kept coming, mumbling something, grabbing her by the waist and throwing her sideways to the ground, following her down and falling on her. Kat used the sideways momentum to continue rolling, taking Justin with her, rolling another ninety degrees left. She got a leg free and jerked her knee up and into his groin, scoring a direct hit.

He grunted and curled into the pain.

She scrambled forward, heading for the front door, but he stretched a leg out and tripped her with his foot, then grabbed her ankle and yanked her back. As he reeled her in, she saw the Glock laying on the floor under the edge of the cabinet, apparently sent flying during their brawl.

She grabbed it by the grip. As he twisted her body and tried to mount her, Kat swung the gun up and fired into the ceiling.

He froze for a second—like a rip in time—and went for her throat.

She swung at him and landed a solid blow to the temple.

He stopped, stunned, looking confused. Kat pushed him back and hit him again with the full weight of the gun.

Justin's eyes rolled back and he fell sideways, unconscious.

Kat resisted the urge to strike him one last time.

Then she collapsed in tears.

Sixty-Two

For the longest time, Kat lay on her back, staring at the ceiling, breathing in ragged gasps, barely able to comprehend the last couple minutes much less the past few hours. A parade of violence she had somehow survived despite overwhelming odds.

She sat bolt upright.

Max!

She crawled over to where he lay. The big mutt stirred and opened his eyes when she stroked his face. Kat leaned in and kissed the top of his head. She would have killed Justin if Max had been seriously injured. She should have shot him anyway. Bastard.

As she got to her feet, Kat surveyed the candlelit room. Justin lay in a heap. Her beautiful kitchen was a disaster. Not that it mattered. She had to get the hell out of there. Just grab Max, her stuff, and flee.

Justin didn't factor into the equation.

Then she glanced at him again, lying on the ground, unconscious and somehow looking angelic. An illusion, but she knew the plume had a clear role in his temporary insanity. Would he recover if she took him away from here? The currents also hobbled her logic as she gazed at the man who nearly killed her with lustful eyes. The cocaine cravings were overpowering. Why hadn't she just killed him? She didn't know.

If she believed in his theories—and she did—the psychotic break wasn't his fault. The irony wasn't lost on her. She had argued against him on that very subject.

But she couldn't trust him. It would be foolish to take any chances. How could she move him safely?

Duct tape.

Kat grabbed a roll from the pantry and bound his wrists together, then performed the same maneuver with his ankles. He no longer posed a threat.

Time was running out. The farm was littered with dead bodies. With all the gunfire, why weren't the police already here? It was an incredible stroke of luck. She couldn't be here when they arrived. Being an ex-con and a parole violator, whether they killed Harven and the others in self-defense or not, the police would never believe her. The victims were drug people. She was a convicted dealer. Nope. The prison gates would slam shut on her forever.

Her path to freedom was clear.

Take Justin's SUV. Go to his place and hide out. Would thirty miles be far enough from the plume? She hoped so, but she first had to eliminate any evidence she had been here.

Kat pulled the key fob from his pocket, slipped a hat on, and ran across the field and through the trees to his Land Rover. The loose ends she needed to consider kept unfolding in her head as she pulled out onto the pavement—gas foremost to set a fire and burn it all down. She passed a black Navigator parked on the side of the road, but scarcely gave it a thought.

She looked in the mirror. Her face was a mess of blood and bruises. How would she pull this off? She couldn't show her face in public. One look and they would call the cops—

Kat slammed on the brakes.

The Navigator had to be Harven's. She knew how he thought. He would have considered burning the place down too.

She backed up level with the vehicle, jumped out, and popped the hatch using a rag to avoid leaving prints. Two big red gas cans sat inside, but she wasn't huffing them through the woods. Nope. Kat loaded them into the Defender and backed up, located the two oaks she knew framed the driveway, revved the engine, and punched through the brush between the trees and onto the driveway.

Justin would have some scratches to deal with later. Only fair for the injuries he inflicted on her.

She drove to his encampment, tore everything down, and jammed it into the SUV. Drove to the house and unloaded the tent and canopy and any other flammable items. Kat dragged all her outdoor stuff inside including the grill and propane tanks. After coaxing Max onto the front seat, she stowed her meager possessions in back and taped her bike and trailer to the roof rack.

The night remained dark and silent.

With a peck on the head, Kat said, "I'll be back soon, buddy. Hang tight."

The last part was the hardest. Justin had to weigh at least one-eighty, all dead weight. She dragged him out to the SUV by his feet, his head thumping down both wooden porch steps. She wasn't yet certain if she cared whether he lived or died.

Stopping to catch her breath, Kat looked up at the stars and realized, as wondrous as it was, the universe was a cold, cold place that didn't care one whit about her or anyone else on the planet. Just like the telluric currents and the glob of magma underground and the horrors that had visited the farm and Walden in the past week. The plume didn't care either. It just was. People were the problem. Primitive creatures who were easily swayed to commit vile acts by insubstantial forces like the gravitational pull of a full moon or surging electrical currents underground.

Kat opened the back door, sat him up, and yanked on his arms using the duct tape as a handle, dragging his torso onto the seat. She climbed out, pulled him across the seat, and slammed the door. Running around the vehicle, she jammed his legs through the other door and kicked it shut, then backed the SUV fifty feet down the drive.

Almost clear.

Sprinting, Kat spread a couple gallons of gas on the backyard dump and tossed a flaming matchstick at it. The gas ignited with a satisfying *whoomph.* The container with the remaining gas went into the fire.

Inside the house, she splashed gas around the first floor, down the basement stairs, and onto the porch. She lit a match and flicked it at the trail of gasoline. A tongue of flame raced indoors and the house erupted in flames as the vapors ignited. The blast seared her face. She tossed the plastic can with the remaining gas onto the burning porch and dashed for the SUV, the old dry wood already crackling from the heat.

The farm soon grew into a blazing spectacle as two huge bonfires lit up the night sky.

Now the police would come.

Kat pulled out and drove toward Sun Prairie, driving along secondary roads and obeying the speed limit. She hoped she remembered the way. Minutes later, three vivid explosions lit up the night sky.

The propane tanks.

Sadness washed over her. What she once viewed as her house was gone. Then she heard sirens in the distance.

Max sat up, tongue hanging out, looking ahead and riding shotgun like a road warrior. She took a deep breath. And another. As each mile passed, another wave of relief and exhaustion washed through her.

It had been one hell of a night. She and Max were beaten and bruised. Tired beyond reason. Kat felt catatonic.

But they were alive.

It felt nothing like victory.

Sixty-Three

Kat awoke at ten when Max nuzzled her arm, a signal he needed to go out.

It took a moment to parse the unfamiliar surroundings of Justin's bedroom before the circumstances of her arrival struck with full force.

Turning, she cried out in pain. Kat froze, uncertain which body part hurt the most. Her face, which felt bruised and swollen? The bump on her head? The cuts on her arms? All the places she had been punched, slapped, and beaten? Everything hurt, as did every action. Breathing. Moving. Grimacing. She eased out of bed.

Kat grabbed the Glock, let Max out, and went to check on Justin in the garage, hobbling like a seventy-year-old. He was still asleep, mouth agape, lying on the floor in her bedroll where she had left him, safely locked out of the house. A bruise darkened his temple. The garage felt warm and stuffy.

Kat held the gun at her side and nudged him with a foot.

"Wake up."

He stirred, shook his head, and looked at the duct tape binding his wrists, confused. "What'd you do?"

"Might want to ask yourself that."

"Huh? I don't remember a thing after I killed that guy."

"Oh really? You went nuts." She spoke with renewed anger. "You were going to strangle me."

He looked horrified and puzzled, apparently unable to believe he was capable of such violence. "Jesus. It had to be the telluric currents."

"Yeah. So much for you being smart and prepared to handle the risks. If I didn't believe your plume theory, I would have shot you and left you for dead."

"Undo me. Please. I have to pee." As he rolled sideways, he grimaced. "Ugh. I have a terrible headache."

"Easy, big guy. And you deserve the headache." She trained the Glock on him one-handed and said, "Stick your hands all the way out and stay still."

She split the tape on his wrists with a box cutter, backed up, and tossed the cutter on the floor. "Free your legs and walk slowly to the bathroom."

"I'm not going to hurt you."

"Really? You see my face?"

"I did that?"

"Half of it."

He looked at her with genuine shame and regret. "I'm so sorry. I really thought I could handle it."

"No matter. Here are the rules. You stay ten feet away at all times. I'll be carrying Ms. Glock until further notice. You sleep in the garage."

"It's my house!"

With a flat, menacing tone, she hissed, "If I shoot you, it's mine."

He hung his head, a look of disbelief on his face. "Listen. Whatever I did, I'm really sorry. I accept the rules. I like you a lot."

"Yeah, yeah."

After he relieved himself, he sat at the kitchen table. "Coffee? Is the prisoner allowed coffee?"

"Yes. And don't get cute with me."

She handed him a mug of coffee, black, and three Advil.

"What about my stuff? Did you leave it behind?"

"No. It's in the truck. The important stuff anyway. You can't go back, you know."

"I'm aware." He held his head in his hands.

"You still seeing red?"

"It's mostly gone."

"That's a start."

She made an omelet and shared it with him, but they didn't talk. Justin brought his gear in and returned to work in his office. He kept a respectful distance and informed her of his every move in advance, as instructed.

Locking the bathroom door and tucking the gun where she could reach it quickly, Kat took a shower and stood under the water forever. The heat and the Ibuprofen she took only dented the pain of the blows and insults her body had taken. Justin had offered her Vicodin, but she didn't want to feel woozy and risk letting her guard down. She ignored the beer and wine in the fridge for the same reason.

She alternately sat on the patio and paced in his garden, reliving moments of the night before and trying to decide where to go from here. Would she ever trust Justin again? Was staying here even an option? For the moment, she and Max were safe. A return to mindfulness seemed best. Just worry about the here and now. Deal with the future as it arrived.

Later, she found a steak in the fridge and made them a light dinner. Kat sat outside watching the sunset while Justin worked in his office.

Mindful or not, she recognized the symptoms of post-traumatic stress from her ordeal: an inability to relax, hypervigilance, a constant need to look over her shoulder. She had frequent and uninvited flash-backs. Harven pinning her down. Justin grabbing her by the throat. Fighting her way through the hawthorns. Setting the farm ablaze.

Walden dominated the evening news. The deaths and the vivid fire at the farm were the culmination of a week of bizarre violence. The police offered no theories about what happened there. Together with the earlier crimes, they were overwhelmed by the scope of the investigations. Kat hoped that lumping the farm in with the other events might obscure their involvement.

At eleven, she watched at a distance as Justin stepped into the garage with his computer, a beer, and a pillow. She hesitated, then locked the door and placed a small group of glasses on the floor. A simple alarm should he try to break in.

Lying in bed, she felt terribly conflicted. When she looked at Justin, she saw a decent, good-looking man. A good-hearted man. She had feelings for him, emotional and physical. Then she closed her eyes and relived the attack in the kitchen.

She put an arm around Max and sighed.

Her life would never be simple.

Sixty-Four

Justin was still sleeping in the garage three days later.

That morning, Kat opened the door without the Glock. She felt a decided difference in herself. The cravings were gone. Some lust remained, but it had been a long time. Maybe that wasn't the plume. He, too, was different. More like the old Justin.

"Rise and shine, prisoner."

He stirred and rolled over. "Where's the Glock?"

"On vacation."

"Is my sentence over?"

"You're on probation. You can sleep on the sofa."

⋆　⋆　⋆

Sitting at a tiki bar in Playa del Carmen, Sam checked for updates on the events in Walden, a story that had gripped the nation for days. It had become clear Mr. Smith was a liar. His picture appeared alongside a news story about a cartel turf war at a location close to where she lost Katrina Lundquist. Identified as drug kingpin Jacob Harven, he was found dead with his head bashed in along with the bodies of three associates.

No mention of Lundquist.

Had she escaped the clutches of Mr. Smith? She hoped so. Sam didn't want the woman's death on her conscience and was grateful Lundquist had eluded her that day and gotten her fired. Otherwise, she might be one of the dead in Walden too.

In the future, she had to be more discerning in her clientele. More idealistic like she once was. She'd had suspicions about Mr. Smith but had ignored them.

Here, it all seemed a million miles away. Sam felt guilty about taking money from a criminal enterprise—a little anyway.

She had gotten lucky yet again. Some said she led a charmed life.

Raising two fingers, she said, "Mai Tai, please."

⋆   ⋆   ⋆

Three months later, as the plume and lava underground receded, life was returning to normal in Walden.

Scientists converged from all over the world to study the strange phenomena. They were officially named microplumes and a new sub-category of geology was born. Justin and Dr. Miguel Carneiro shared credit for the discovery. Dr. Carneiro had long passed, but Justin was a bona fide celebrity in the world of seismology.

The second of his theories was still under intense scrutiny and the subject of great and prickly debate. The surge in crime in and around Walden was well documented, but to blame it on seismic activity? Much harder to accept. Near impossible to prove.

Included among the inexplicable and violent events were the deaths of four drug cartel members on a farm outside Walden. Given that violence was endemic in the drug business, they excluded the deaths from the Walden incident list. Beset by so many crime scenes, the case on the farm was closed without resolution. It was thought to be a battle between rival cartels. Police assumed the perpetrators had fled the state.

The morning the case closure made the news, Kat and Justin were eating breakfast. Max lay sprawled out after devouring a plate of bacon and eggs. The day outdoors was grey, rainy, and cold.

"You're off the hook," Justin said.

"We're off the hook. You were there too."

"I only killed a guy with a rock. Self-defense. You shot two people."

That number was a curious business. Denny hadn't been shot but had died from a stab wound to the throat. Had Gina done that? Another thing she would never know.

"You lied to the police about your sensors on the farm."

"Apparently, they bought the story that I had already left."

They ate in silence for a minute. Kat sipped on a mimosa.

One of the lesser stories, buried by the headlines, was a missing person case. Natalie Schaal had been reported missing by her mother. There were no official leads and Kat felt guilty that she couldn't offer the mother peace of mind in the matter. Maybe some day, far in the future. But what would she say? The vision of Natalie's face was still vivid and forever burned into her memory. Nothing would ever explain the expression of terror.

A peculiar news item, one Justin found fascinating, was the saga of Timmer Welding. The business had just reopened after an extended closure. Apparently, the employees had quit en masse claiming the building was haunted by dozens of ghosts. They agreed to return only after a priest performed an exorcism.

Playing with his eggs, Justin said, "I spoke to an attorney."

"I asked you not to."

"I didn't give him your name or mention any details he'd recognize."

"And?"

"If you explain your fear of the cartel, they would probably go easy. Home arrest or an additional period of parole, especially if you have a stable life situation."

"No guarantees though?"

"No."

"I'll think about it."

But Kat didn't know if she would act. She feared prison. Feared the cartel and the reach of the Campo brothers. Feared losing the semblance of sanity she was building with this science geek and her rescue dog. And while she mostly trusted Justin now, she still slept with the Glock in the nightstand and he knew it.

He put his hand on hers. "I support you either way."

She glanced at him and smiled.

Her life would never be easy.

But she could handle tough. Kat felt a spark of hope as she embarked on this new chapter in her life.

It felt like a second chance.

Sixty-Five

Adam Laskin clicked *Send.*

As the email disappeared into the night, he leaned back and rubbed his neck to massage tense muscles.

His laptop sat atop a two-hundred-year-old cherrywood desk in an office lit by an art deco desk lamp. The house was otherwise dark. That email closed the book on the farm and the horror that had visited there so long ago. After the police released the scene, he signed papers to sell the eighty-acre lot to Henderson Coop, a large farming operation in the area—everything but the quarter-acre plot where the house once stood. Then he hired a company to bury the basement, level the property, and plant trees. Next summer, he would visit one last time to place a small memorial for his brother.

For some serendipitous reason, the police never found the bootleg-ger's room under the basement during an investigation after four drug people died at the farm—nor the gory crime scene from a fall evening many years before.

A widower in his sixties, Adam hadn't visited Walden since the death of his family. He hated the place. Always had. The farm felt like a prison, a place that seemed to drag him deep into the throes of depression and stole his joy. He had considered suicide more than once.

After he went on to college, he saw the world anew, like having a blindfold removed. Adam began to see the house as the problem, the source of some dark, oppressive influence. His last summer there, even his father and mother had acted strangely. Only Mikey seemed unaffected by it.

When he went home to visit, the dark feelings returned with a vengeance. Trying to recall his last visit, he still couldn't remember how things went so terribly awry that night. Events came to a head during dinner. That much he knew.

Fighting a migraine, he suffered through Dad quoting scripture and Mom nagging him about leaving the farm behind. He didn't want the farm or their life. It upset them to no end. Adam tried to shut them out but couldn't.

You have to carry on the family tradition, blah blah blah—

He snapped.

Adam stomped off to his room and grabbed the Springfield pistol he used for plinking cans and marched them down to the bootleg cellar. His great-grandfather had apparently built the room to distill bathtub gin. He also hosted a weekly poker game. He sounded like a cool dude. According to Grandpa Laskin, he hated the farming life too.

Things grew hazy after that.

When Adam came to, Mom and Dad were dead. He hated to hurt Mikey, but the kid wouldn't stop screaming and the hammer was just lying there.

He panicked and rearranged the scene. Placed the hammer by his mother and the gun in his father's hand so it would look like a murder-suicide. The Tarot cards were a ruse. If the bodies were discovered, he hoped people would draw crazy connotations about the murders. The cross had been a confused symbolic effort to create a memorial. Why? He no longer remembered.

Unable to afford them a proper burial, Adam left the bodies as they lay and concealed the trapdoor beneath a pile of junk. He shuttered the house and walked away.

Adam understood his family wouldn't be missed if he handled things right. Mikey was home-schooled. Adam settled the bill with the seed company and told them the family was moving. Paid the bills and shut off the utilities. Signed the title to the farm over to himself and paid the taxes every year. There was no family to speak of. Mom was an only child and Dad's brother died in Vietnam. Their parents were dead. Curiously, Adam had long suspected his father killed his grandmother. The fall down the stairs had been suspicious and too convenient given all his grumbling about her.

The murder of his parents did not trouble him. Killing Mikey haunted him to this day. A constant source of nightmares, Adam had endured several bouts of alcoholism before confessing to a priest, who refused him absolution unless he turned himself in.

Adam wasn't stupid. That would solve nothing.

Then chaos came to Walden again. The farm was part of it and more people died. He should have burned the place down when he had the chance. A scientist said the problems were caused by something called microplumes and telluric currents—surges in underground voltage that compelled people to do bad things.

Was that it? Evil currents in the soil? Did the farm sit on haunted ground?

Did it matter?

His brother and parents were still dead.

He wished he cared more. But he embraced the idea of an invisible and malevolent force. If he had been driven to kill by such a thing, then he wasn't a monster.

Or was he?

He never quite escaped the feeling that he was.

Despite his troubled and fractious childhood, Adam succeeded in life. He evaded discovery and arrest, got married, and became a successful author. Not even his wife suspected he had once been a killer.

Adam had written it all down in a fictional portrayal, a thriller. A memoir for him. The book was a national bestseller.

One could argue some good had come of it all.

But that was a terrible take, a symptom of some depravity still lingering beneath the surface of his placid demeanor.

He really had lost his soul on that farm.

Adam drank the remaining scotch in his glass, turned the light off, and went to bed.

Thank you!

Thank you for reading *Haunted Ground*. I hope you enjoyed it. As an independently published author, I rely on all of you wonderful readers to spread the word. If you enjoyed *Haunted Ground*, please tell your friends and family. I would also sincerely appreciate a brief review on Amazon.

Again, thank you!

Cailyn Lloyd

www.cailynlloyd.net

Acknowledgments

No book is published without considerable work by people behind the scenes. For *Haunted Ground*, those people were:

Paul Martin of Dominion Editorial who read and critiqued the first draft which lead to significant improvements in the story. Lucy Snyder who read and critiqued the second and third drafts, pointing out weaknesses in the narrative. Jennie Lloyd who read each draft and offered many useful insights and ideas. Fran Lebowitz who read and pointed out the errors and weak or poorly executed ideas in the pre-final draft. Sean Leonard copyedited and proofed the final draft and helped sharpen the prose. Katie Lloyd who proofread the final manuscript. Sherry Docta, a retired prison guard, for her insights on prison life for women. Denis Caron, a marketing specialist who assisted in the release of the book. My sincere thanks to all of you.

About Max. His story is mostly true. He was a stray who jumped into a neighbor's pickup truck. He had no tags, just the blue and white collar with his name inked into it. A golden retriever and St. Bernard mix, we adopted him and gained a warm and loving companion every bit as smart as the fictional Max. He passed years ago but we still miss him.

Books by Cailyn Lloyd

Shepherd's Warning (2019)
The Elders Book 1

Quinlan's Secret (2020)
The Elders Book 2

Hayward's Revenge (2021)
The Elders Book 3

The Mill (2022)
Haunting at Rock River

Haunted Ground (2023)
The Ghosts of Laskin's Farm

9 798218 174651